s applied to Dominic
s family has ruled the
dreds of years, guiding
Unspeakable loss drove
.... ody can tame. Now he's

...... g ...., ... a
war.

At best theirs seems like a desperate alliance, but when their mate bond turns hot and fierce, there's no end to the questions and the doubts. Neither of them expects to fall in love. But sometimes people don't know what they're looking for until they find it.

THE LEOPARD KING

Ann Aguirre

For Karen, Fedora, and Pam.
Your passion fuels my courage.
Thank you, always.

Acknowledgments

First of all, thanks to Bree Bridges for giving me the courage to try. She held my hand from the first scary steps all the way to the end, and now I'm exhilarated by the possibilities. There has always been such joy in writing, and romance is my first love, so I'm thrilled to be back.

Thanks to Sasha Knight, my editor. She polished my prose and asked the hard questions, so readers could enjoy the fruits of our labors. I also need to thank Karen Alderman for devoting so much time, love, and expertise to this project. Thanks to the phenomenal designer Kanaxa, who knew what I wanted before I asked for it. She did a splendid job of bringing my ideal to life.

In general, I couldn't write or work without support from my friends and colleagues, who inspire me, fill me with warmth and admiration, and push me to aim higher. In particular, thanks to Donna J. Herren, Lauren Dane, Megan Hart, HelenKay Dimon, Tessa Dare, Courtney Milan, and Yasmine Galenorn for the friendship and sisterhood. I mentioned Fedora Chen and Pamela Webb-Elliot in the dedication, but they deserve another mention here. My beta readers excavate time in their busy schedules to read my chapters, and for that I couldn't be more grateful. They also brainstorm with me, cheer me on, and fuel my writing engine with their love of romance.

For my family, I have only boundless gratitude. My husband and children never question that important work is, in fact, occurring when I'm in my pajamas on the porch swing. Thank you for your patience and understanding and for accepting that I cook more between deadlines.

Readers, I appreciate you saving a space for me by the fire. I have wandered through other genres and come home weary, ready to write about love and sex and happy endings. I hope you enjoy the Ars Numina series as much as I do.

Thanks for supporting me, and as always, read on.

1.

THIS LONELY MOUNTAIN was where the leopard king had come to die.

The house built atop the desolate aerie might as well be a fortress, as the only land approach came by way of the steep, foreboding steps carved into the cliff, worn smooth by decades of wind and rain, green with moss. Overhead a leaden sky threatened to dump a deluge on her, and Pru shivered. It might even be cold enough for sleet or snow.

Hunching deeper into her down jacket, she started the long climb. The Ash Valley pride hadn't seen their reclusive leader in almost three years. When he delegated day-to-day affairs to his second, Slay, they'd all expected Dominic to grieve and return. So no one had protested when he packed his things and left his quarters at the hold, eschewing companionship in favor of the solitude at the retreat ancient seers had used for meditation.

But true to his nickname, Slay didn't excel at diplomacy, and with the conclave approaching, they couldn't afford to have him in charge of peace talks with the Golgoth and the Eldritch. There was resentment over the way the territories had been divided, and border skirmishes since then had claimed lives on all sides. Delegates from the Pine Ridge pack and the Burnt Amber clan were already waiting to discuss strategy, concerned that the Animari would lose ground in the coming negotiations. So far, Ash Valley had avoided any admission of how completely Dominic had withdrawn, but she only had a few days, a week at most, to accomplish the impossible—to bring him home.

Pru understood why he'd left. The hold echoed with emptiness for her too. Dalena had been her best friend, and the silence after her death sometimes seemed unbearable. She hadn't wanted this mission, either. In fact, she'd argued with Slay when he ordered her to go.

"Why does it have to be me?"

"You know why."

Then Slay had given her a look that made Pru wish she hadn't asked. Heat washed her cheeks, and she dropped her gaze. *Two reasons, then.* As Dalena's closest friend, she had the best chance of reaching Dominic, and if she couldn't, if he'd gone feral, well... As a Latent—one who'd never mastered the art of changing forms—she was also the most expendable. So if she pushed their grief-maddened leader too far, Ash Valley could afford to lose her.

Still, she'd tried to protest. "You should go. Dominic trusts you, or he wouldn't have made you second."

"If I go, we'll fight. And we both know how that ends. I don't want to kill my best friend. I want to lead Ash Valley even less. Please, Pru. Do this for me?"

Slay had known she couldn't resist a pleading look, not that he deployed it often. He also knew she was weak where he was concerned, a truth she could neither change, nor deny. As his golden gaze softened, she remembered how her parents had attempted to match them and he passed. She couldn't face Slay for a month afterward, and he was the first of four rejections. After that, Pru had begged her parents to stop trying. Her heart pinched.

Of all potential partners, he was the only one whose answer had truly mattered. It was also why she'd reluctantly agreed to this fool's errand—because she'd do anything for Slay. So she'd sighed.

"Fine. I'll go."

Slay had smiled. "It's been more than long enough. Cats don't mate for life, so he needs to stop wallowing. Bring Dom home, all right?"

Easier said than done.

Pru's thighs burned as she approached the summit. The air was thin and crisp. A panoramic view offered some compensation as she gasped for breath, then she turned to study the house. Built of ancient stones, it looked about as inviting as the stairs leading up to it. There were no lights on, no signs of life within. Nobody had seen Dominic in six months, the last time Slay had come to report, though he sent guards to stock the fridge regularly. Setting her shoulders, Pru hurried toward the heavy front door. There was an actual brass knocker, so she slammed it repeatedly against the wood.

No response.

She hadn't expected it to be that easy. The door was locked, naturally, but circling revealed two more entrances. They held firm too. Someone else could have kicked down the door, but she had only human strength, a result of Latent status. The first shift enhanced speed, strength, and agility, but she'd never joined that elite group. She'd nearly killed herself more than once, trying to force the change.

The stinging cold reminded Pru of the slap Dalena had

delivered, knocking the razor out of her hand. Metallic clink as the blade tumbled across the bathroom floor—Dalena was strong enough to leave Pru's head ringing. Firm fingers settled on her shoulders, shaking her.

"You may not care about your life, but *I* do. Understand? I won't let you kill yourself. You're too precious. Please, please stop this. Shifting doesn't matter. *You* do."

Tears burned in contrast with the bitter wind as Pru wrapped her arms about herself, just as Dalena had done, rocking her on the bathroom floor. She'd cried a lifetime of tears into her friend's shoulder, letting go of an impossible dream. After that, she loathed her Latent status but she didn't carve any fresh scars. *Dalena saved me. I wish I could've done the same for her.*

Now she accepted her limitations, but she was still shivering in the cold when she should be inside, starting her well-rehearsed speech. She banged on all the doors for an hour. By this time, the threatened rain arrived, only it came in a mixture of water and ice, lashing at her like stinging needles.

Desperate measures it is.

Pru grabbed a stone from the rock and topiary garden and chucked it through the nearest window. She expected an alarm to sound, but after the shattering glass, there was only silence. Dread rose in her like floodwater as she reached over the jagged shards and unlocked the frame; she lifted it easily and scrambled over the sill onto the counter, toppling the stacks of dirty dishes piled everywhere. You could tell a lot about a person from their kitchen, and it looked like Dominic was in disarray that bordered on complete destruction.

Other people expected him to be recovered by now, but

she understood how much he'd loved Dalena. Not every Animari was lucky enough to find their fated mate, but Dominic and Dalena's magnetism had been instantaneous. Though Dom had gone to her parents for permission, if they had objected, Pru had no doubt he would have carried Dalena off and started his own pride. From the moment their eyes met, their love was magical... legendary, even. Dominic and Dalena weren't just perfectly matched; they were also the ideal leaders of the Ash Valley pride.

And then everything ended.

The kitchen reeked of rotting food. She stepped over the glass fragments and picked a careful path into the next room. Overturned furniture, more broken glass, and claw marks made the place look as if a fight had gone down, but she didn't smell blood. Some of the damage was obviously days or weeks old with dust settled on the wreckage. Her pulse kicked up a notch when she glimpsed a flicker of movement farther into the gloom.

She steeled herself. "Dominic...?"

At first, he didn't answer, but she recognized the sound of him prowling closer. Once she'd spent almost as much time with him as Dalena. Pru's first glimpse of the leopard king in exile stole her breath. He'd always been lean, but now he'd dwindled to gaunt with pain lines carved into a face that looked more like granite than flesh. Sunken eyes gleamed with a febrile light, glinting citrine from beneath heavy brows. At his best, Pru wouldn't have called Dominic Asher handsome, but he'd radiated a certain calm strength, and his smile could quicken anybody's pulse. Now, he was all angles and anguish. Not long ago, he must've shaved his head, resulting in ebony and silver bristles. Her throat closed at his aura of pure intimidation.

"What the hell are you doing here?"

AT FIRST, DOM thought he was hallucinating.

As much as he'd been drinking and as little as he'd eaten in the last five days, it wouldn't surprise him. Sometimes, if he fasted and downed enough liquor, Dalena came to him. Not in her last moments with blood trickling from her mouth, but the smiling Dalena with twilight eyes and hair like a swathe of midnight. He wished he had the courage to just… let go and follow her. For the last three years, he'd been working up to it. The real world seemed ephemeral now, so he'd been about to shift for the last time and let himself go feral.

On the cusp of his final farewell, Pru Bristow had the nerve to break into his sanctuary, standing before him like she had every right. It summoned such a wash of rage that he took a step back as his hands curled into fists. *It's not her fault. Dial it down.* Controlling such raw fury came at a cost, however. He swayed a little and caught himself on the wall. Inwardly he cursed as Pru rushed to his side, offering her shoulder.

Dom shook her off with a snarl. "You didn't answer me."

She stumbled a bit, a round little woman made more so by the puffy jacket she wore. Dom probably should care that her lips held a blue tinge and that her red-brown hair had bits of melting ice in it. He didn't. As he watched, she shrugged out of her coat and hung it on a hook near the front door. Her heavy boots were sodden too, so she stripped out of them. Beneath, she wore striped socks with bright colors on each separate toe. Dom twitched and fought the urge to eject her forcibly. But he hadn't fallen so far that he'd treat a pride mate that way.

Not yet.

Finally, she replied, "Beren from Burnt Amber is waiting for you at the hold, and we had word from Pine Ridge just before I left. Raff will have arrived by now."

"So?" He bit off the question as if he didn't know damn well what she was driving at.

Her freckled throat worked visibly before she managed to say, "Slay has carried on without you for as long as he could. It's time to take care of business."

"You're wasting your time. Ash Valley should've ousted me officially two years ago, so let's cut to the chase. What will it take to make you give up and tell Slay to accept his role as pride leader?"

Pru lifted her chin slightly. "I can't go back without you."

"Then I suggest you shovel out the guestroom. And don't expect me to take care of you."

Dom slammed out of the den, but his keen hearing still picked up her soft response. "Why would I? When you can't even look after yourself."

Stinging hard from sympathy that felt so much like pity, he downed the remainder of the fifth he'd been nursing, but due to an accelerated metabolism, he had to drink *so* much to feel it, that he needed his own still. Dom hurled the bottle at the wall and took faint satisfaction in the glass pile he had going. If Dalena knew how he was treating the woman who had been like a sister to her, she'd be beyond furious.

And that's the problem. She's not here.

Yet seeing Pru after so long brought back a rush of good memories. He couldn't count the nights the four of them had spent laughing until the sun came up. Dalena had been protective of Pru, conscious that she couldn't accompany everyone else on regular hunts. No, Pru was left behind at the hold with the handful of other Latents, ostensibly holding down the fort, but he'd always secretly pitied her yearning eyes as she watched the rest of the pride shift and run, a sweet freedom she could never experience. Now that *she* felt sorry for *him*, it burned like a bitch, and he wanted to tear this place apart with his bare hands. The only reason he'd lasted this long without Dalena was the faint hope that he might someday take revenge on the unidentified devil who'd executed her in cold blood. His wife had died trying to give him a clue, and like a useless bastard, he'd only held her in stunned, uncomprehending silence.

As the days after her murder turned into weeks, the trail went cold and he lost hope. He couldn't stay at the hold without her, and he didn't have the fortitude to die. *Welcome to purgatory.* At first, visitors from Ash Valley came and went, most bearing gifts or sympathetic words. In time that number dwindled to an occasional call from Slay, allegedly looping him in, but Dom knew his friend had really been checking to see if he was still alive.

And now he's sent Pru. Fucking prick.

Pacing—with a door between them—Dom tried to ignore her, but she didn't make it easy. He picked up the sound of her cleaning: first the scritch-scritch of the broom against the tiles of the kitchen floor, then the off-and-on hiss of the water as she washed dishes. The smell of cleaning products wafted through the rooms between them, prickling his nose. This place hadn't been lemon-fresh in years, and he couldn't just hide while she brushed away the cobwebs he'd been cultivating. While he couldn't throw her into the icy rain, he could make her choose to go.

But it took another bottle to give him the resolve to face her again. As he got a decent buzz on, she tidied his kitchen, put away all the dishes, and cleaned the floor. It smelled so much better that he stopped to breathe in the freshness. Dom hadn't even known there was an apron anywhere in the retreat, but she had one, a yellow thing with ruffles that made her look like a half-drowned buttercup.

"How long's it been since you had a proper meal?" she asked.

"Fuck off."

"That's not part of the four food groups. I'll take that to mean it's been a while."

It had been over a week since he went hunting, and he couldn't remember if he'd eaten that night. Loss felt better as a leopard, muted and distant. Since he hadn't bought provisions in forever, he didn't expect her to find anything. But Slay must have sent shit behind his back because she found meat in the freezer and got it out with a smile so strained that he could've passed pasta through it. Pru ignored his scowl and got to work defrosting, like he had been waiting for somebody to take charge.

"I need you to get the hell out. Right now." If she didn't, he had no idea what he'd do.

"You don't know what you need." She sliced the steak into strips without looking at him.

For a moment, he was speechless. "Pru. Watch how you address me."

Dom had grown accustomed to a certain amount of respect as pride leader, and now he wasn't used to people talking to him at all. So this much defiance made his scalp prickle. She smelled like fresh air and goat milk soap, plus a touch of pine from the long walk up here. Her heart was beating fast, but she didn't back down.

In fact, she even folded her arms, staring up at him with narrowed eyes. "You can't have it both ways, Dom. Not long ago, you said Slay should lead permanently in your place. Which means you're not above me, you're just a pride mate being a dumbass."

His jaw clenched so hard that it might crack. "*What* did you say?"

"Until I hear otherwise, Slay is the only one who can give me orders. Cats don't mate for life, and you have a responsibility to Ash Valley. You need to move on. So I'm here whether you like it or not. Once you come home, I'll apologize for my disrespect."

"You want me back so bad?" He shouldn't say this, but she'd goaded him past the point of any pretense at being polite. If he let her, she'd dig at his wounds in a clumsy attempt at lancing them. "Fine. Here are my terms. I'll return when *you* can shift and take me as a mate."

Her reflexive flinch said she couldn't brook his current level of cruelty, and Dom smiled. *Sorry, Dalena. Pru is sweet as honey-butter biscuits. Breaking her won't take long.*

2.

PRU NEVER WOULD'VE imagined that Dom would use her greatest weakness against her, but at the moment, he was an injured beast, so she breathed through the pain of that challenge. He knew perfectly well how hard she'd tried, how much she'd suffered for repeated failure—and how impossible his request was—yet she couldn't return to Slay, defeated by a few harsh words. So she waited until the pain subsided while considering the gauntlet he'd thrown. One impossible thing added to another, so why not become Dom's mate if she could shift? She might as well wish on a star for a solution.

So she said, "Deal."

He cocked his head. In leopard form, his ears would be swiveling. "We both know you can't do it, no matter how much you want to."

"That doesn't mean I'll give up." She turned away before he figured out one critical fact.

It hurts me too, asshole. Seeing you, without her.

Mechanically, she went about searing the steak strips, leaving them oozing blood on the inside. It was ironic; she preferred her meat that way too, even if she couldn't change like everyone else. He cursed as she plated the food with artful care, and then she carried their dishes into the ruined dining room. Dom probably didn't expect her to right the table and two chairs, but she did, and then she sat down.

"You expect me to have dinner with you?" he demanded.

"It's the sensible option. Or you can starve yourself until you're too weak to resist when I force-feed you."

A muscle ticked in his jaw, but he slammed into the seat across from her and grabbed his food like she might fight him for it. He devoured her cooking with a ferocity that yielded to simple hunger; Pru registered the moment he stopped pretending to savage her with his teeth. She didn't speak again until their plates were clear, and then she washed up in the kitchen. Since she'd expected him to retreat, his silent departure came on cue.

Proud, arrogant, and a touch vain, but also kind, generous, and protective—for years she'd witnessed Dom's devotion to Dalena, and now she had to add selfish and self-absorbed to that list. If he didn't care about Ash Valley anymore, if only *his* pain mattered, then he was more of a bastard than anyone could've predicted. Pru controlled the urge to slam around the kitchen; that would reveal too much about her state of mind.

By then, exhaustion had her in a chokehold, so she switched off the lights and went down the darkened hall toward the stairs. Ruined furniture made her feel like a squatter as she used her phone to avoid pitfalls. On the second floor, the first bedroom had no mattress, just padding and foam that had been clawed to shreds. Likewise, the second room offered no shelter, so she made a nest in the third. While the bed was broken, Dom had left the mattress amid the wooden shrapnel.

If the retreat had central heating, he didn't have it on. Undressing in the austere bathroom, she shivered in stepping into the shower. The water never warmed properly, either, and Pru's teeth chattered under the chilly spray. Cold and miserable described her situation all right; it was like Dom denied himself creature comforts as penance. It wouldn't surprise her to learn that he wore a hair shirt like a self-flagellating monk beneath the tattered sweater that looked like he hadn't taken it off in weeks.

With her confidence at low ebb, she crawled beneath a mound of musty covers and tried to sleep. At some point she must've, but guttural cries jolted her awake. It sounded like Dom was being strangled as he wept, and she hesitated. If he was awake, he might pull her head off for stepping over the line. On the other hand, nobody should fight nightmares alone.

She followed the sounds to the end of the hall. He hadn't spared this room either, and Dom sprawled amid the wreckage, long splinters of wood and shards of glass that glimmered in the moonlight streaming through the window. No furniture remained intact, and he lay curled on the bare floor, which wouldn't be so pitiful if he'd shifted.

Carefully Pru knelt and set a hand on his brow, which was cold as ice but clammy with fear sweat. He'd hate like hell for anyone to see him like this. Yet her touch seemed to settle him a little; it wasn't natural for a cat to hide for so long. While many enjoyed solitary hunts, there was also plenty of close contact and camaraderie. Even the fiercest cats needed to purr.

Half holding her breath, she eased from the crouch to sit beside him. Tentative as a first kiss, she petted his head as her mother once did to lull her back to sleep after a bad dream. Awake and alert, he'd chew off her fingers before allowing her to comfort him. At first, he was restless, thrashing as if he fought unseen enemies, but she maintained a soothing rhythm and his breathing steadied. His vulnerable, sleeping features showed even more clearly how he'd suffered since Dalena died.

"I'm sorry," she whispered. "But I have my orders... and she wouldn't thank me for letting this go on. She'd hate this, all of it."

Dom reached out and locked long fingers on her wrist. "You can't be in my bed unless you can shift."

Pru laughed. "What bed? And don't flatter yourself."

Letting out a faint sigh, he let go of her and folded his arms beneath his head. "How come I never knew that you have claws?"

"It was never my place to use them on you before."

"It still isn't," he muttered.

Changing topics, she ignored his anger; it was easier to handle than his anguish. "First thing, we're cleaning this place up. Do you have a heater? It's freezing."

"You're soft, that's all."

"Dom."

"If I turn it on, it'll only encourage you. So find it yourself."

"Okay. I will."

Oddly, she found his behavior less painful in the middle of the night, possibly because he struck her like a wounded child. Smiling, she went back to stroking his head and felt mildly astonished when he didn't threaten to bite. Instead he remained quiescent, staring into the darkness, until a long, heavy sigh slipped out of him.

"That feels good. I hate that it does... and that I'm too tired to fight you right now."

"I won't quibble over victory by attrition."

Thus encouraged, she let her fingers say the things her mouth couldn't, like, *I miss her too* and *I'm sorry I left you alone for so long.* Once, apart from Dalena, Dom had been her closest friend. As if his mate had been the glue holding everyone together, the center couldn't hold without her. Disintegration came in slow sobs and hands clutching empty air. His shorn hair scraped her palm like the bristles of a brush.

"I really hate you," he said then.

But there was no heat in it, only sorrow. Pru tipped her head back. "I hate you too."

"As long as we're on the same page." He sounded exhausted.

She planned to linger only long enough to make sure he settled, but even after his breathing leveled out, he reached for her when she moved. His big hand splayed over her knee and she just... stayed. Pru's back was aching by the time the sun came up, but Dom seemed to be sleeping peacefully for the first time in gods only knew how long. When she finally crept out, it was well into the morning.

First thing, she taped some plastic over the broken kitchen window, as that wasn't helping the arctic front sweeping the old house. In daylight, her explorations revealed a number of old-fashioned radiators, so there must be a furnace somewhere. Pru found it in the basement, but the pilot light had gone out, and it took a solid hour of tinkering before she got it running. The resultant rumble-roar filled her with satisfaction.

Maybe I can't shift, but I can fix things.

DOM HAD NO idea how long he'd been out, but clearly he'd lost control of the situation. Not only had he failed to drive Pru off, but she'd somehow managed to clean his room *while* he slept in it. If she'd come to murder him, he wouldn't be alive or pissed off. He went for a cold shower to settle down, and the damned hot water kicked in.

What the hell.

A savory smell bubbled through the house: roasting meat, rosemary and sage, a touch of something earthy. Best guess, she was probably making stew out of the groceries Slay had smuggled in. After he dressed, he strode through the house, agitated by the changes she'd wrought in such a relatively short time. Gone were the ruined fixtures and broken glass. His rampage had left the retreat nearly unfurnished, but she'd dragged a few old things in from somewhere, either the attic or basement, and somehow, impossibly, made the place livable again. He wanted to strangle her.

"You think this solves anything? You tidy up, cook me a few meals, and somehow I'm magically fixed?" His voice came out rough and tight with fury.

"No." She didn't look at him, but he could tell from the slant of her shoulders that she was fucking exhausted, as one would expect, after all that heavy lifting.

"I don't need a goddamned maid. I need my wife, and you will *never* fill her shoes, you're not even her shadow anymore, so get that through your thick head and crawl back to Slay. Oh wait." Dom snarled deep in his throat. "He doesn't want you, either." When her breath hitched, guilt slashed at him, but the discomfort was so faint that he swallowed it.

Too far? She should be running out in tears in 3-2-1…

But when she spoke, her tone was level. "Slay chose not to be my mate, but he respects me. That's why he sent me to retrieve you."

Reluctant admiration boiled up from the emotional volcano seething inside him. With every word she spoke, Pru tethered him tighter to the real world. Problems and responsibilities hammered at him, the echo of voices he'd nearly managed to forget. Memories crashed like waves on the shore, endlessly repeating, and for the first time in months, he wondered how his father would feel, knowing he'd abandoned Ash Valley and everyone who depended on him.

He'd be so ashamed of me.

But he couldn't admit she was getting to him. "You know my terms. Better get to work."

Dom imagined she'd have a snappish retort, and he almost wanted to hear it. So it startled him when she took off that damned buttercup apron, turned down the heat on whatever she was simmering, and quietly left the kitchen. Questions pecked away at his composure, but he pretended like he wasn't interested in whatever Pru might be doing. That mock indifference didn't last as long as he wanted. Eventually curiosity overwhelmed him, and he went looking for her. He prowled the house, growing steadily more irritated.

I should be drunk by now. Working on it, at least.

At last he tracked her to the basement, where she'd curled up next to a box of glass fragments. He had no idea why she'd saved them, but that puzzle dropped out of his head as he breathed in an unmistakable coppery tang. Most likely he should've caught it sooner, but drink, isolation, and inactivity had blunted his senses. *Some apex predator I am.* He switched on the light and closed the distance between them, his heart lurching in his throat.

"What have you done?"

She tipped her head back, her eyes glassy with pain and grief. Her hair fell down her back in a messy tumble as he reached for her arm and saw that she'd carved eight lines, shallow cuts that marched over her wrist and toward her elbow. The trickling red connected in his head like a dreadful map navigation, arrowing toward Dalena's death. Dom gave her a little shake.

"Pru!"

"Pain is supposed to prompt the first shift. Fear. Anger. Passion. Any strong emotion, really. But I don't feel things properly, huh? I'm not enough, I never will be. I'm broken."

A litany of curses escaped him as he bundled her close. The shard dropped from her bloody fingers, and he laid into her as if she were a kit who'd wandered into Golgoth territory. Her lax expression troubled him. This idiot would probably die for Slay if he asked nicely. In his rage, in his wretchedness, he'd forgotten how close to death Pru used to skate in trying to force the change, and how hard Dalena worked to haul her back from the brink.

Swallowing hard, he closed his eyes briefly and then raced upstairs with her. She fought him as he wrapped her wounds, but she never flinched. He held her close and tight, wordlessly demanding that she settle down. *Breathe,* he told her silently. She didn't smell like goat milk soap anymore, but whatever cheap stuff was currently in his shower. When she met his gaze, her eyes were dry. That look caught and clung, a silent clash that ended in him noticing how the freckles she'd always hated stood out in sharp contrast to her sickly pallor.

Pru didn't seem grateful as she shoved him away. "The food is ready."

"Would you really die to bring me back?" he asked softly.

Her chin came up in a gesture so familiar his heart ached. Though he'd never had eyes for anyone but Dalena, he'd grown up with Pru. Her face—he knew it like each of his own scars—each freckle, each of her eyelashes had once been so dear. Mentally, he begged his mate's best friend for mercy. *Don't do this. Don't make me survive losing Dalena.*

Monotone response, a sign that Pru was hurting so bad she couldn't process it. Anguish overload, Dalena used to say. "I was prepared for that when I came."

"To *die*?" he demanded.

She shrugged, like her life was nothing. Dom clenched his fists, drowning in the desire to discipline her properly. But he couldn't do that unless he meant to take up the mantle of all his old obligations. So he savaged his lower lip instead.

"As you said, you set the terms. If my shifting will get you off this mountain—"

"Don't hurt yourself again." He was almost begging.

How did things turn out like this? At this rate, he'd be afraid to leave her side for even a minute. *If she dies...* His stomach turned inside out. From birth he'd been reared to carry the whole pride on his shoulders, and he never forgot his role... or all the burdens that came with it.

Until Dalena died.

"I can't promise that. I wanted to shift before, enough to do practically anything. But now, the stakes are just too high. Don't you get that? The alliance with Burnt Amber and Pine Ridge could dissolve, leaving us to face the

Golgoth and Eldritch alone."

"Pru—"

She clenched her good hand and waved her fist in his face, as if she might punch him. "I love Slay, but without you to check him, he will *start a war*. Yet you've got me playing games, testing me. So fucking fine, Dom. I'll do anything. Do you get it now? The minute your back is turned, I'll figure out how to activate my defective ass or die trying."

"That's where we are?"

"I hope I was clear."

"Crystal," he growled.

"Then eat your fucking stew."

In all the years he'd known her, he'd never heard Pru swear so much. Her color was better at least, as she slopped some brown food into a bowl and practically threw it at him. Honestly, he'd always thought she was sweet but somewhat timorous, following Dalena like a faithful sidekick. This stubborn streak astonished him.

"I am. See? Eating." He raised the spoon in a placating gesture.

"Good." That was all she said for a while.

But he couldn't let her rant stand unchallenged. "You know this won't work, right? I won't let you push yourself."

I'll watch you like a hawk.

She offered a tight smile. "We'll see."

Damn her, she was right.

When he went to the bathroom an hour later, she vanished again, and he might lose his mind before he hunted her down.

3.

COLD GNAWED THROUGH Pru's flesh and down to her bones.

She shivered and her teeth chattered until she ran out of steam. It was bad enough without a coat, but when the sleet started, it got worse, glazing her hair, which felt like she had icicles growing out of her head. Her body went numb and heavy, and it would've been too much work to get up. The house seemed so far away, well beyond her reach. She'd thought that the threat of freezing to death might do the trick, but her genes remained stubbornly locked.

There should be some fear or alarm, but she'd passed beyond that point. Distantly she wondered if Slay would care, if he'd blame Dom. As she closed her eyes, the wind carried a voice to her. Pru didn't call back; the great leopard king could do his own tracking. She wouldn't give up, no matter what it cost her.

A sleek and gorgeous snow leopard raced toward her, and then he was Dom, clutching her with frantic hands. She stared up at him with wide eyes. They might be frozen open because she couldn't even blink, and her voice felt like a ghost in her throat. The worsening storm stole his words, sweeping them away, but she could guess what he was saying. Then he swooped in a furious pounce and ran with her to the house. She could feel his shoulder bones beneath her cheek, but despite how thin he'd gotten, he still held her easily.

"You're driving me crazy," he snapped as they slammed into the retreat.

Pru didn't protest when he stripped off her clothes; Dom had as much interest in her naked body as he had in modern art. Averting his eyes, he wrapped her in a blanket. That wasn't enough, but she did start shivering again. She couldn't remember Dom taking care of her before. Nobody had since her mother died. Her dad was taciturn and gruff, preferring to spend his nights prowling as a lynx. Before she came to the retreat, it had been a month since she'd seen him.

"Hang in there. I'll be right back."

Drowsily she watched him tear his closet apart, and then he returned with socks, a knit cap, and mittens. For some reason, the idea of wearing *only* those three items struck her as hilarious, so she couldn't stop giggling as he tried to dress her. But Dom hadn't practiced on dolls, so his normally deft hands fumbled, especially when he knelt at her feet.

She could scarcely feel his fingers and there was something magical about this numbness. A hateful inner voice pointed out, *It'll be worse than dying if you lose extremities. Then you won't just be defective... you'll also be the fool who maimed herself.* That killed the laughter, and she swallowed the lump in her throat without weeping.

"It didn't work," she told him.

"Why the hell did you think freezing yourself would

accomplish anything?"

"It's about the only thing I haven't tried."

With a muttered curse, he cupped her cheek in his big palm. "You're still too fucking cold, and taking you down the mountain would only make things worse in this weather."

His touch burned her skin, so she flinched away. In weary astonishment she watched as he shucked his sweater and the white T-shirt beneath, revealing his bare chest. Even with clothes on, she'd noticed how gaunt he'd become, but his ridged abs had yielded to a concave belly, a hollow beneath his ribs, and the jut of his bones made her want to cook him something right away. Except that her legs wouldn't hold her when she tried to stand.

"Don't worry about me," she mumbled.

"Like that's possible. I think Slay sent you as my punishment. Come here."

But she couldn't even grasp what he wanted, let alone comply with his request. So he lifted her into his lap, her freezing back against his bony, fever-hot chest, and then he wrapped them both up in multiple layers of blankets. When he shifted so they were near the radiator, the blast of warmth hurt. The agony of her thawing flesh finally gave Pru an excuse to cry, and she could pretend her grief stemmed from something other than the fact that she'd failed.

Again.

Great sobs wracked her, and the entire time, Dom held her like she was fragile and precious, like nobody ever had. His arms tightened on her until it hurt almost as much as the sensation returning. When she shifted to complain, the tear tracks on his grim face silenced her. He needed to grieve more than she did. Whatever he'd been doing the past few years, it wasn't mourning. At no point had he accepted his loss or let any of the pain out. It seemed more like he'd been nursing it, letting a broken heart fester into a soul-deep wound.

Clumsily, she shifted and wrapped her arms around him. Pru expected him to shove her away; maybe because she was still so cold, he didn't. A shudder ran through him, and then he tucked his painfully warm, damp face into the curve of her neck. She cradled his head in her mitten-covered hands, closing her eyes so she wouldn't fixate on how strange this was.

They stayed that way for what felt like forever. His breathing went deep and slow. She registered the moment when the tension slipped out of him, and he leaned on her to the point that she had to exert herself to keep him from falling. *He's not as strong as I thought.* But he'd done a good job of warming her up gradually. Now that her head was clear, she understood that he'd done things that way to avoid plunging her into shock or causing arrhythmia. Yet now she was naked in his arms, conscious of where his bare skin touched hers.

And he's sound asleep.

On some level, she should probably be insulted, but he needed rest so much that Pru didn't even mind. Carefully she stripped out of the mittens and brushed her fingers through his prickly hair. A rumble of unmistakable pleasure escaped him, startling her to stillness. She'd heard him make that sound a thousand times, usually when Dalena nestled close.

Maybe it's a good dream this time.

He nudged her hand like the great cat he was, and she

didn't have the heart to wake him on a wave of disappointment when he realized she was the wrong woman. In secret and in silence, Pru comforted him the only way she could. Gently she dug into the neck muscles where he hid his tension, and he rewarded her with a noise that was nearly a purr. Encouraged, she worked down to his shoulders, and he responded with an unexpected nuzzle to her throat.

I can't let this escalate. He'll be mortified.

Yet he resisted when she tried to escape. Though he wouldn't admit it, Dom must be starved for physical contact. Sometimes it wasn't about sex, just a need to hold someone close and know you weren't alone. So she ran her nails over his back in a soothing tickle, quietly wincing when she realized she could count his ribs. She remembered how Dom had sprawled on his stomach and demanded that Dalena use her "claws" on him. Their happiness had been palpable, golden and glowing, and he squirmed with pleasure beneath her hands until Pru had to leave the room. It was too much like spying on foreplay.

Now, though, little shivers twitched through him each time she dragged her nails up his back. The downward stroke seemed to soothe him, so he arched against her with increasing friction, tense and relax, until she had no idea if she was consoling Dom or teasing him in his sleep. When her hand stopped, he grumbled an incoherent complaint. She'd never considered the back an erogenous zone; Slay definitely didn't react this way. When she shifted, trying to withdraw a second time, she realized two things.

He was awake. And he was hard.

DOM BATTLED EQUAL measures of bewilderment and guilt.

This was, he figured, the normal reaction to cuddling with a naked person. Nothing to be ashamed of. He'd fallen asleep, and his defenses went down, but he had *no* idea how to extricate himself without making it awkward or awful. She solved the problem by putting a hand over his eyes. To his vast relief, Pru didn't say anything about… that.

"I'm taking a shower."

The least she could do was thank him for saving her life, but she didn't seem grateful. He averted his gaze as she pulled one of the blankets loose. His cock throbbed with an ache so long unfelt that he'd almost forgotten it. While his heart might be buried, his body wanted to fuck.

"Be careful," he said. "Use lukewarm water in case your body temperature is still low."

"I will. One near-death experience a day is my limit."

How could she take this shit so lightly? It rankled, but before he could lay into her, she was gone. Realizing he couldn't let her out of his sight, he followed her to the bathroom, where she shut the door in his face. He paced the whole time. She might try to drown herself in the bath or open up a vein with his razor. Before he knew it, he was banging on the door.

"Hurry up, I don't trust you."

"Still alive." She emerged in a cloud of steam to tease him.

To *tease* him. Like there was anything funny about their situation.

Pru stood there, still dripping wet, and wrapped in a towel. Much to his frustration, his cock held firm at half-mast, and so much dewy, freckled skin didn't help. Dom didn't know where to look and finally settled on her injured arm. Her bandage was soaked, and he clenched his jaw over how little she cared about her own welfare. *Maybe Slay really did send her to die. Unless he guessed I couldn't just watch it happen.* But in all honesty, he wasn't sure his second had the cunning to come up with such a Machiavellian plan.

"Put some clothes on, then come to the kitchen for hot tea and dry bandages."

Her brilliant smile actually made him back up a step. "You're getting bossy again. That's a good sign."

"Don't," he said, unsure what he was even protesting.

"Okay. Do you have something I can put on? I only brought one change of clothes."

Dom didn't want to share his things because the intimacy seemed overwhelming, but he couldn't leave her in a towel or blanket indefinitely. Begrudgingly, he found a ratty shirt and briefs, then offered them to her, and when she emerged from her room a few minutes later, he could only stare, transfixed by the thought, *Pru is wearing my underwear.* She looked small and disarmingly feminine. None of this felt real, as prior to her arrival, his existence had dwindled into a predictable nightmare of loneliness and liquor.

She followed him to the kitchen, where he filled the kettle and turned it on. While they waited for the water to boil, he checked her cuts, then cleaned and wrapped them. Afterward, in silence that was both awkward and not, they drank tea together.

She's winning, he thought. Like he'd forced warmth back into her chilled body, she was reviving him, one provocation at a time.

"My heart can't take any more excitement," he said, once they finished. "I want a shower too, but I'm afraid you'll do something stupid."

"You already took one."

His mouth flattened. "And then I nearly froze looking for you."

With dawning chagrin, she seemed to realize that *he* might need warming too. "Sorry."

"The problem is, the last time I left you unsupervised—"

"I'll stay outside the bathroom while you shower. I'll talk to you, so you know I'm still there. Is that good enough?"

"I suppose it has to be," he growled.

Dom set their cups in the sink and took Pru by her unwounded wrist. If she'd fought him on the way to the bathroom, he might've lost control because while they sat, innocently sipping tea, that insistent need wouldn't go away. He didn't want to shower for warmth, but he desperately required privacy. *Just five minutes. Damn.* The way he felt, so tight and sprung, it might be less.

"What should I talk about?" she asked, as he shut the door between them.

"I don't care. Tell me a story. Tell me a secret. Whatever you want."

Since he was already half-undressed, he only had to shuck his pants and briefs. To lend credence to his claims, Dom turned on the water and stepped under the spray. His cock leapt before he even touched it, anticipating his intentions. *It's been so fucking long.* Shuddering, he took himself in hand as Pru started talking.

"It's strange how life never works out like you expect."
Surreal.

Her chattering outside the bathroom should've slowed him down, but now that he'd started, he couldn't have stopped if she'd opened the door. He used rough strokes, just wanting to quell the beast, and she kept talking, telling some story about how she'd gotten lost on the way to visit the Burnt Amber clan. He remembered that, actually. His father had been pride leader back then. Golgoth raiders had been sighted just beyond the borders, and they'd feared she had been taken. In particular, Slay had been frantic, though once rescuers located Pru, he'd acted like he didn't give a shit.

For some reason, Pru's monologue made him tug harder. Her words blurred into aural ribbons, warm and sweet; he couldn't focus on what she was saying, but he knew she was safe, and he relaxed a fraction. The feeling built in his lower back, spiraling outward, and the hot water stung his sensitized skin in a good way. His hand moved faster. *Almost there. Need to*—he huffed out an urgent sound, and she heard him—she must have—because she paused.

And said, "Dom?" in a tender, quizzical tone.

He came.

Immediately, shame overwhelmed him, and he crouched beneath the warm water to wash it away. Such a visceral reaction, it was inexplicable. Somehow he struggled upright and switched off the tap. In the aftermath, he braced on the wall, unable to steady his breath.

"Yeah?"

"You okay?"

"Fine," he got out.

Actually, he was dizzy as fuck and oddly grateful. There were no bad pictures in his head, nothing but a kind of fuzzy stillness, and that was so much better than it had been that he throttled the impulse to hug her as soon as he put on his clothes and opened the door. Her smile made him look away.

"Feeling better?"

There are so many ways I could answer that.

"Let's talk about sleeping arrangements."

Her brows shot up; they were darker than her hair, nearly black, and their pride mates used to tease her about dyeing them. Russet hair, eyes like a winter sky, so many freckles that nobody had ever counted them. Her nose was short and tilted; like an ass, Slay had once said that if Pru ever shifted, it would probably be into a Persian house cat. Dalena didn't stop hitting him for like five minutes.

Pru cried, he remembered then.

Though she'd forced a smile, Dom caught her later, curled up in tears. She never did it where anyone could see, not that he knew of anyway. *Until today.* He didn't know why that mattered, or if it did. Suddenly he kind of wanted to punch Slay.

But that would mean returning to Ash Valley.

"I'm listening," she said.

"We're both bunking in your room for two reasons. It has the only surviving mattress, and you might wander off somewhere. For the record, I'm tying you to me with a length of string. I'll sleep closest to the door, and if you try to get past me—"

"World of hurt, I know. I'm familiar with your rhetoric."

"My *what?*"

"Bombast. Grandiloquence. Orotundity."

"You're just making up words now." Dom smiled, despite the fact that she was clearly insulting him. Normally, the pride didn't give him shit like this, part of being the exalted leader.

He didn't hate it.

"False. I'd tell you to get a dictionary, but I'm sure you

shredded all the books here and then burned them in a fit of rage."

"I… don't remember."

"It doesn't matter," she said gently. "Things are replaceable. You are not."

He had no words.

It wasn't late enough for bed, so Pru found a deck of cards and made him play some ridiculous game. She told him the rules, then changed them to suit her, but she had a terrible poker face. They gambled with matchsticks, and she pouted when he collected all of them.

It was only when they headed to her room that he realized he hadn't taken a drink all day.

4.

PRU STUDIED THE length of twine that bound them, wrist to wrist, then shook her head with a faint sigh. *How am I supposed to sleep like this?* Though she had three feet of slack, she was on the wrong side of the mattress, but he'd insisted on putting himself between her and the door. Now he lay facing away from her, the curve of his back like a wall between them. As if that wasn't enough, he'd also rolled up a blanket and used it to divide the space.

Judging by his breathing, he wasn't asleep yet. He'd actually laughed a couple of times during their game of Follow the Queen, surprising the shit out of her. Maybe if she wore him down enough, he'd change his mind about the stupid terms he'd set. Pru understood that it was an impossible bar for her to vault over, but she still had five days before the Eldritch and the Golgoth representatives arrived. Raff and Beren wouldn't be pleased over cooling their heels, so she hoped Slay's stalling tactics had improved.

Since her brain wouldn't stop ticking over, Pru found it impossible to sleep. The bolster also pissed her off, as if she couldn't be trusted not to molest Dom in the night. In furtive motions, she slowly unspooled it and drew it on top of the rest of the covers. Eventually, the extra warmth made her sleepy, but she couldn't figure out how to roll over without getting tangled in the string, and she usually slept on her left side.

"Why are you sighing?" Dom asked, sounding exasperated.

"I can't get comfortable."

"Then go back to the hold. Your own bed is waiting."

"Like you'd let me leave. What if I do something dangerous on the way home?"

He glared at her over his shoulder. "You don't ever want me to sleep again, do you?"

Pru couldn't restrain a quiet laugh. "I'd apologize, but—"

"You're not sorry."

It felt strange to lie here talking to Dom as drowsiness tiptoed closer. He was asking something about Ash Valley when she passed out. Later, she woke to find him curled around her, his chin against the top of her head. *Spooning. We're spooning.* Pru stared at the lean arm curved across her waist, the fingers splayed low on her abdomen.

I'd give a lot to be like this with Slay, just once.

But while he was open to having fun, he never stuck around afterward. *Anything more is a bad idea,* he'd always said. Because of how the mate bond formed, she guessed. Sufficient sex could jumpstart it, or a couple could choose each other, then the emotional connection developed over time. Slay couldn't know that she'd always considered herself his, whether he chose to keep her or not. So it was beyond fucking ironic that Dom would be the first person to snuggle with her so intimately, his heart drumming a lullaby against her back.

But she didn't think it was his closeness or his heat that

had roused her. Something else... but though she strained her ears, she didn't catch any alarming sounds. Her sense of smell wasn't sharp enough to detect trouble, either. *I'm probably imagining things.* Yet she couldn't get back to sleep. Dom was strumming her belly slowly now, like she was an instrument he could play. Despite her best intentions, his gentle touch sent a shiver through her.

It's fine. He doesn't know what he's doing.

When he eased his hand lower, Pru caught it and held it still. These were the two arms that he'd tied together, so she was literally bound to him. It wouldn't be hard to untie the knot and slip away, but she lacked the energy to attempt shifting again so soon. Each failure drained her and left her feeling like shit. Not to mention, she hadn't been joking when she said she had tried damn near everything else.

Burn scars marched up her inner thighs, ten years old and faded, a testimonial to a lifetime of quiet desperation. Pain did nothing, so maybe she had never been sufficiently frightened. Passion didn't work either, as Slay once made her come five times and then walked away with an odiously self-satisfied smile.

If I was meant to shift, it would've happened then.

Amid her depressing reflections, a floorboard creaked. *That* definitely *was not my mind playing tricks.* She sat up and shook Dom, who roused with a sleepy glare.

"What now?"

"Someone's here," she whispered.

He froze, head cocking, and then he ripped the string off. "You're right. Stay here."

With a speed and grace she envied, he slipped into leopard form, perfect for prowling a dark house without alerting his prey. Whoever was skulking about, they couldn't have good intentions. What *wouldn't* she give to help with defense instead of hiding? Anxious, she crept to the door, listening for combat, but the enemy must be elusive. Then she caught a furious snarl and the sound of battle. After what she'd put Dom through, he'd probably disagree that obedience was her strong suit, but she had no intention of stirring, until a shadow slid through the open doorway.

By moonlight, she recognized the intruder as Eldritch, mostly by virtue of height and build. The silver of his hair gleamed in the dark, contrasting with the black silk mask that identified him as a Noxblade, an elite order of assassins. A silver blade slashed the air, so close it lopped off a lock of her hair. Somehow she bolted past him toward the smashing glass downstairs, knowing she had no hope of defeating a killer who began training at five and according to legends, likely used poison weapons as well. Under normal circumstances, that would only weaken an Animari, but it also made them easier to defeat in an extended battle.

In the past few years, Dom had gotten thin and weak, so the venom might impact him more. Shifted, he might be able to compensate, but his endurance... Fear took hold of her like she'd never known, especially when she cleared the stairs to find him pinned, snarling, with two Noxblades closing in. She also smelled the richness of Dom's blood. From behind, she heard the whisper-soft footfalls of the one who had tracked her down. If an Animari who could shift and fight had come to fetch Dom, they might stand a chance. Desperation and adrenaline flooded her, and she launched herself at the one coiling his arm for a killing strike.

I don't care, it doesn't matter. I'll bite with my stupid human teeth—

Only as she leapt, her whole body shuddered. *The pain, nobody ever told me about the pain.* It was like being cut open and reassembled with knives, all in the space of an instant. Then she flew toward her target with a grace she'd only dared to dream before. Pru landed on the Noxblade's back and clamped down without hesitation, her sharp teeth savaging the side of his throat. The blood palate like freshly fermented wine, and as her enemy twisted and slashed, he couldn't reach her with his terrible knives. As he fell, she bounded away, small and nimble enough to disappear on the beams that framed the ceiling.

Dom destroyed the other one, first with a claw swipe and then with a lunge and bite that cracked the Noxblade's skull like a dry nut. *Much better odds, now.* Which left a shadow prowling near the stairs. Pru could see in the dark like it was day, and she watched as the sole surviving assassin melted toward the side door instead of pushing his luck. It seemed highly probable that someone had been spying on Dom and gauged him an easy mark. *His defenses are down, drunken stupor. Take him while he's weak or in his sleep.* Imagining those instructions, she let out a quiet snarl and Dom rumbled in response. When he padded after the intruder, she followed. The scent trail led off property and though they patrolled for hours afterward, there was no sign that the killer had lingered, looking for another opportunity.

Finally, he signaled with a toss of his head that they should turn back. Joy suffused her because even following orders felt better in feline skin.

DOM SHIFTED AS soon as they stepped through the kitchen

door, but Pru frolicked at his feet, rubbing against his legs like she *never* intended to change back. Before, there had been no time to reflect, but there was no doubt now. *She saved me. Such a fearless little cat.* Her ambush had been exactly the distraction he needed to get out of that corner and turn the tide. He ran a hand over her back, admiring her markings. Like her mother before, she was an ocelot, larger than their non-shifting cousins but small by Animari standards.

But she did it. She shifted.

Kneeling beside her, he stroked her head and whispered, "Come back now, Pru. It's been too long already."

She vibrated a little, maybe in protest, but then she toppled into his arms, all woman, all naked. Blood smeared her face, especially around her mouth, caked and dry now. Normally, her parents would've talked her through this, but because she was twenty-seven—incredibly late for the ability to kick in—the charge fell to him. Tears streamed from her eyes, and she trembled all over, so hard that he had to hold her close and press her face to his shoulder to keep her from biting her tongue. He took a moment to be grateful that she'd cleaned the kitchen floor.

"Everything hurts," she got out from between chattering teeth.

"I know." He stroked her back. "The older you are, the more your bones have fused. So shifting is tough. And it feels worse than it does for someone who started around puberty."

"Will it al-always be this bad?"

"I don't know anyone who broke through past twenty-five, so I'm not sure. But Arran was twenty, and he said it got better, slowly. So give your body time to adapt, yeah?"

"I feel like I'm dying."

"You're not. Breathe for me."

Her lips parted against his bare shoulder, rousing unexpected chills. If she didn't need soothing so bad, he'd suggest they put some clothes on. Hers lay on the floor in the next room, but she was too shaky to separate yet. After his first shift, Dom recalled clearly how he'd felt, almost eighteen years ago now, clinging to his father, sick with exhilaration and a bewildering, brand-new biological cocktail.

Pru wound herself around him, arms so tight about his neck that he had a hard time getting oxygen. He didn't try to detach her; instead he massaged her biceps in turn, then he rubbed her all over as he'd never touched any woman but Dalena. First-generation kin and mated pairs—they were usually the only ones to see somebody after an initial shift…and this was why.

In time her shivers subsided enough for her to say, "They thought you'd be alone. But… why do the Eldritch want you dead? There are four days before the new negotiations begin and a full two weeks until the old treaty terms expire."

It had been so fucking long since he turned his mind to such questions, but the answer came nonetheless. "Guessing here, but… I'm more moderate than Slay. If he becomes pride leader, it'll be easier to provoke a fight."

"Between the Golgoth and us?" Pru guessed.

He smiled against the top of her head. "Exactly. If we battle the Golgoth to the point of exhaustion—"

"The Eldritch sweep in and conquer both our territories. They're not much for open warfare, so this sort of shadow play is precisely their style."

Her excellent, concise summary startled him so much

that he tipped her head back to study her face. "Since when do you know so much about politics?"

"Since always. I've spent my life studying since I couldn't take patrols, couldn't stand watch, couldn't scout, couldn't fight, couldn't—"

"Hey." He set a finger against her lips to stem that bitter tide.

"Sorry. I still can't believe it. I don't even know how I did it or if I can do it again." She dropped her head to his shoulder, hiding her face. "I'm honestly afraid it was a fluke."

Dom laughed. "Silly kitten. I've never heard of anyone shifting just once. You either can or you can't. It'll be easier next time. I promise."

For some reason, his words seemed to reassure her. She let out a sigh, and her lashes drifted down to create dark crescents on her freckled cheeks. Now that he'd seen her cat form, he probably should've guessed she'd have spots while shifted too. She still hadn't let go of him, like he was the only solid ground with water rising all around her.

Then she sat up abruptly, and he wondered if it had hit her that they were curled up together, naked, again. But no, she pulled his arm up to the light so she could inspect the wound. He had another puncture in his side, and from the heat radiating from it, the dagger had been coated with something because he felt distinctly woozy.

I'll run a fever for a few days, feel like shit. No permanent harm done.

"I'm so sorry. I forgot that you're hurt."

Somehow she found the fortitude to make her legs work, and he watched in stunned amazement as she prowled the kitchen bare-assed in search of the first-aid kit.

I'm not even a man to her. Dom didn't *want* to get pissed off, but her complete indifference rankled. And fine, Ash Valley wasn't a particularly modest pride; they shared communal bathing facilities, but that didn't mean her behavior was normal. But for reasons he couldn't even explain, he didn't say, *Put a damn shirt on.*

My *shirt.*

Maybe it was because she had such pretty tits. *Oh, what the hell.*

Annoyed with himself, he scowled the whole time she ministered to him, washing, fussing, wiping, poking, rubbing him with allegedly healing unguents. By the time she got the bandages on, it felt like his skin was too small. Dom reminded himself that she'd saved him.

And I didn't even say...

"Thank you," he said.

She tilted her head, looking puzzled. "For what?"

"You kicked some major ass tonight... and right after your first shift? I'd have shit my pants if I'd faced a Noxblade on my first go."

Astonished and rapt, he watched the rosy flush that started at her chest, crept up her neck, and colored her checks, making her freckles stand out coppery in comparison. *Didn't anybody compliment her before?* Absurd. Pru had so many good qualities, but she always... blended in. Probably because she didn't want people talking about her, judging her, but that camouflage seemed to have left her hungry for praise.

Her wintry eyes sparkled like the sun on clear water. "I want to be modest and say it was no big deal, but... even I think that was pretty fucking awesome."

A laugh burst out of him, unexpected and liberating. His

chest felt a little looser too, even if his side still stung like a bitch. "No arguments. We should wash up and then get some sleep. They won't try again tonight, but that doesn't mean we're safe."

She nodded. "I was just thinking the same thing. But... I'm *so* hungry. Is that typical? I mean seriously, I could eat a moose."

"Shit, yeah. You just burned like a week of calories. Let's get you fed."

If Arran, the pride seer, had predicted he'd be sitting, naked, on the kitchen floor, eating cold stew out of a pot with Pru, he would've suggested early retirement. As they ate, he reminded her of the changes she could expect: additional muscle mass, increased appetite both for food and sex, across the board sensory improvements, greater speed and strength. She listened, starry-eyed, making him feel like he'd done something to deserve that. Eventually they scraped the pan with their spoons, then she fed him the last bite with a happy smile. And it wasn't strange. Dom had no idea what this was, but when she stretched and rubbed her stomach, he had the sudden thought that it was... good.

"I can live now," she mumbled, dropping their dishes in the sink.

Gratitude welled up in him, so strong he couldn't fit in one word. But he tried anyway. "Thanks."

She turned with a quizzical look. "You already said that."

"Not for that. For... everything else."

For coming. For staying.

For saving me.

"Then there's only one thing left on my to-do list." With an enigmatic smile, she sauntered out of the kitchen.

Out of habit, Dom rushed after her, not realizing until he hit the stairs that there was no reason to stick so close anymore. He hesitated. *No reason to go to Pru's room. No reason to tie her to me.* That insight left him feeling oddly aimless. Then he heard the water running, sounds of her brushing her teeth, and since he needed to rinse off the blood as well, he went up. After taking his turn in the bathroom, he found her waiting in the hall. She looked— well, there was no way to describe it except determined.

"I've met your terms," she said softly. "I shifted. Even killed for you. Only one requirement left, so now... I'm taking you on."

When she touched him, there was no mistaking what she meant.

5.

S HOCK AND DISMAY warred for dominance in Dom's expression.

Not the reaction I want when I'm trying to seduce somebody. But it also seemed impossible that Pru had her fingers on Dom's cock and he didn't take her hand off at the wrist. Instead he stared at that point of contact, and then his expression melted into a sort of helpless regret. She worked not to show how nervous she felt and how *wrong* this seemed.

He belongs to Dalena. Always has.

But when she said he needed to move on with a new mate, he'd replied that when she could shift and take the role herself, then he'd come home. Only then. While Pru grasped he'd meant it as a *when-hell-freezes-over* sort of reply, the pride needed him bad enough that she had to try. If he rejected her, she'd have to crawl back to Ash Valley without him, and the Eldritch might send more Noxblades next time. The consequences of failure scrolled through her head until she trembled.

I'm sorry, Dalena. It's for the pride... and for his benefit. I've never fucked somebody for their own good before. Without the adrenaline left from her recent shift, Pru wouldn't have the courage. It took all her self-control to pull back and smile at him. An answering flicker deep in his eyes told her she hadn't lost him completely. Over the past couple of days, they'd established a connection, so if she could just forget… everything, it might work. She tried to erase the memories of him with Dalena, of the way they were together.

Breathing deep to steady her nerves, Pru set a hand on his shoulder. "You have to keep your word and let me try. Just a kiss, okay? If it's awful, we'll stop."

Like Dom had gone nonverbal, he lifted his chin slightly in reply, but he didn't bend to make it easier. But she knew quite a lot about him, so when she cupped her hand around the back of his head, he dipped reflexively, his mouth close enough for her to take. He tasted of toothpaste with just a hint of Eldritch blood sweetening his tongue.

She pulled back to assess his response. He touched his lips, staring back at her in silence.

"Was it awful?"

Slowly he shook his head. "But—"

For the first time ever, she kissed someone to shut him up. Pru already knew what he would say, and she didn't want to hear it. *Yes, you're still in love with Dalena. And I wish you were Slay. But the pride needs you, and you… you need a reason to live. If not love, maybe I can give you purpose.* Her heart ached a little because part of her wanted to run home and tell Slay:

I shifted. We're not impossible anymore.

Except it was, now. For different reasons. She'd committed to bringing Dom back, no matter the cost, and he'd set the terms. Even if he'd spoken the challenge in a fit of rage, he would keep his promise. Plus, she railed at the idea of being accepted *because* she could shift; Pru would rather make this bargain with Dom.

With effort, she banished all thoughts of Slay. He was her past, and Dom, her future. Pru gave everything to this kiss, delicate pressure, advance and retreat, teasing away to nibble his lips. At first he was so still that she thought he was humoring her, and she expected him to break away with a sympathetic look. *Sorry, Pru. You can't start my engine,* he might say. Except that he finally moved, and *not* to set her away. His arms came up like he was swimming through deep water, and then he tangled a hand in her hair, the other splaying on her back.

Elated, she went for a longer kiss, and he made a low sound in his throat as their tongues flirted. With each flutter, he hardened against her belly until he burned her, hot and throbbing. She wrapped her arms around him in an excuse to get more friction. He especially liked it when she sipped at his tongue, and he actually moaned when she pulled it between her lips.

Mouth-fucking.

When Dom broke away, panting, she thought they were done, and she couldn't even argue that he hadn't let her try. For a few seconds, he only stared down at her with a fevered, incredulous expression, and then he went back in for another kiss. This time, her toes curled because he ate at her lips so hungrily, all teeth and tongue and vicious need. Without breaking the kiss, she pulled him to the bedroom.

As they tumbled to the mattress together, he seemed to startle, like someone waking from a dream. But his cock was still hard, so she nuzzled a trail of kisses along his jaw, skirting his mouth, and then she went for his throat. A muffled groan escaped him, and heat flooded her pussy. *He wants me.* There was something irresistible in that.

Rubbing her wet, open mouth over his chest made him jump and shake. On some level, Pru couldn't believe he was still letting her set the pace. She straddled his hips and lowered her head to lick his pectorals. Other than the hands in her hair, he didn't react, but she felt the tremors working through him. Just like hers, his nipples were hard, and his whole body twisted when she kissed one. Silently he pushed her head down until she sucked and licked to the point that he actually raised his hips, grinding against her.

Impossible to get a breath. On fire and a little dizzy, she slid lower, licking a path over his ribs to nibble the curve of his hip. He fisted his hands in the covers, feverishly silent. Now it wasn't enough that he wanted her. Pru needed him to talk—to make sounds—and it seemed like he was strangling them. Only the rapid rasp of his breath made it out.

"You have to tell me what you want next."

This was a gamble. He might be pretending she was someone else; this could shatter illusions and interfere with his fantasy. His eyes were closed, and his expression radiated a complex pleasure-pain. But she couldn't do this if he wasn't with her.

Dom opened his eyes, and he jerked when he saw how close her face was to his cock. The tremor deepened into a full shudder. She'd never heard his voice sound like that when he said, "Suck me."

She took him without further teasing; he lifted his hips with an alacrity that made her mouth water. No pretense now, no hesitation. He tangled his hands in her hair and urged her on. Pru swirled her tongue beneath the head and grazed him tenderly with her teeth. That made him thrust faster, not even trying to throttle his moans anymore. Like an animal, he hunched upward, and a snarl escaped him when she pulled back. But he couldn't finish like this; that would leave him an escape clause.

Her breath came in soft whines. "It's time, Dom. You promised you'd come back when I could shift, when I became your mate. I'm offering myself now. Will you be mine?"

Something flashed in his face, not reluctance exactly, but he didn't want to say it. He *had* to say it. She squeezed his cock.

"Yes," he bit out. "Fuck yes."

Pru held him still as she mounted. His eyes just about rolled back in his head when she sank down on him. From this angle, he felt massive inside her. She paused to adjust, but it wasn't fast enough for him. He framed her hips in his big hands and lifted her, then dropped her down, fucking up into her with uncontrollable need.

"You feel so sweet," she whispered. "Talk to me, Dom."

A desperate, strangled laugh escaped him. "Nothing to say. Just have to come."

"You want to come for me." Some devil drove her as the pleasure spiked. She had to keep him fastened tight in this moment. He had to focus on who was making him feel this.

"Pru..." Her name slid out of him, part moan, part protest.

"That's good. Do it. Faster."

"You like it." Suddenly, he was talking, just as she'd asked.

"I love it."

"Harder. Like this." He pulled her down to punctuate

his words. "You feel so…oh, *fuck*."

With a moan, he lurched upright and wrapped his arms around her, so they held each other and worked in quick, tight pushes. She dug her hands into his back. As he came, he kissed her, wet, sloppy and open-mouthed, and that was enough to finish her off. It was a light orgasm, but he felt it as he shuddered and filled her with heat.

Afterward, she expected him to disengage and make her feel shitty-guilty about the whole thing. Instead he stayed close, hands gliding over her sweat-slick back, so unexpectedly dear that tears prickled her eyes. She dusted kisses over his chin, his shoulders, and nuzzled him until he kissed her back, a sweet little thank-you of a caress.

"It wasn't awful," he said with a thread of laughter in his tone. "You win, Pru. We'll go home in the morning."

DEEP IN DOM'S gut, guilt had both claws and tentacles, chewing and lashing until he could hardly stand it. But when she threw herself on him like he was a sex grenade, he fucking lost his mind. Now, the truth gnawed at him—after the Noxblade attack, he'd already made up his mind to go with her. In his defense, he *had* tried to speak.

And now the die was cast. She'd offered and in the heat of the moment, he had accepted. The emotional aspect of the mate bond might take a while to form, but he couldn't go back on his word. People paired up for all kinds of reasons, and he could do a lot worse than Pru for a lifelong companion. *But what the fuck am I going to tell Slay?* He knew damn well his best friend had been waiting his whole life for a miracle. *Now that it's finally happened, I get the girl?* Even to Dom, that seemed ten kinds of jacked up. Though he didn't approve of how Slay protected himself and kept Pru at arm's length, he'd seen his second's eyes, how he watched her when he thought nobody was paying attention—so much longing that it hurt him to log it.

Though Pru winked out, likely exhausted by her first shift and then fucking him into submission, he couldn't sleep. Partly because the Noxblade might circle back and partly because he was weighing the variables. *I could tell her I was just being an asshole when I offered that deal.* All of that was even true. But she'd take it wrong, as people had been making her feel inadequate her whole damn life. As Dom recalled, she stopped eating for three days when Slay turned her down. *No, it's done, agreement made.* In all honesty, returning to the hold with Pru at his side pushed his reluctance to the fair side of bearable. Maybe she could prop him up long enough to keep the pride from figuring out that he was an empty husk.

Fuck it. I'm a terrible person, and Slay let her go.

He held her until dawn when he roused her with a kiss to the temple. "Moving out."

"Hope my clothes are dry. I really can't travel in your underwear."

Laughter startled him. It had been years, so he'd almost forgotten he could make the sound, but she'd amused him so many times already. "Have you always been this hilarious?"

"I think so."

Fortunately, her things were ready to wear, if somewhat crispy. He liked that she had no shame around him, no awkwardness. You'd think they had been waking up together forever. Dom dressed in a hurry, then they layered up. Pru led the way out of the retreat, heading down the steep steps like she'd never doubted she would drag him home. In fact, she was even humming, some cheerful little song.

"Did you bring the Rover?"

"Yep. It should still be powered up enough to get us back, unless…" She trailed off, and he could guess what she was thinking.

"The Noxblades disabled our vehicle."

Without replying, she quickened her pace. It was only an hour and a half driving, but if they had to run, it would change the scale. Plus, it would mean arriving in cat form, which he supposed was a hell of a way to announce her new status.

Just then, her foot slipped, so he grabbed her arm. "Hold up. See the melting ice? You could break your neck."

And that… no. Just, no.

Her pale gaze seemed to see everything, even the quiet dread he'd rather not acknowledge. "Sorry. If the Rover's broken, rushing won't fix it."

The view during the descent awed him all over again. A snowy valley spread before them, filled with evergreens frosted white. Cold and crisp, the air sparkled in his lungs, until he wished he could bathe in it. Dom couldn't remember the last time he'd paused to appreciate the beauty of the territory he had been appointed to protect. Pride leadership didn't always pass down by bloodline. If they'd found him weak or wanting, they would have chosen someone else after his father died.

Golgoth bastards.

She seemed to sense his anger, but she didn't flinch from it. When she took his hand, all the badness flowed away, leaving him calm and focused. Dom felt fucking bulletproof, like words and ammo alike would bounce right off. The stairs yielded to a rocky path that wound through the trees to the clearing where she'd left the Rover. As he'd half-suspected, their ride was smashed to shit, wires cut, solar panels broken into shards.

Pru sighed. "Good thing I can cat up, huh? Otherwise it would take us forever."

"Go for it," he said.

After taking a deep breath, she closed her eyes. But he could see that she was tense and scared, the prospect of failure practically immobilizing her. Dom had no idea if this would work, but it couldn't hurt. He pulled her close and rubbed her back, like he had right after her first shift, right after their first mating. As he whispered nonsense, tiny reassurances into her ear, she eased against him. A little shiver ran through her, and then he was holding a squirming ocelot, tangled up in her clothes. When her head popped free, her sparkling eyes seemed to say she hadn't expected it to be so sudden. Laughing, he extracted her.

She bounded around in the snow, tail lashing, as he stripped, chucked their things into the defunct Rover, and changed. For him, it didn't hurt, more like diving into deep, cold water. A shock, holding his breath, and then he could run like the wind. He had no worries that she'd keep up; she might be small, but she was quick.

The ground spoke of various animals that under other circumstances might be prey, but he didn't intend to spend the night in the wild. Like she'd said, Pine Ridge and Burnt Amber were already waiting for him. Delaying would only make it worse. Now and then, he caught a whisper of Noxblade, but that trail led away from the hold.

He's returning to report, not hunting us down.

Pru's rumbled growl said she smelled it too. She gave him an inquiring look, but he pushed on. *No time for a detour, and we're not a raiding party.* Since he'd been waiting for an ambush, he relaxed a fraction. Not completely, of course. While there should be nothing but wild animals and Animari between the retreat and the hold, complacency could be catastrophic.

I was sure. So sure our borders were secure.

Never again.

Tension made it impossible for him to focus on anything but guiding them safely to sanctuary. Pru, on the other hand, made it clear that this run was the most fun she'd ever had. She frolicked in the snow, scratching at trees and generally acting like he had at the age of twelve, all brand-new in leopard skin.

It was...

Fucking adorable.

For her sake, he even regretted it a little when they crested the final rise and Ash Valley lay before them like a jewel. An ache started in his chest. *How did I stay gone so long? How?* His grandfather had designed the town, and that fact only increased his pride in its beauty. The pale, perfectly mortared stones of the wall gleamed in the late-afternoon sun, nearly blinding him when it reflected on the snow. Beren from Burnt Amber always called this the city of bone because of that ivory gleam, but there were no dead hidden beneath their streets.

Dom greeted the guards on the intercom, ignoring their amazement as they opened the gates. Pru wouldn't know how to go about this; it was her first time. Inside, he took her to the changing room, applicable in more ways than one. Since it wasn't always possible to bring back the clothes you had on when you left, they kept the shelves stocked with basic attire in varying sizes. He slid back into human form and slipped into a tunic and trousers, wondering if he'd have to shift-whisper her again. But no, she only seemed to have a hard time with going cat. She'd worn human skin for twenty-seven years, after all.

"I never even knew this was here," she said in a marveling tone.

This stone chamber wasn't anything special, but until now, she'd had no cause to use it. For that reason, it must seem magical. He could almost hear her thinking, *I lost my clothes, so I need this place. Just like everyone else.* That wonder kindled in her eyes and illuminated her smile, so radiant that it drew an answering look from him, irresistible as breathing.

The moment shimmered between them, fragile as spun glass.

"The fuck is going on here?" Slay snarled.

6.

THE TIMING COULDN'T be worse.

In contrast to Dom, Slay was burnished and strong with a mane of dark hair that tumbled past his shoulders. Sharp features, high cheekbones, a divot in his chin, and thick-lashed golden eyes. Always, always, it was his eyes that seduced her, time and again. A storm was building in them as he stared at her naked body.

It wasn't like Slay had never seen her this way, but everything was different now. A muscle ticked in his jaw when Dom stepped between them to shield her. Looking ready to kill, Slay strode forward, but Dom didn't give ground. To diffuse the tension, she went ocelot and darted around Dom's legs. Her tail high, she showed off a little, and Slay stilled.

Slay murmured, "Beautiful. You're so beautiful."

His eyes glinted, as if he might be on the verge of tears. Then he knelt and reached for her with a shaking hand, a smile brightening his face like sunrise. Pru only let him graze one of her ears before backing off. Wearily, she returned to human form. *Dom was right. It's easier.* The pain no longer dizzied her, at least, but she wasn't looking forward to this exchange.

Slay beamed at her, all sparkling joy that she was about to crush. "So that's why you're naked. For a minute, I thought…" He laughed and shook his head.

When he reached for her, Dom blocked him again as she dressed. "We should talk."

It would be easier to let Dom take all the heat, but that would imply they weren't equal partners and she needed him to sort her issues. Plus, she owed Slay one last conversation and a proper good-bye. Of course she'd still *see* him, but things could never be the same. Their failing relationship had been on life support for years, but it shuddered and died the day he decided she was expendable. For all he'd known, Dom might've turned into a killing machine, left alone for so long, and she'd lacked both claws and fangs.

So she tapped Dom's arm lightly and shook her head. "Go greet our guests. I need to take care of things here."

"You sure?" Dom brushed her shoulder in passing, support or reassurance.

Slay's brows shot up, over the touch or at her use of "our", but he had to suck it up. For better or worse, she'd be leading Ash Valley alongside Dom from this day forward. That would take some getting used to, but she intended to be a strong, reliable partner.

No matter what.

She traded a look with Dom and then tipped her head toward the door. With his eyes, he asked if she was all right on her own. Faintly surprised Animari silent communication had already developed, she nodded. Slay balled up a fist as Dom left.

When the door clicked shut, Slay punched it. "I *really*

don't like this vibe. Since when am I a thing to take care of? Clue me in before I lose my shit."

Part of her wanted a better setting than bare gray walls, plain shelves, and benches, but did it really matter *where* she said this? While she wrestled with the kindest way to break the news, he settled his agitation. One breath, another, and then he was smiling again.

It would be better if you were angry.

"Never mind." Typical Slay, he didn't wait for explanations. Instead he pounced, buried his face in her hair and then recoiled. "You smell like Dom. Why the fuck—?"

"I made a deal," she said softly.

"Don't jerk me around, Pru. It's not funny."

"I'm not. Dom and I, we're mated." There was no way to be gentle. Best to drop the truth like a bomb and deal with the fallout.

Baring his teeth, he snarled, "You went away mine and came back his? How does that make sense? Especially now. You know—you fucking do know—that I've been waiting."

Closing her eyes briefly, she sucked in a sharp breath. This was the first time he'd ever said anything remotely like that, and it didn't soothe the bitter sting since it came *only* after she'd shifted. Mostly she recalled the shape of his back as he strode away. She also remembered the brutal humiliation of his rejection five years ago, sitting across from Slay and his parents as her nails cut crescents into her clammy palms. Her mother wore a determined smile as she made small talk, and then her father carved through the chatter with his customary bluntness.

"From what I know, these two want each other. We're here to put our stamp on the match, if your family's willing."

Pru had watched the rebuff forming in Lorelle Slater's eyes, but to her eternal shame, Slay spoke first. "I need a stronger mate, someone capable of fighting beside me. Sorry."

That old hurt broke wide open, bolstering her resolve, and she shook her head. "I wasn't yours, and you were never mine, either. You made sure I knew that. I can't even count how many times you said it... *This was fun.* As you left."

"So you fucked my best friend to get even?" Like somebody taking a punch, he rocked a little as he said it, hands opening and closing as if he didn't know what to do with them.

"That's not why. Dom needs me, the pride needs him, and you? Don't deserve me."

"When did you start hating me?" he whispered. "And why didn't I know about it?"

"I don't. I'm just... done. You had ten years of my devotion, and you rewarded me by weighing the odds and deciding the pride could afford to lose me."

"Fuck, no. I never thought for a minute that Dom would hurt you." Torment kindled in his lambent eyes, as if she'd cut out his heart and eaten it in front of him.

Pru didn't let his pain weaken her when she had truth-ammo left to fire off. "We were attacked by Noxblades. If I hadn't managed to shift, they would've executed both of us."

His legs seemed to give out, and he collapsed onto the nearest bench. "So this is for real."

"It is. I think... it'll probably be easier if we put some space between us. Eventually I'm sure we can—"

"Be friends? Screw that." Slay let out a bitter laugh.

"You weren't alone for the last ten years, sweetness. Did you ever see me with anybody else or even hear a whisper of it?"

"I figured it was only a matter of time. I've heard your mother talking."

He sagged forward, elbows on his knees, and he couldn't meet her gaze for a few seconds. "It's not like I haven't been ignoring her for years."

"Now you don't have to." That response came out quiet and cold.

Slay swallowed hard, gazing up at her with pleading eyes. "Well, shit. I never imagined you'd give up on me. I always..." his voice hitched, "...thought we were forever."

She considered saying, *I wanted us to be.* But it wouldn't change anything. *I won't cry. I won't.* Instead she took a step back.

"Everything changes. And love doesn't survive untended."

The next words he spat at her through clenched teeth. "Fine, I'm a dumb shit and I didn't make it clear how I feel, but whatever I did wrong, it's hard not to feel like you traded up. Why settle for second when you can fuck your way to first?"

That poison verbal dart landed. "I finally understand how you could treat me like Latent was the worst thing I could be. You're just fucking *small*, Slay."

"That's not what you said a couple of weeks ago."

"And... I think we're done here."

As she turned for the door, suddenly he was there, wrapping his arms about her from behind. His familiar scent dizzied her: sage, cedar, and sandalwood. "I'm sorry. I lost my mind for a minute. Please don't leave me. I don't care what happened on the mountain. Just... tell Dom it was a mistake."

Tears burned in her eyes and the back of her throat. It was too late; she'd made a promise, and Pru took her vows seriously. Besides, love wasn't everything. Respect and friendship mattered too. If she could keep Dom on a steady keel, Ash Valley would be better off. She let Slay hug her for a moment longer and then she broke his hold.

"You were never strong enough to do that before," he said in a soft, shattered voice.

"I'm different now." And it was true. She wasn't the woman who had waited for his love endlessly, wishing she could command it.

With that, she put Slay behind her and didn't look back.

MORE THAN ONCE, Dom was tempted to double back because Slay had looked murderous.

Only the certainty that his second wouldn't hurt Pru kept his feet moving in the opposite direction. The hold bustled with activity as he strode down the main thoroughfare. All the buildings gleamed with the same stone that formed the wall. A few things had changed in his absence; they had torn down the old repair center, and there were three new shops. Belatedly, he wondered how the factories were doing, as when he'd left, he let go of the reins completely. Members of the pride greeted him with varying levels of disbelief, excitement, and relief. Two of his father's friends hugged him and pounded his back so hard that he'd probably have bruises.

"You were missed, son." Caio had been his father's second, and he'd declined the role of pride leader when

Dom's father passed.

"Thanks."

"Get to the hall before Beren flips a table. He's not happy about the delay, says he's got some disturbing news about the Golgoth. But Slay has been plying him with liquor while betting his whole hand on Pru."

It wasn't a bad move. She came through.

"Raff?" he asked.

"Busy flirting with Magda. You know how that wolf is."

"Thanks for the update."

"We'll talk more soon." With a pat in parting, the older man went about his business, leaving Dom to do the same.

After making the bear and wolf leaders wait this long, ten minutes longer wouldn't hurt; it would be bad manners to greet them dressed in what amounted to pajamas and slippers. He got stopped twice more before he reached the residential annex. Outside the apartment he'd shared with Dalena, he hesitated. Finding everything exactly as she'd left it would cut him wide open, but it might be even worse if all her things were gone. Briefly he rested his brow against the door. But it wouldn't do for anybody to catch him being weak. The pride needed to believe he could steer them through the coming crisis.

On a bracing breath, he entered the pin; the lock clicked open and he stepped inside. Somebody had obviously been cleaning, as the furniture shone, not a speck of dust anywhere. Same gray sofa with burgundy pillows, same overstuffed armchair, but the blood-stained carpet had been removed and replaced with a fluffy rug patterned in black and gray. Their wedding portrait still hung, and Dalena's smile hammered him until he couldn't breathe.

This is where she died.

He skirted that part of the salon and went to the bedroom, pulse pounding in his ears. But she was gone from here; his clothes hung alone in the wardrobe, and none of her powders or lotions remained on the shelves. For a moment, he breathed in and imagined he could smell the honey and lemon of her skin. But the room only gave back clean linen and chamomile soap.

With effort, he forced down the sadness and got ready as quick as he could. Half an hour later, Dom inspected the loose fit of the charcoal suit he'd chosen. Still, with a fresh shave and proper clothing, he no longer looked like a scarecrow. As he left the apartment, he felt lighter, hurrying toward the main hall.

Slay must still be talking to Pru because he only found Beren, Magda, and Raff in the lounge, which was now decorated in russet and gold. They had been offered drinks and refreshments, and he felt sure they both had been allotted private quarters where they could rest and curse him. Beren was an enormous man with a shock of silver hair; the years since Dom had seen him hadn't been kind, weathering his face and giving him a perpetual air of irritation. Raff hadn't spotted him yet, but the way he was smiling at Magda, he didn't seem to mind the wait.

"I apologize for the inconvenience," Dom said smoothly.

"Finally stopped contemplating your navel?" Beren rose and offered a hand for a crushing shake.

Typical of the bear boss.

"I thought you went up the mountain to die," said Magda, slapping Dom's shoulder.

Mags had been chief of security since before his father died, and she was taller than Raff by a couple of inches, but the differential didn't dampen the wolf lord's interest. Raff came over to greet Dom; his dark hair was longer than it had been at the last meet, and he'd grown a full beard, shaped to partially hide a fresh scar on his right cheek. Dom didn't ask; unless it impacted the alliance, he had no interest in wolf pack or bear clan affairs.

"Good to see you. Finally," Raff added.

It seemed best to play host. "Have you eaten?"

"Several times." Beren waved an impatient hand. "There are far more important matters to discuss."

Nodding a dismissal at his security chief, he led the way to a cluster of comfortable chairs. This part of pride leadership didn't trouble him. "Tell me."

"There have been skirmishes on the northern border." Beren seemed sure he would immediately grasp the severity of the situation.

"Golgoth?" he guessed.

The bear leader nodded. "The same. Raff hasn't spotted any yet in the east, but my scouts are picking up a lot of activity, troop movements and supplies being shipped."

Dom sighed. "That doesn't bode well."

"They'll wait for the treaty to expire," Raff predicted. "If I had to lay odds, I'd say they'll send someone to stall during peace talks and strike while we're focused here."

"But where?" He didn't necessarily expect an answer.

"I've assigned my best to find out," Beren said.

"What do we know about the delegate the Golgoth are sending this time?" he wondered.

Beren had the answer. "Alastor is the youngest prince, old King Theno's get. I don't think he's set foot outside Golgoth lands before."

"Personality?" Dom glanced between Beren and Raff,

but both men shrugged.

Past precedent suggested this Golgoth prince would be brutal and bad-tempered; otherwise, he wouldn't have survived the abattoir he called home. Now and then, captives broke free and crawled back to their clans, but they were never the same afterward, scarred in every conceivable way. Ash Valley had one such survivor, and he never left his apartment. Both Magda and Arran had visited Eamon often, as of three years ago. On a surge of guilt, Dom wondered how he was faring.

I let so much shit slip, like I'm the only one who matters.

"I have some news about the Eldritch." Dom offered a concise version of the Noxblade attack at the retreat.

Beren scowled, standard for the old bear, and Raff rubbed at his beard like he wasn't used to it. "No disrespect to Slay," said the wolf lord, "but I'm glad as hell to see you."

"I'll have some hard questions for the Eldritch when their party arrives."

"They'll deny it to the death," Raff muttered.

That sounded about right. While he could probably smell a lie under normal circumstances, the Eldritch had witchy ways and dark magic. Everyone in Ash Valley would be on edge until the two emissary groups departed, and it fell to him to avoid mortal insults and an escalation to bloodshed on their home ground. The prospect made him tired.

"Unless either of you have pressing business, I'd like to defer more detailed discussion for when we're all fresh in the morning. It's been a hell of a day."

Since he'd told them about the sabotaged Rover and running from the retreat, he got understanding nods from both Beren and Raff. A few more formalities, clasps on the back, and Dom made his escape. By this point he was sweating, and he really fucking wanted a drink. *Talk about being thrown into the deep end.* The Golgoth threat swam in his head like carnivorous fish, devouring all other thoughts.

Which was why he didn't see Slay coming. When his second grabbed his lapels, the murderous expression he'd noted before hadn't faded any. If anything, Slay seemed like he planned to pull Dom's head off and punt it.

"You backstabbing sack of shit. How could you take her from me?"

Despite knowing honesty was probably the wrong move, Dom answered, "Look, you've got it the wrong way round. I didn't steal her, *you* sent her to me. So... respect Pru's wishes. I promise I'll look after her from now on."

"Tell that to Dalena," Slay snarled, before punching Dom in the face.

7.

WHEN PRU TRACKED Dom down between the admin center and the residential annex, he had a split lip that was already swelling. Her mouth compressed. "Slay?"

"I gave him one free shot." He also carried a palpable air of fatigue, with lines bracketing his mouth and shadows beneath his eyes, but she didn't think that weight came from his second.

"You shouldn't have. I'm sorry he's hurt, but we didn't do anything wrong." Stretching up on tiptoe, she inspected the damage. "Let's get that iced down. The last thing we need is for the other leaders to carry tales about dissent in our ranks."

"Beren wouldn't do that."

With a faint smile, she noticed he didn't vouch for Raff in the same way. "It's been a hell of a day, huh?"

Dom answered with a sigh that said he was burnt to a nub. "No arguments. But we haven't talked about... much of anything. I should've asked your father first, made sure he has no objections. And I need to make a formal announcement—"

"He'll be so happy I can shift—and I look so much like

Mum when I do—that he won't care about anything else. Don't worry about acknowledging me right now. Save your energy for strategizing with Raff and Beren, and then the conclave, of course."

"Why do I suddenly think that arguing with you will prove impossible?"

Pru grinned. "Just accept that I'm always working for your welfare, and there will be no need for troublesome independent thought."

Delight spiraled through her when he laughed. "So I'm to become a puppet monarch?"

"It will only hurt a little when I attach the strings." Teasing, she dug her fingers into his back, momentarily forgetting how much he liked being touched there.

"Mmm." He arched, eyes drifting half shut. "Keep doing that, and I'd probably let you."

For a moment, she worked her hand up and down his spine. "There *is* something we need to discuss, though."

"Hm?"

"I don't want to move into your old apartment. It would be better to have a fresh start."

Anxiety percolated because he might think she wanted him to forget Dalena, but it was only that she couldn't stand living where her best friend died. *That's not healthy for him either.* Scrubbing away the evidence of the most horrific crime in Ash Valley history? Pru had done it, sobbing so hard she almost threw up. It had been hell taking care of the place in his absence. Pru had boxed up all Dalena's things because Dom was too mad with grief, then she secured them in storage. Afterward, she'd aired the flat, dusted, and polished once a week.

But I can't live there.

"What do you have in mind?" Dom only hesitated slightly, making her think he was open to the idea.

"My place would be better. We can redecorate completely so it feels like ours, if that's all right with you."

"I don't have the mental energy for lamps and cushions, but I appreciate the offer. What about your father, though?"

"He's almost never home. Will you mind when he is?"

Dom shook his head. "It'll be nice, I think."

"What?"

"Being part of a family again."

After Dalena's murder, her family moved out of Ash Valley, leaving Dom alone. Pru understood why they'd want a fresh start, but maybe he wouldn't have spent three years in seclusion if the pride had tried a little harder to support him. In retrospect, she squirmed over how she'd let him down.

"Well, I have two aunts and an uncle, plus like ten cousins. I can invite them all over regularly to pester you."

"You're threatening me with your extended family? I say bring it on since I'm not the one cooking all that food."

"We'll see how cocky you are when my little cousin is climbing you." Smiling, she took his arm. "This way. Second floor, next building."

"Why do you think I don't know where you live?"

Color washed her cheeks. "Sorry. Force of habit. To be honest, I don't expect anyone to remember anything about me."

"I'm not just anyone, Pru. Not to mention, we've been friends forever. For instance, I remember how often Slay made you cry pulling your hair."

"Good times," she said wryly.

Dom looked like he wanted to say something else, but

in the end, he swallowed it. "Will you help me pack?"

"Of course."

Stepping into his old apartment sent a shiver through her. *How would Dalena feel about this? Does she think I'm stealing him?* But since it was for the pride, her friend would probably understand. Still, she couldn't look long at the photo of Dom and Dalena, so perfect together, so in love. Her chest tightened as she went to the bedroom. Half an hour later, Pru carried two bags to the front door, and Dom caught up with a couple more.

"I think that's everything I need in the short-term. Eventually I'll give this place back to the pride and let admin assign a newlywed couple here or something."

"Sounds good."

They walked in companionable silence to her flat. At the door, she paused. "The pin is my mother's birthday, 3105."

"I'll make a note."

His eyes flickered, likely remembering that the code to his old apartment had been Dalena's. But he only nodded as she punched in the numbers and ushered him in. Pru couldn't remember the last time he'd been here, or if he'd seen the place since she rearranged the furniture. Done in earth tones, it was a cozy place with lots of pictures commemorating their happiest moments. Her mother smiled from the shelves beside the tan sofa.

"How is it?"

"I never want to leave."

At first she thought he was kidding, but when he pulled off his jacket and fell onto the couch, loosening his shirt collar, it seemed he did feel at home. With a soft smile, she carried his belongings to her room in two trips. Since he'd closed his eyes, Dom didn't appear to realize she was unpacking for him until she was half done.

Looking abashed, he hovered in the doorway. "That's daunting efficiency, Pru. If you keep this up, you'll spoil the shit out of me."

"Somebody should," she said.

"I feel like I ought to make some compelling arguments otherwise, but all I've got is this stupid smile." Dom did look softer than she'd ever seen, except when he'd forgotten about pride business and played with Dalena. "How much longer will you be on vacation?" At her surprised look, he went on, "You must be on winter break, unless the school schedule has changed."

"It hasn't. I've got almost three weeks to help out with the conclave." Pru couldn't hold his gaze, as it felt strange to be the sole focus of his attention. Everything happened so fast that it didn't sink in before, but now realization settled on her like a slow-falling snow. Guilt swept her in a suffocating wave, and for a moment, she couldn't breathe, seeing only Dalena's eyes and imagining how her friend would feel.

"I'm glad," Dom said. "I'll need you to get me up to speed."

Pru nodded. "Why don't you take a bath? I'll finish up in here, find you some pajamas, and then get started on dinner."

He shook his head, laughing quietly. "Shower, yes to clothes, and I'll help you cook."

God, this is strange.

But not in a bad way. It didn't take long to clear out space in her drawers to put away the rest of his clothes. She left loose drawstring pants on the bed, along with briefs and a thin, comfortable shirt. For obvious reasons, she had no idea what Dom normally wore to bed. Pru could hardly believe he was here for good; they'd be sleeping together from this day forward.

When he came out of her room, dressed and drying his hair, she was slicing meat for a fry-up. At least that was what her mother had called it when she cut up whatever was in the fridge and sautéed it together. He took the knife from her and made short work of the few vegetables that were still good. It turned out fairly tasty, she thought, and he didn't complain.

As they ate, he filled her in about the Golgoth activity in the north. "Hard not to worry about that," she muttered, once he finished.

"Don't. That's my job."

"Mine is to halve your burdens, however I can."

His gaze locked on her, all citrine intensity. "When you say shit like that, it is impossible for me to fathom why Slay didn't lock you down years ago."

"Funny, huh."

Though he doubtless intended his words as a compliment, they stabbed her in the squishy bits. Tears threatened, so she gathered their plates and retreated to the kitchen. Pru thought she'd have a minute to compose herself, but when she turned, Dom stood there with a penitent look.

"I'm so sorry. I shouldn't have said that."

"No, I don't want you to be guarded. Dalena and Slay were part of our lives for so long… it doesn't make sense for us never to mention them. It's critical that we stay honest, if we're building something together." That sounded wrong, but it was the path they'd both chosen.

He nodded. "Just know… if it was me, I'd have claimed

you regardless."

DOM CURSED HIMSELF inwardly. Throwing Slay under the bus was a shitty thing to do, and he'd hurt Pru with his careless tongue. His conscience might be technically clear, but he also felt like a backdoor man who crept around while the husband was away. *They weren't bonded,* he told himself. *It's not the worst thing anyone ever did.*

His mouth smarted, reminding him that Slay felt otherwise. *Gonna be a while before he forgives me. If ever.*

Pru studied him for a long moment, then her expression brightened to a willingness to tease. "Easy for you to say. I can shift, so you won't be tested."

"You have a point. Wash up if you like. I'll clean the kitchen."

Given what she'd said about helping him, Dom didn't expect her to accede, but she smiled and thanked him. They hadn't made a huge mess, so he made short work of the dishes. By this point, it was late enough that he felt like going to sleep, but it seemed wrong to retire without Pru on their first night together. So he got a random book from the shelf and was dozing with it on the sofa when she finally came out of the bathroom.

"Sorry I took so long. Ready for bed?"

"More than," he answered.

She crossed to him and took his hand, tugging him to his feet. "Don't be polite. This is home now."

"I know." He followed her to the bedroom, where they worked in tandem turning down the covers.

It's been forever since I slept in a real bed.

As Pru eased under the blankets, she said, "I think it's

natural for it to be a little strange at first. But… we have a lot going for us. Friendship. Respect. And we're definitely… compatible." By the look she slid from beneath her lashes, Dom took her meaning.

Despite his general exhaustion, a flicker of heat shimmered through him. "True."

"So as long as we communicate well and remember to ask for what we want and need, I'm sure we can make this work." This sounded like a pep talk she had been giving herself, so he didn't poke holes in it.

Besides, she made some fair points. "I can't promise I'll be good at any of that. Hell, I didn't talk to anybody for quite a while."

"I won't expect immediate perfection," she said, smiling.

"Thanks." Dom pulled the covers over him and settled in.

When she rolled onto her side, facing him, he did the same, because it seemed like she had more to say. Hopefully the conversation wouldn't run long, as he had no idea if he could stay awake, and it'd probably piss her off if he drifted while she was talking. At least that had been the case with Dalena.

Reaching over, she switched off the light, plunging the room into shadow. "This next issue is a bit more complicated. I mean, if we'd been lovers for a while it'd be different…"

"Just tell me what's on your mind. Honesty is our motto, right?"

"Definitely. At first, it might be difficult to come out and say that we're… in the mood. So I propose some kind of signal."

Suddenly wide-awake, Dom realized she was talking

about sex. *Yeah, I can't grab Pru and growl, "Let's fuck."* Part of him still couldn't believe they'd done that. It was odd enough being in bed with her when he only meant to sleep. During the daylight hours, his mind had skittered away from the heat that sizzled between them. *Probably because I was starved for it, and she was riding an endorphin wave.* Even so, they'd both want more sooner or later, as it wasn't like orgasms came with a warranty.

Good for six months or six thousand miles.

He thought for a moment. What would look innocent to anyone else? "Like, if I kiss your neck, it means—"

"Yes," she whispered. "And if I run my nails down your back..."

Dom barely checked a moan. The idea of a secret sex signal turned him on something fierce. He imagined her coming to him in the middle of the conclave with some innocuous excuse while her fingertips whispered filthy things in a slow slide down his spine. With no further prelude, his cock stirred, half-ready to play.

Somehow he managed a sensible response. "If you don't pick up the cue, I'll know it's not in the cards."

"Saves us both some embarrassment," she said.

At the moment, he didn't know if he could sleep because his dick just kept getting harder, and they'd only had this sweet, awkward little conversation. Dom weighed the odds. *She may not want to, but...* he leaned over and brushed his lips against her throat. Her eyes widened in the moonlight, but she scooted closer, no more than a whisper between them. A light shiver worked through him as he remembered the feel of her coming on his cock. Last time, he had been so shocked and passive that it was a miracle she'd gotten anything out of their encounter.

This time I'll make her moan.

Like they were petting furtively, he touched her over her pajamas, running his hands down her body until she arched and sighed. Then she pulled his palm to her breast, and a hard little nipple nudged for attention, so he lowered his head. Dom licked until the fabric clung to her. Through her top, she gasped at the pressure of his lips and teeth.

I wanted to die until you came to me. The thought crystalized as he nuzzled her shoulders and collarbone, and the anguished sweetness of needing Pru, even this much, made him want to drive her out of her mind. He teased her with forays to her bare belly until she squirmed against him, her breath coming in soft gasps. She smelled of hot, willing sex to the point that he went lightheaded, and he must be hitting her exactly the same way.

"Please take my clothes off." Her voice sounded husky.

"Right after mine."

Dom just about shredded what he had on, wanting to be closer to her. Pru didn't wait for him, however. By the time he was done, she'd flung her pajamas all over the room. *Why didn't I notice how sexy she is until now?* He couldn't stop looking, tracing a path with his eyes over the swell of her breasts, the indent of her waist, the faint curve of her stomach, and the delicious roundness of her ass—all of her dappled beautifully. A full day wouldn't be long enough to lick every place he wanted.

"Why are you staring?" She didn't try to hide, but he spied the first hint of shyness, endearing after her determined seduction.

"Because you're eye candy, and I've got a sweet tooth."

Obviously delighted, she giggled. "I can't believe you said that with a straight face."

Her laughter went to his head like the strongest liquor.

No more provocation than that, and suddenly he was shaking. Another minute and he might combust. "Pru..."

"Yes?"

"I don't think I can wait. Is it okay if we skip a few steps?" With unsteady hands, he stroked her pussy, once, twice, and his mouth watered over finding her wet.

In response, she fell back and opened her thighs, but he wanted something else, *had* to have it. Snarling a little, he flipped her and lifted her hips, then he slid beneath her, face first. She startled when he licked her; there was no strangling her moans as he tasted and sucked. When his tongue grazed her clit, she rubbed against his mouth in reflex. He didn't know how long he could control himself, so he grabbed her hips and rocked her on his face. Pru took the rhythm and ran, gasping in helpless pleasure.

"I can't," she moaned.

Only she didn't stop riding his chin, squirming until he could drown in her. Her orgasm astonished him since he felt crazed instead of skilled. In the midst of it, he pounced on her and took her from behind in a hard thrust to savor the last few pulses of her tight, slick pussy. The melting bliss nearly made him come, so he held still, shivering and swearing.

"I'm okay. I'm okay. I just need a minute." He didn't even know what he was saying, and then she started pushing back on him, demanding more.

"Oh, fuck." She squeezed down on him, and it actually felt like she might be going again.

"You can't, you can't be—" Only she was. Her pussy did magical things to his dick, and again, until he couldn't breathe or think or even thrust.

Dom came so hard he almost passed out.

8.

YEARS AGO, DALENA had whispered, "Mating frenzy," and Pru gave her a look.

"You're making that up," she'd replied.

"No, I'm serious. It's a real thing. You think sex was good before, but when you've just agreed to be bonded, it's wildly intense. You'll find out for yourself."

Now, lying in bed with Dom, she wondered what her friend would say now. *But of course, if she could comment, I wouldn't be here. I might never have shifted and I'd still be waiting for Slay.* It seemed ridiculous that she was discovering the truth of the mating frenzy with Dom.

She sighed faintly, and he shifted to settle her head on his chest, his hand playing idly in her hair. "You okay?"

"Just… surprised," she said.

"By what?"

"The fact that our bodies communicate so well." There, that was clear, but she still blushed over saying it.

"It's a little unexpected. But I'm glad you want me. I'd almost forgotten how it feels."

Pru shied away from that admission; it skirted too close to forbidden territory. She'd made peace with the idea that some parts of him would always be off-limits. Since Slay had been partitioning their relationship for years, she was used to that, and at least Dom wouldn't treat her like a dirty secret or hide her from his family.

Her silence seemed to trouble him, however. Because he touched her cheek and prompted, "You do, right? While we're together, you're not thinking of…"

Slay, her mind supplied the name he didn't say. Pru shook her head quickly. "Of course not. When I'm with you, I'm *with* you."

She could have said that he was different than Slay, wilder. Slay prided himself on how crazy he could make her without letting his guard down. Maybe that had been because he didn't want them to get attached, even accidentally. That was also why Slay had doled out their physical encounters like starvation rations. But Pru refused to open the door to comparisons; there was no way she'd win against Dalena, and she didn't want to.

"Glad to hear it." He sounded sleepy, so she let him drift off.

Once he winked out, she breathed him in with a sort of bittersweet bewilderment. He smelled of fresh mint and aspen wood, delicious to the point that it was hard not to nibble him. Lying beside him, Dalena must have felt exactly this way, and Pru fought tears that tasted of betrayal. Pru had spent her life trying to work hard enough to make up for the fact that she was defective, and she didn't know how to stop that anxious *trying*. In time he might find her bothersome or overzealous. The day would probably never come when the shadows left his eyes, but maybe he could be content with her.

Eventually, she slept.

She dreamt of a particular autumn afternoon, of golden sunlight, crisp air, and the fluttery of orange and crimson leaves. The four of them on a picnic, Dalena and Dom had gone cat, tumbling each other and snarling with mock ferocity, while Slay rested his head in Pru's lap and lazily demanded she pet him, like some kind of emperor. Pru sank her hands into Slay's hair, as she had a thousand times before.

"This is perfect," he purred.

SUDDENLY, THE SCENE soured—and Dalena shifted back to human form, her eyes tricking blood tears. Though Pru didn't recall them moving, Dom and Slay had swapped places and he was *touching* her while Dalena watched. He nuzzled her thigh with his cheek, then moved so he could kiss higher, and she squirmed, pinioned between pleasure and shame, and it was like she was the only one who could see Dalena anymore, a sorrowful ghost fading in the sunshine.

"How could you?" her best friend wept.

Dom was gone when she started awake, her entire body trembling. It took Pru a long time to settle down.

After she gathered herself, she got out of bed. Dom must have picked up her pajamas because they were no longer strewn about the room. Abashed, she got dressed and discovered that he'd left tea and toast on the table for her, a kindness that made her misty as she ate breakfast. Before she could tidy up, a knock sounded at the door. Pru checked in case it was Slay, come to fight with her some more, but she brightened when she spotted her cousin, Jocelyn. As usual, Joss only waited a few seconds, then let herself in.

"Rumors are rampant," Joss said with a grin. "So I came straight to the source."

"Good morning to you too." Sighing, she put her dishes in the sink and got a sponge.

"Don't be grumpy. I've got juicy gossip. Slay got seriously shitfaced last night and had to be thrown in the drunk tank until he settled down. I'm willing to bet a week of patrol duty that it's related to the whispers I'm hearing about you."

While she washed her cup, she summarized the current state of affairs for Joss.

"Holy shit, you can *shift*. You realize you just doubled your workload, right? In addition to teaching, you'll also have guard rotations, and... I suspect you're too happy to care about that." With this reaction, Joss established why she was Pru's favorite cousin and closest friend since Dalena died. "Congratulations, copper top."

Anyone else would be fixating on the mess I've made of my relationships.

"Don't call me that."

"You prefer carrots?"

Pru sighed. But she knew exactly why Joss was acting this way. "It's all right. You can ask about Dom and Slay if you want."

"Whew. I thought I might die of curiosity. So...?"

Joss listened with occasional nods, but she didn't interrupt. When Pru ran out of words, she glanced at her cousin, who was now sitting at the table with her chin propped on her hands.

"I don't know if you want my actual opinion or unconditional support."

"Honesty is best."

"Considering how long you and Slay did that dance, it's a little shitty you didn't break it off clean first, but there were extenuating circumstances, and I've never liked how Slay treats you, so it could be argued that he deserved a hard lesson. All told, my vote goes to Dom." Joss offered an impish grin. "Of course, that might be because I can say that my cousin leads the pride. What kind of perks can I expect, huh?"

"You're ridiculous," she said, laughing.

Joss tossed her hair, which was curlier than Pru's, and so dark that unless the sun hit it, you wouldn't realize how red it was. She'd also escaped the freckles and gotten green eyes like a mossy pond. The fact that she hadn't chosen a mate related directly to the fact that she refused to settle down. There had been two or three contenders, but when Joss laughingly challenged them all to a series of quests to win her hand, they backed off so fast it had been embarrassing.

"Seriously, though, all I care about is that you're happy. You'll be surrounded by the patter of little paws in no time."

"I doubt it. We've barely talked about where to live, so I won't flip the fertility switch until we agree it's time.," she said, recalling how Slay's mother hinted she had inferior genes.

Wandering to the kitchen, Joss helped herself to leftovers. "I've heard that human women have *no* say over when they get pregnant or if they do."

"That's quite a design flaw. But I think maybe the Eldritch have the same problem."

"Golgoth?" her cousin asked.

She shook her head with a half-shrug. "Can you imagine someone sending a survey to investigate their reproduction? I've never even seen one in the flesh."

"They do seem like stories we're told to keep us from roving too far from the hold, but come to think of it, our curiosity will be sated in a few days." Once Joss scarfed down the food, she tossed her dirty dishes in the sink. "More importantly, I can't *wait* to patrol with you. Have you talked to Caio about getting on the roster?"

"Not yet. As you can see, I'm still in my pajamas."

"Well, put some pants on. Let's take care of business."

Thus motivated, she rushed through getting ready and followed her cousin to the cramped office that completed admin-related tasks like housing assignments and guard duty. Caio glanced up and then rose when he recognized her. To her astonishment, he executed a half-bow, the like of which she'd seen old pride mates use with important guests.

"Er—"

"Welcome, matron."

Pru traded looks with Joss, who was wide-eyed and failing to quell a bad case of the giggles. "You don't have to be so formal."

Caio ignored that. "What can I do for you?"

"I want to join the rotation. Do I need to fill out a form or prove that I can shift…?"

The old man opened the security assignment log book and perused it with complete focus. "Not necessary. I'm checking to see where you'll fit best. I understand you're an ocelot?"

"That's right."

"There's a recon mission needing one more. Would you like to join that team?"

"Please," Pru said, ignoring her cousin's disappointed huff.

Caio wrote down the pertinent details and handed them over. "Good luck and congratulations. Your achievements enrich the pride—on all levels."

"Well, that was weighty," Joss muttered as they left the admin office. "I thought he was about to genuflect."

"He's old school. You know how seriously they take everything."

And then Pru noticed the crowd gathering in the square, all eyes focused on her.

WHEN PRU TOLD Dom, *don't worry about an announcement,* he heard, *I'm not important enough, don't bother.* And fuck that.

So between strategy sessions, he spread the word among the guards, who were the biggest gossips in the pride. He didn't need to do much to assemble an audience, and anyone who missed out would hear the story soon enough. Pru froze on the steps of the admin building, and he had to go fetch her. She even resisted a little when he took her hand. It seemed better to go back up the stairs, high enough that everyone could see him.

"I'm sure you've already heard some speculation, so I'm here to confirm. Pru has consented to be my mate and to lead Ash Valley as my partner."

Resulting whoops sounded from the crowd, and some-one shouted, "When's the party?"

"That has to wait until after the conclave, but I wanted to clear up any doubts. Please congratulate us and spread the word." Dom lifted their joined hands over his head and then carried Pru's fingers to his lips.

Congratulatory roars rang out in response, but one

angry face leapt out at him. Slay glared from the back, simultaneously homicidal and heartbroken. After another moment, he wheeled and stalked off. Pru withstood the wave of good wishes, but she didn't look happy, and her nails dug into his hand. After a while, he extricated them from the thinning throng and led her toward a quiet niche. On closer inspection, he saw that her face was red to the point that it looked painful, and she was trembling. Tears stood in her eyes as she jerked her hand away.

"I can't believe you ambushed me like that," she snapped. "What's *wrong* with you?"

This wasn't the reaction he'd expected. "But I did this for you."

"Didn't you realize that I hate being the center of attention? It makes me want to throw up. I don't know what you were thinking, but—"

"Sorry. I'm so sorry. I should've come up with a better way. But you have to understand, I want you beside me. I didn't want you feeling like you have to hide." Dom tried to pull her close, and she flattened her palms on his chest, preventing him from completing the embrace.

"That grand gesture would've delighted Dalena," she said quietly. "But I'm not her."

"I'm sorry." Dom didn't know if he should push, but he had the feeling he'd stepped on a butterfly. "What should I have done, then?"

"I told you clearly not to worry about it. I mean, I just explained to my cousin Joss, and she'll tell everyone she knows. I don't have to stand on a stage with you to legitimize our relationship. Honestly, it feels like showboating."

He dropped his hands, feeling like she'd produced a

scorpion tail and stung him. "You think I arranged this to... rub us in Slay's face or something?"

"That's not what I said. Or meant."

"It looks like I misjudged the situation," he said.

Pru let out a slow sigh and knuckled tears from her eyes. "Look, I don't want to fight. You're just used to pleasing a different kind of woman."

There was no way to keep from flinching; it felt like he'd given her Dalena's clothes to wear. "I'll work harder and figure out what makes you happy."

Finally, she let him draw her close. "Maybe you thought I was being a martyr when I said to focus on other issues. But I meant it."

"Noted. Will it bother you to attend the next session with Beren and Raff? They want to meet you, and your perspective will be helpful."

She shook her head. "I'm fine in a professional setting, and small groups are no problem either. The surprise today, I would've done better if I had a chance to brace for it. Some people thrive on attention, but for me, it's like diving off a high board. I can do it, but it requires time and preparation."

I should've remembered how she preferred being invisible to people gossiping about her Latent status. That won't change overnight.

"Is there anything else I should know? So I don't hurt you again with good intentions."

"Off the top of my head, I can't think of anything. I appreciate that your heart was in the right place." She put her arms around him gently. "And... I'm happy you're proud to be with me. If I hadn't been so upset, I would've said that first. I'm sorry I started out scolding you."

"Don't apologize. If you don't tell me, how will I learn?"

Now that the first sting had faded, gratitude trickled in. She could've pretended everything was fine until a knot of resentment developed. Her honest anger meant she trusted him enough to work through it, together. That, more than anything, gave him hope for their future, and it shone in him like the brightest evening star.

"You make a good point," she admitted.

"Am I allowed to kiss you before we go act like authoritative leaders?"

The furious color had subsided, and she smiled, a dimple cutting into her left cheek. Her lower lip was fuller than the top one. Even her smile seemed different, a touch secret and just for him, but also delightfully crooked, as one corner of her mouth pulled higher than the other.

"That can be arranged."

She went up on tiptoe; Dom met her halfway, framing her face in his hands. She tasted of salt and jam. *Tears and the toast I made her. I have to do better.* As he fought the urge to pull her even closer, someone cleared their throat behind him. Turning but not letting go of Pru, he recognized her cousin, Joss.

"So this is where you disappeared to. You can't keep your hands off each other, huh?"

"Joss," Pru chided.

Dom chuckled. "That was more like a kiss of peace. Don't ask."

"Wasn't going to. Welcome to the family."

Joss astonished him with a warm hug and a sloppy kiss on the cheek. Laughing, he had no idea how to react. Pru had threatened him with her effusive extended family, but this was starting sooner than he'd envisioned.

She pulled Joss away with a dark look, whispering, "I'll

deal with you later." Pru turned to him, a blush rising, though she tried to play it cool. "Shall we go talk to Raff and Beren?"

After checking the time, he swore. "They're expecting me back in two minutes. I only asked for a short recess during the last meeting."

"Come on, then. We'll talk more soon," she added to her cousin.

They rushed to the conference room, where as he'd predicted, the wolf and bear leaders were already waiting. Beren had taken a chair, but Raff paced like the generous-sized space couldn't keep him from feeling hemmed in. The wolf lord scowled as Dom stepped in.

"If I didn't know better, I'd say you're *trying* to insult us."

"Your father never would have treated his allies this way." That judgment, delivered by the stone-faced bear chief, cut deep.

He would never have failed on other levels like I have, either.

Before he could apologize, Pru stepped forward and bowed low to each man in turn. "This is my fault. You may not have heard, but Dom and I are recently mated. In fact, we were together at the retreat when you arrived, and just now, he held a brief assembly for my sake. So I must beg your pardon for any slight you may have suffered. I promise, going forward, we'll treat you as the most honored of guests."

"When you put it that way, dear lady, it would be most churlish of me to deny you goodwill and my warmest wishes for your happiness." Raff took her hand and pressed a kiss onto its back.

Her smile quivered at the edges, but she conveyed a

compelling impression of delight. Still, Dom wanted to knock the wolf's arm away because it took him *far* too long to let go. When Raff finally retreated, he had a snarl lodged in his throat.

"We didn't know," Beren said. "And it explains much. I'm glad to meet you. May Ash Valley prosper for your partnership."

I'll be damned.

With a bow and smile, Pru settled their raised hackles, and talks regarding the imminent negotiations resumed smoothly.

9.

P RU WISHED SHE could retire, but after her big talk
about halving Dom's burdens, it seemed wrong to tap
out so soon.

If Beren and Raff had brought their women, she would
be entertaining them, but Beren's mate had passed on two
years ago, and Raff had yet to settle down. It was nearly
midnight, and they'd eaten in the conference room.
Smothering a yawn, she put on the kettle for the third time.
They were currently arguing about where they needed to
increase patrols, as the one thing they did agree on was that
the conclave offered the perfect opportunity for the Golgoth
to strike.

"We're the ones who will suffer," Beren said, slamming
a hand on the table. "We share a border, and I've *shown* you
the troop movement reports that are coming daily."

If Dom had looked tired before, it was nothing compared to tonight's exhaustion, and the conclave hadn't even
started yet. "I can send twenty guards to augment security
in the north. Any more and I risk leaving the hold vulnerable."

"I'll match that," Raff said.

Finally the bear leader seemed appeased. "Then let's end things here for tonight. We can't afford to be sleep-deprived when the enemy arrives."

"Assuming they have any interest in renewing the Pax Protocols," Dom muttered.

Raff sighed. "That attitude will make negotiations break down before they get started."

"You two are young," the bear said. "And you don't remember what it was like before, but that makes it hard as hell for me to take either of you seriously. Fucking cubs."

Pru put a hand on Dom's shoulder to keep him from snapping in reply, but Raff had nobody to check him. She tipped her head toward the exit, suggesting silently that they should escape while the other two argued. This wasn't pertinent, just wolf and bear blowing off steam. There was no reason to watch or mediate.

Dom seemed to agree because he padded out on silent feet. In the hall, he popped his neck and groaned. "How did my father do this? I'm out of patience with our *allies*."

"Practice, I expect."

"I can't shake the certainty that shit is about to go horri-bly wrong."

"Not tonight. Let's get some sleep. Tomorrow is the last day to decide how you'll vote in response to the Golgoth and Eldritch requests for concessions."

"You don't think I can persuade them to sign an identi-cal agreement…?"

Pru laughed. "Doubtful."

Because he really seemed to be dragging, she took his hand, and he managed a smile. "Thanks for going the distance. Believe it not, that's their best behavior, so it would've been worse if you weren't there."

"No problem." Belatedly she realized she hadn't shared the result of her trip to the admin office, so on the way home, she told him about the recon mission tomorrow night.

Dom paused in entering the pin. Already he remembered without hesitation—3105—and that gave her an odd, happy flutter. "Are you sure you're ready?"

"Please don't tell me you want to lock me up for my own protection, now that I can finally shift." That would spark a bigger fight than the one they had earlier.

"No. I'm just... worried. Not about your ability, just the timing. If that Noxblade finds you or the Golgoth snatch you—"

"Is this because we're recently mated, because I was Latent until a few days ago, or some combination of the two?" Pru studied his face as they went into the apartment.

Whatever Dom might have said, he didn't complete the thought. Instead, they found her father drinking at the table. A tall man with silver hair and deep-set eyes, he was thinner than he had been the last time she'd seen him, an echo of the way Dom mourned for Dalena. Blearily he glanced between the two of them and raised his brows.

"It's late for visiting," he pointed out.

But Dom stepped up, saving Pru the worry. "I'm sorry I didn't ask your permission first, sir. The truth is, I'm not a guest since Pru and I have agreed to share our lives. She's shifting now, not sure if you heard." Dom wrapped an arm around her shoulders, adding, "Prettiest ocelot I've ever seen."

That startled her dad so much he tipped over the tumbler of amber liquid. With shaking hands, he righted the glass and then lurched toward her. "Just like your mother...

Is it true?"

"It is. Do you want to see?"

"If you're not too tired."

As she stripped, her father averted his eyes. It was weird since most Animari started changing much earlier in life, so she shouldn't be doing this for the first time at her age, which made it a little awkward. But his reaction when she went cat made the minor discomfort worthwhile. His bloodshot eyes teared up as he knelt to pat her back.

"You do look like her. I'm so glad you're not a mangy lynx like me."

Bending down, Dom scooped up her clothes. "Do you mind if we get some rest? We have another long day tomorrow."

"Not at all." Her dad was smiling, happier than she'd seen him in six months.

Pru followed her mate into the bedroom and shifted back with an audible groan. "I shouldn't have done that. Feel like passing out."

"You were right about his reaction. I think you could've brought a Golgoth home and he'd have only seen an ocelot."

"Told you. I know people and I pay attention."

Muscles sore, head fuzzy, she brushed her teeth and crawled into bed, not waiting for Dom to finish his routine. By the time he joined her, Pru was already half-asleep. It surprised her when he spooned up behind her; he'd done it on the mountain, but this time he was awake and presumably knew what he was doing.

"This okay?" he whispered.

"Mhm. But... can *you* sleep?"

He hesitated before replying, "It's the only way I can.

When I'm touching you, I don't dream, or at least, I don't remember any nightmares."

Nobody had ever said anything like that to her before. The flutter she'd felt earlier twisted into a shimmering bluefish, and it felt like it was leaping against a line tied directly to her heart. Pru put her hand over his where it rested on her stomach, quietly delighted by the heat of his skin. He answered the touch by kissing her temple, *not* the sex signal, thankfully, because with her dad in the next room crying into his liquor, she wanted to sleep more than fuck.

"Night, Dom."

"Sweet dreams."

In the morning, she got up early enough to fix a good breakfast. Her dad hadn't passed out on the couch last night at least, so maybe her shifting milestone would help him turn the corner on his grief. He came out bleary-eyed when he smelled hot coffee and frying meat. She didn't have the heart to scold him when he plucked a slice off the platter and nearly swallowed it whole. From the look of him, he hadn't hunted enough to stay healthy as a lynx.

"When did you decide on Dominic? I thought you were holding out for the other one. That hothead jaguar." After their failed pairing, her father always pretended he couldn't remember Slay's name.

There was no point in telling the story like she had with Joss. Her dad wanted to hear one thing only. "It happened pretty fast, but I'm happy."

"That's all I care about."

Impulsively she hugged him and then wrinkled her nose. "You reek. How long has it been since you washed up?"

"I don't remember."

"No breakfast unless you shower."

Dom sauntered out of the bedroom with wet hair in time to catch that. "Looks like I'm in luck. Okay for me to go ahead?"

"Of course. You only have twenty minutes."

"*We*," he corrected. "Unless you plan to leave me hanging today?"

"No, but I may not be able to stay as long. Recon mission," she reminded him, bracing for him to list the reasons why it was dangerous.

But as Dom tucked into the food, he said, "I've been thinking about that, and you have my support. You can't live in a cage, just to ease my mind."

MUCH AS I wish you could.

But if Dom limited Pru because of his own fear, that would make him a shitty excuse for a leader. Not to mention, Dalena had been "safe" at home when she died. So avoiding potential danger wouldn't guarantee Pru's safety. What Slay had said gnawed at him, and sometimes he wondered, *What makes you think you can keep her safe? Especially now.* But she was the first person to break through and make him care again—about her, the pride, and himself.

Her reaction was everything he could've hoped. She stilled for a second, her eyes brightened, and she threw herself at him, locking on to his neck in a fervent hug. Laughing, he caught her and then wouldn't let her up when she realized she was sitting on his lap. As Dom tried to get her to feed him—just one bite—her father came out of the bathroom. Deep eyes took in the scene, and then he smiled.

"That takes me back." Without telling Dom to unhand

his daughter, he helped himself to a generous portion of breakfast.

Pru startled him by stuffing bacon in his mouth, then she squirmed away to scarf her own food quickly. She still needed to wash up, and things were pleasantly chaotic as they got ready. As they tussled over who would clean the kitchen, her dad laughed.

"I'll do it. There are no important meetings on my schedule today."

"Thanks, Dad." She kissed his cheek and grabbed Dom's arm. "Hurry, we only have four minutes now, and we promised not to keep them waiting again."

It turned out that she'd adjusted the clocks, so when Pru said "only four minutes", she really meant, *We'll get there fifteen minutes early.* For the first time, they arrived at the conference room with time to spare. Dom wavered between amusement and irritation, but at seeing her relief, his sense of humor won out.

"Are you this earnest about everything?"

"Pretty much," she said, smiling up at him.

Somehow he restrained the urge to kiss her. He'd never hear the end of it if Raff caught him going at his mate in the conference room. So Dom contented himself with brushing his knuckles against her cheek. Because his people knew their business, the table had already been set with tea and sweets. He didn't have a chance to sample any, however, because a messenger burst through the door, breathless, and tried to speak.

"Easy." He recognized the young guard, an eager puma. "What's happened?"

"The... the Eldritch party, sir. They've arrived early and will be here any time."

Dom swore. Those witchy assholes wanted to catch the pride flatfooted and force them to start the negotiations in the red, especially in regard to hospitality. But... it could be worse. *If the Golgoth show up too, for instance.*

He gave the orders at once. "Convene an honor guard. Whoever's on duty, get them in formal dress."

As he said that, his clever mate had her phone out and was already dialing. "Beren? This is Pru. The Eldritch have preempted further discussion. If you could collect Raff and head for the gate—oh, you're with the wolf already?" A pause. "Excellent. Then summon your men so you don't lose face during the welcome ceremony."

The messenger nodded and raced off.

Fortunately, his father had set a precedent for formal attire, even during ally talks, so he had on a decent suit, and Pru looked lovely in a dark blue dress. She smoothed it over her hips and tugged at the bodice with an expression he recognized as sheer nerves. Dom stroked her arm in passing as he headed for the door.

"Come along, clever cat. Your habit of arriving early may have just saved us a great deal of embarrassment."

"That's a coincidence," she mumbled, hurrying after him.

He set a cracking pace to get to the gate by the time the Eldritch party requested entry.

The plaza was full of pride guards in dress black while Beren's crew stood behind him in matching mahogany, and Raff's retainers were lined up in heather gray. Despite a few breathing hard here and there, nobody would ever guess how wildly they'd just scrambled.

"What are you waiting for?" he called to the guard on the wall. "Invite our guests in."

The Eldritch came thirty strong, at least five Noxblades among their number. At their head, a tall, lean man strode through the parted gates garbed in scarlet and silver. His guards were likewise dressed in red so dark, it likely wouldn't show bloodstains. It was impossible to gauge an Eldritch's age just by looking, as most of them had hair so fair, it could be ash blond or silver with age. Dom had heard that the Eldritch inspired old legends in humans to the south, tales of long-lived elves and immortal fey folk.

Dom stepped forward. "Welcome, Lord Talfayen. It is our pleasure to greet you."

The Eldritch lord had sharp features and eyes like twin coals. He raked a contemptuous glance around. "Perhaps it would be best if *we* hosted the conclave next."

Since they'd showed up early, none of the preparations were in place. There were supposed to be dried herbs on the ground and wreaths hung, woven of hothouse flowers that reflected a desire for peace. If Talfayen wanted proper royal treatment, he should've stuck to the timetable. With some effort, he locked his annoyance down.

Pru was right to drag me back. Slay would already have laid this asshole out.

His mate bowed low, both hands pressed to her chest, and Dom caught a flicker of surprise from one of the guards up front. *That must be an Eldritch custom. She's saving my ass.* Talfayen returned the gesture with one elbow, which meant...hell if he could remember what. He'd studied all this shit endlessly, but then—

Murder.

Exile.

And so much liquor. It would be a miracle if he recalled half of what he needed to know.

"Welcome to our holding," she went on. "May our shadows bind as one and no disharmony sour our song."

The Eldritch wore a faint smile. "You know our ways?"

"A little," she answered.

"Burnt Amber greets you." As the elder Animari at the gathering, Beren inclined his head instead of bowing. Judging by his expression, he wasn't inclined to kowtow to a group he called war-holes in private, a contraction of warlock and asshole.

"Likewise, good health and tidings from Pine Ridge." Raff didn't hesitate, but the glint of his eyes as he swept low told Dom this was polite bullshit.

An awkward silence crept up—with Talfayen stone-faced and seeming as if he might snub the other two lords. *Not an auspicious beginning.*

But Pru stepped into the breach with a smile that looked sincere even to Dom. "Will you accompany us to break bread and thus formally accept our hospitality?"

"Certainly. Are my men welcome?" This appeared to be a test of some sort, and Dom realized he couldn't let Pru carry this encounter on her own.

He shook off his quiet amazement and offered his own bow. "Of course. Our meat and drink we offer freely." The words tasted odd and archaic on his tongue, but the Eldritch cleaved to old ways more than any other faction. *Probably something to do with their long lives.*

With Pru beside him, Dom led the way to the hall where kitchen staff worked feverishly to lay out a feast that they were woefully unprepared to serve. Possibly he could delay—but his mate was already whispering to the guards, to Raff and Beren. *She's an effective leader, all big-eyed please and thank-you.* All the men looked like they'd cut out a kidney if she asked for one. Which should please him greatly.

It didn't. Their mate bond was too fresh and fragile for him to be comfortable with seeing so many other males casting their gaze at her.

Once everyone settled—the most important dignitaries at the head table—each squad of Animari guards ran drills to show their readiness. It wasn't much of a dinner show, but it was the best they could do on short notice. From across the table, Dom caught Pru's eye and lifted his chin in thanks. The mood softened slightly as their guests sipped at the good wine he kept flowing during the soldierly display.

"It's delicious," Talfayen said, raising his glass to study the ruby liquid.

"We have a small winery. I could give you a tour if you like." That proved to be a safe offer when the Eldritch lord nodded with apparent interest.

Taking that as a cue, Pru got up and topped everyone's glasses off, circling the table with a friendly air. As she reached Dom, she bent and whispered from beneath her curtain of hair:

"I smell him. He's here, the Noxblade who tried to kill us."

10.

MUCH LATER, ONCE the welcome party ended and after the guests were settled, Pru finally got a moment alone with Dom. He waited until they reached the sanctuary of their apartment, but first took the precaution of checking each room. Her father wasn't around, which was just as well because she didn't want him involved in anything this dangerous. Pru didn't speak until her mate signaled the all-clear.

"Well?" she prompted. "He was seated at the next table, the Noxblade with the red eyes. What are we going to do?"

"For now? Nothing. We have no proof. It's not as if we inflicted an injury we can point to and say, 'A-ha!' when it's revealed."

"They'll probably try again. Maybe that's even why the Eldritch came early."

"I'll quietly spread the word among the guards. We should consult with Magda and Slay, too, provided he's calmed down enough."

Pru nodded. "I'll call them."

"You call Magda. I've got Slay."

With a tilt of her head, she wondered if he could possibly be worried about her talking to her former love. Pru decided that was absurd and dialed up the security chief. "The sooner you get here, the better. We have a situation."

Magda's sigh came across loud and clear. "Can't you tell me now? I'm up to my ass in minutiae since the war-holes showed up early."

"In person, please. It won't take long." She could've mentioned Dom or Slay, but it bothered her to think she needed backup for a short conversation.

"Fine. Where are you?"

"My place. See you soon."

She and Dom both disconnected at the same time. "Slay's on the way."

"Magda too."

The first knock sounded five minutes later. Pru had the kettle on by then, not that she really expected anyone to want tea. She let Magda in with a smile, but the other woman looked too harried to respond. Her frown expanded to include Dom as well.

"You two think I don't have enough to do?"

"This is important, or you wouldn't be here," Dom said. "And when Slay gets here, I'll clue you both in."

A minute later, he opened the door for Slay. At first Pru had a hard time looking at him, but she squared her shoulders and resolved not to make things weird. Briskly she set out four cups and poured a splash of tea into all of them. After trading glances with Dom, she decided to start by filling the security chief in on what happened at the retreat.

By the time she finished, Magda was spluttering. "Why wasn't I informed *immediately*? I need to adjust everything, and now we've already got the enemy inside our walls."

"I should have briefed you sooner. Sorry." Dom inclined his head, but from where Pru was sitting, it didn't seem to appease the other woman much.

He took up the narrative from there, explaining how they'd both scented the surviving assassin. Slay finally stopped looking sullen. "He's actually here? Ballsy."

"We're not sure what the Eldritch are planning. I have no intel on whether they're going to escalate. That attack may have been a solitary effort, and since it didn't pan out, they may see how it goes with the Golgoth while waiting for another opportunity. Any questions?"

Magda shook her head. "I'll circulate information among the guards and tighten patrols."

"I think we should pull some men from the external rotation. Our focus should be here, not making sure there are no trespassers in the wood." To Pru, Slay's strategy seemed solid, but Dom reflected for a minute before nodding.

"Sounds good. Two teams can be spared from recon and scouting runs."

She waited until the others left to say, "That better not include my group tonight."

"You still want to go?"

"Why wouldn't I?"

For a long moment, he stared at her, visible conflict warring in his gaze. But at last he let out a sigh. "Never mind."

Holding eye contact, Pru acknowledged Dom's misgivings scattering like startled birds, but she appreciated that he trusted her to decide what was best. She wouldn't let fear define her.

At the appointed time, she presented herself at the changing room; relief trickled in when she realized Magda would be leading the mission. She recognized Arran, the pride seer, and one of the guards. But when the last member of the team arrived, she clenched her jaw.

"Is it wise for both of you to go?" she asked.

Magda grinned, seeming to find the question funny. "Asserting yourself as pride matron? Don't worry, I swapped with Slay. I have too much work here, and he volunteered to take over."

I bet he did.

"Sorry," she said.

"Not a problem. Your opinion matters, and you'd be right if we were both going. Stay sharp, everyone."

There was no point in complaining. If Slay wanted to witness her shifting, let him. He said a few words about their unit goal, something about tracking unreported Golgoth movements, but Pru couldn't focus. *Stop it. Don't let Slay screw this up for you.* She waved when Magda took off and made small talk with Arran. No amount of composure could erase the weight of Slay's gaze. It was so awkward stripping down in front of him. He watched her remove each article of clothing with a stare so intense that she fought the urge to turn away. *I have no reason to hide. No cause to cower.* Nobody else seemed to clock the tension, and if they did, they were kind enough not to mention it. Pru put away her clothes and went ocelot; this time, the discomfort was more akin to unexpectedly slamming an elbow against a table. In fact, she could picture the day when it wouldn't pain her at all.

The group fell in behind Slay. Instead of going out the main gate, they circled through a passage built in the wall and slipped out a concealed side exit. At first she wondered why Dom hadn't come this way when they returned from the retreat, then she guessed that he likely didn't want to give away pride secrets on the off chance the Noxblade was still tracking them.

Pru had never been part of a patrol before, but she emulated the others. It was impossible not to notice that she was the smallest cat. Not the size of a human pet, no matter what Slay had said, but definitely not on par with Magda in terms of combat ability, either. She admired Slay's jaguar form as they prowled away from the hold, and then wondered if that could be construed as disloyal to Dom.

Darkness cloaked the forest, but it also brought new clues. Sensory input nearly overwhelmed her, scent trails wafting to her. Part of her wanted to chase them—to explore—but the group's focus didn't permit kittenish behavior. Since this was a recon mission, they had a clear goal. *I just wasn't listening when he explained. That's on me.* At this point, she could only do her best not to be a liability.

Snow in the air.

The wind tasted crisp, laced with complicated messages that she could only half-decipher. She padded behind the others, listening now and then, but so far, she registered normal night noises. As the group novice, however, she might not notice subtle yet crucial clues. For hours, they ran as a group, steadily pushing north, and Pru restrained the desire to play. Since the Golgoth were supposed to arrive in a few days, the official convoy must be on the move. It would mean trouble if they found any sign of additional troops inside the borders.

Slay angled his head, an indication they were breaking right. A peculiar smell laced the ground. It carried a chemical tang, but it didn't smell like any fuel she'd ever encountered. The others circled, appearing equally perplexed. Whatever this was, it scraped the trees and broke branches on the way in. From the depression in the ground, some kind of machine sat here for a while, and it scorched the earth. Her nose whispered of carbon and charred vegetation.

Definitely not our tech.

Animari machines ran on biodiesel. *Plus, we respect the environment far too much to create anything that could do this.* As Pru studied the site, pain pinched her shoulder, and the world went fuzzy. The last thing she saw was Slay's back as something dragged her away.

LORD TALFAYEN HAD been talking for forty minutes. Once, the Eldritch leader took a long breath, and Dom thought that meant he would have a chance to respond to the litany of complaints. No such luck. Talfayen resumed, and Dom went back to taking notes. From their expressions, Beren and Raff were no happier about the state of this meeting.

"Lord Talfayen," he cut in at last. "I'm aware that the Eldritch have many concerns about the current accords, but official talks don't commence until the Golgoth arrive. Any concession we make now would be denounced as unjust."

"That… is true," said Talfayen in his measured way.

"Perhaps we could change the tone. It's time for a break, and you mentioned your desire to tour the winery?"

"Another time." The Eldritch lord rose with a dismissive gesture. "I hadn't realized the hour was so late. You'll be wanting your evening meal and a rest."

"You're welcome to join me," he invited.

Please, no. If I have to eat with him—

"Very kind, but I need to go over some private matters

with my nephew. I'll see you in the morning. With respect, please see that the meeting is more productive."

As Talfayen sailed out, Dom snapped his teeth at the air. It would give him great satisfaction to let diplomacy explode like a grenade, but the pride would suffer. Beren made a noise that sounded like he might be strangling on a beehive as Raff paced the length of the room.

"How can fate be so cruel?" Beren wondered aloud. "That I should survive long enough to suffer through this a second time. I'd prefer a quick death in combat."

"That can be arranged, old bear." Raff didn't seem to be joking, either.

"Enough." Dom sighed, wanting only to get back to Pru and find out how her mission went. But if he left these two so riled, there was no telling how things would play out tomorrow. "Let's have a drink to settle our nerves. Talfayen is a harmless blowhard, and if he *wasn't* whining, then we'd really have something to worry about."

Raff went to the sideboard and poured three shots. "I thought he'd never shut up about that pastureland. Supposedly your grandfather stole it from his old man?"

"Ah, but that land is magical," Beren mocked. "Their goats must eat the white flowers specially pollinated by consecrated bees and then they can make sacred cheese, or some such."

Dom rubbed the bridge of his nose. "The Eldritch live a long time, and apparently they don't forget grudges."

"There's probably a ledger. 'On this day the first of May, eighteen hundred and eight, the Ash Valley pride, in collusion with Burnt Amber and Pine Ridge, did swindle from us two hectares of pastureland.'" Wearing a disgruntled expression, Raff passed out the drinks.

Despite himself, Dom laughed as he swore. "Can you believe it? All of that wind over…" he quickly did the math, "…not even five acres of land."

"Those are mine now," Beren said. "And after making me listen to all that moaning, he'll have them back over my dead body. Cheers, you rotten cubs."

After clinking glasses with the other two, Dom drank up. The liquor burned pleasantly on the way down. Another glass tempted him, but he'd only just climbed out of a bottle, so he covered the top of his when Raff tried to pour more. Between Beren and Raff, they emptied the decanter, and both of them were steady as rocks when they left the conference room.

Though he wanted to head home, work still beckoned. Mentally grumbling, Dom found Magda poring over surveillance footage. He hadn't even known they had cameras near the retreat. Due to an old seer's edict, the lodge itself was off-limits, but the approach and surrounding terrain had hunting cameras posted, and from her cranky face, Magda had been watching the feeds for a while.

"Anything?" he asked.

"Shadows. Wildlife. The Noxblades are good, so it was a longshot that I'd find actual evidence this way."

"What about the bodies?"

"I sent a team to investigate this afternoon, and the place has been sanitized. We found broken furniture, but the corpses are gone, along with all trace evidence."

Dom swore. "If I'd acted sooner…"

"I won't say you handled things right. You made my life harder, no exaggeration. But I'm willing to cut you some slack. You're rusty as hell, and at least you kept yourself safe." Magda gave his shoulder a bracing pat. "Along with

Pru."

"Yeah, but now we can't lodge a formal complaint about the attack. If I hadn't dropped the ball, we'd have two dead Eldritch on ice, and I'd get to see Talfayen's face when I confronted him."

Losing that opportunity pissed him off. The Eldritch leader couldn't control all his physiological reactions, but it would be an empty accusation without proof to back it up. Talfayen could even allege that Dom was lying to gain traction in negotiation.

"Crying, spilled milk," Magda said with a dismissive shrug. "If you feel bad, do better."

"It's taking me longer to remember how to lead the pride than I'd like to admit."

Magda turned from scrutinizing the three screens before her. "Never thought I'd hear you say that. But... in my book it's enough that you're aware. The rest of us will pitch in until you're completely back to your old self."

Is that possible? Or wise?

Dom figured he'd shown enough weakness for one day. "Status on the assassin?"

"He went into his room an hour ago. Still there, according to the guards." She flicked a few switches, transferring focus to the external corridor in the guest wing.

Courtesy prohibited monitoring equipment in private areas, but Dom wished he had access to the room the red-eyed Noxblade was using. As he watched, the footage flickered. Puzzled, he leaned in at the same time as Magda. On the surface, it could be nothing, but then precisely thirty seconds later, it flickered again.

"Something's not right," he said.

"I'm on it."

The security chief tapped at the keys. A moment later, Magda snarled a curse. "It's looping. Someone's tampered with our equipment."

His first impulse was to sound the alarm and alert all personnel. There could be no good reason for a Noxblade who had already tried to kill him once concealing his movements. Magda sat rigid, awaiting orders.

"We can't let this blow up, can we?"

She shook her head. "Definitely not. Even worse, there's no evidence the Eldritch did this. They'll argue it could've been our own people or a traitor in the Pine Ridge or Burnt Amber camps. In this scenario, there are *so* many ways an angry accusation breaks bad."

"Then I'll hold it in until we know more. Find out what you can. Quietly. Talk to the guards assigned to that corridor personally, and report back here."

"On it."

Magda raced out of the control room, leaving him to scrutinize the footage. He didn't have her way with tech, so Dom didn't learn anything new. His stomach growled, reminding him that he hadn't eaten since lunch, and then, not much. He went back to the records his security chief had been inspecting and found where Pru arrived at the base of the mountain.

On screen she hesitated and then started the long climb, a small woman in a puffy jacket, her head bowed against the wintry wind. She couldn't have had any clue how things would turn out—that she'd learn to shift and swap her love for Slay for the good of the pride. *Wait, what was that?* He paused the feed to be sure. An icy chill crawled up his spine when he realized he was looking at two shadows on the stone steps.

Two shadows?

Pru... and a Noxblade nearby, maybe. So they were watching? She could have died on the way to me, and I wouldn't have known. Dom clenched the edge of the table until his composure returned. Checking various camera angles, he couldn't see much of the retreat and the range didn't extend to the clearing where she'd left the Rover. Hunting cameras weren't meant to provide high levels of surveillance, but he swore regardless.

When the door banged open, he expected Magda with an urgent report.

But it was Slay, wild as Dom had ever seen, too winded to breathe properly. Somehow he got the words out. "Pru... Pru..."

Fear went needle sharp inside him, and he grabbed his second. "Speak. Now."

That touch seemed to take Slay's knees out from under him. "She's missing."

11.

"WAKE UP."

The lilting accent in conjunction with an acrid snap catapulted Pru back to consciousness. Someone waved the stink beneath her nose, and a deep inhalation stung her sinuses. As her eyes watered, she struggled to make sense of her surroundings—rough walls and a dirt floor. This seemed to be an outbuilding, nowhere she'd ever been before. The place smelled of moldy grain, spider webs big as a bed canopy overhead.

At some point after passing out, she'd reverted to human form, and someone had wrapped her in a man's overcoat. Fear spiked when a shadowy figure resolved into the sharp features of the red-eyed Noxblade that had tried—and failed—to kill Pru before. Crouched before her and clad in black, he was the stuff of nightmares, the goblin king from an illustrated storybook that gave Animari children delicious shivers. Pru fought to keep her breathing steady. Whatever torture he intended, she wouldn't crack.

"You must be wondering why I've taken you, if I plan to play."

She swallowed and tried not to show her fear. "No."

"My name is Gavriel. Not so vicious now, hm?"

"I...what?" If she thought it would work, she'd go cat and try to escape, but in the gloom, she couldn't find any gaps that she could slink through, even as an ocelot.

He ignored the question. "Listen carefully, we don't have much time."

"Is my murder on a tight schedule?" She didn't mean to respond at all; the words just burst out.

"If I wanted you dead, little cat, you would be."

It was hard to argue that. In fact, Pru didn't understand any of this. "Then...?"

"I bear a message for your mate. You will reveal it only to the master of Ash Valley, or the consequences could be unthinkable. To the rest of the pride, you will apologize for getting lost on your first patrol. Do you understand?"

"You expect me to pretend that I've been wandering aimlessly for this long?"

"If you don't agree, I'll end you and find another way. Butcher."

Provoked, she curled her hand into a fist. "You invaded our sanctuary and nearly opened my throat. Trust me, you don't occupy the moral high ground here."

"Think twice about our first meeting. If I meant to kill you, how did you get past me? Do you truly believe that your pathetic reflexes bested me?"

Pru froze, trying to remember. He'd lashed out, clipping a lock of her hair, and then she made it all the way downstairs on human feet, at human speed. *How?* Now that he'd spat words limned in mockery, underscored with grief, she couldn't get it straight in her head.

"If you have any doubts, try now." He stepped back so they were equidistant to the door.

Though she knew it must be a trap, she threw herself toward the exit, and he was there, so swift she sensed rather than saw his movement. Shaking, she dropped into a crouch. Close up, he smelled of cinnamon, cloves, and blood. His skin gleamed pale as a pearl, and his lashes were white, so they disappeared into his skin, leaving only the crimson of his gaze.

"I don't understand," she whispered.

"We weren't there to kill the master of Ash Valley. In fact, we were sent to *warn* him that an attack was eminent, but our rescue went wrong. Probably because you were there, he didn't seem to hear us, only fought harder, and the sleep serum on our weapons didn't function as predicted. He shook it off and then you... *you* murdered my brother. I watched you tear his throat out with your teeth."

No, this isn't true. It can't be.

"Why would Talfayen send Noxblades to save Dom? And from what? This is insane."

"He didn't. This is the warning you must carry—at cost of your life, if necessary. Talfayen has turned traitor, and he is working with the Golgoth. There *will* be blood spilled at the conclave. Now it is only a question of how much."

"Why didn't you just pull me aside? This is absurd for a simple meeting."

"The hold is full of eyes and ears, you stupid cat. But please, test that privacy. You'll be stunned at what you discover. This way, if Talfayen learns of our meeting, if you betray me, I will know precisely who to blame. And can act accordingly."

"I don't believe you." But it was a rote objection as grains of the explanation accrued, coalescing into an undeniable truth like a picture layered in colored sand.

The assassin clenched his jaw. "That's your choice. Trust me, I long to kill you myself. Because of you, I will never see my brother Oriel again, never drink with him or share a laugh, or..." Gavriel's voice broke.

Suddenly, she had no doubt he was telling the truth. "I'm sorry. But... they had Dom cornered. He was *bleeding*."

"That didn't strike you as odd? Why would two fully trained Noxblades have difficulty dispatching one weakened Animari? If they had come at him with full skill, you would have found his corpse. Yet he suffered only superficial wounds."

Much as she hated to admit it, his words rang true. Dom had predicted he would fall sick soon after the attack as a result of poison blades, but that never happened. In retrospect, she should have noticed the inconsistencies. Guilt settled in her stomach like a heavy meal.

"But you didn't say a single word, only hunted me down."

"I was trying to subdue you. I had no orders where you were concerned," the Noxblade bit out. "Prior intel reported that he was alone. We were to extract the master of Ash Valley and bring him to this location for a private meeting."

"With who?"

"Suffice to say, we are working to unseat Talfayen and restore peace to my people."

Desperately she sorted the influx of information, still sifting for inconsistency. "If Dom was in danger, why did you sabotage the Rover?"

"The brakes were already disabled," Gavriel snapped. "I only made sure you couldn't careen into a tree. You really should thank me. By that point, I wanted both of you dead myself." His calm tone sent a shiver down her spine. "I still do. Without my current instructions, this story would have a much different ending."

"Your orders... who gave them?" Pru didn't know enough about Eldritch affairs to speculate who might be acting in opposition to Talfayen, assuming he truly had turned traitor. What that meant for the conclave, she couldn't fathom yet, but the idea of all the accords dissolving and returning to chaotic days of constant war—

No, I can't let that happen.

"You must earn more information."

"Do you think we'd side with Talfayen and the Golgoth?" Pru asked, horrified.

"I have no idea about your pride's politics. The important issue here is that your mate is still in danger, and his second's temper is well-known."

Her whole body iced over. "You have a deal. I'll repeat what you've said—only to Dom—and let the rest of the pride think I'm incompetent. If you're telling the truth, let me go. I'll need to run for a while in ocelot form to purge your scent."

To her surprise, Gavriel nodded. "We can't let anyone connect me to your absence. I risked much joining Talfayen's entourage and stand to lose more than my life if I'm unmasked."

She didn't ask what he meant by that; presumably he had loved ones who would suffer. "I'm so sorry about your brother. If I'd known..."

"I carry my share of the blame. I misjudged your ferocity. If I had called out to you instead of giving chase, Oriel might be alive. Yet we are shadow warriors, not diplomats. It would have been better to send emissaries versed in such, but they would've lacked the skills to remain hidden and could not have fought if we arrived late. Thus, it was judged best to extricate the pride master first and explain the particulars later. That miscalculation proved... costly."

"So if the sleep serum had worked properly, you'd have removed Dom from the retreat and had this talk with him instead?"

"Precisely. But you thought we were the assailants and responded accordingly."

"You *are* assassins," she muttered.

"You dare? *You?*" The Noxblade leveled on her a look so full of anguished rage that her heart crumpled. For a moment, Pru suspected she might die anyway and damn his orders. Then he let out a long breath. "Get out before I change my mind about killing you." Gavriel moved away from the exit.

Pru didn't ask him to avert his eyes when she dropped the overcoat. He did so naturally as she shifted. When he opened the door, she raced into the night.

SLAY IS MY friend. I will not kill him.

But with each passing hour, the urge to choke the life out of his second increased until Dom could hardly contain it. Multiple patrols searched for Pru quietly, and each time they reported nothing, he fought panic that made it hard to breathe, let alone think. *This can't be happening. Not again.*

But I can't let on. If Raff and Beren find out, they'll blame the Eldritch. He'd already hunted down that damned red-eyed assassin, who'd turned up in one of the lounges. The bastard claimed no clue as to the video tampering, and Pru—

Pru is still missing.

His chest ached. "Tell me again how you lost her."

Before Slay could reply, the radio crackled. Dom grabbed it with desperate speed. "Give me some good news."

Magda's relief came through bright as sunrise. "We've got visual on her. She's approaching the side gate. All ocelot, all healthy from what I can see."

"I'll be right there."

He ran through the rush of relief, despite weak knees and the echo of fear that tasted like copper in the back of his throat. When Dom arrived, Pru was getting dressed. She didn't seem worried or shaken, and she kept apologizing for getting separated from the group. With obvious skepticism, Magda eyed him above Pru's head, and Dom shrugged. For this moment, he only cared that she was back.

She's home. She's safe.

Ignoring the cluster of security personnel, he scooped Pru into his arms and headed for their quarters. He drew a few eyes that way, and at first she struggled. "I need to tell you something. It's urgent."

Dom didn't hesitate or put her down, despite the shiver her breath against his ear roused. "I don't care."

That startled her to silence long enough for him to get inside the apartment that already felt like home. Her father wasn't around, just as well, given Dom's current mood.

"Seriously, this is—"

He interrupted her with a ferocious kiss. Pleasure surged like a night-kissed ocean around the iceberg of terror his heart had become when she parted her lips and wrapped her arms around his neck.

"Really important," she said against his mouth.

"Still don't care. Give me an hour. Right now, let me be your man. Do you understand that I need you?" The admission hurt, but it got easier when her body softened against his.

"All right. You have me."

"Good."

Finally, Dom could breathe again, and he put his face in her hair to savor the sweet essence of her: crisp wind and balsam wood, an echo of cinnamon. Raw longing boiled over as he swept a hand down to the flare of her hip. Watching Pru's eyes go smoky-hot was one of the sexiest things he'd ever seen. Instinctively, he pulled her arms up and pinned her wrists overhead with one hand. Her back arched to hold the pose, and suddenly he wanted her naked, exactly like this, up against the door.

"Can we go to the bedroom...?"

"No. Take your clothes off."

Pru started to protest; he clicked the manual override on the lock. "Anyone could hear us, passing by."

"Maybe that's the point. Maybe I want everyone to know I'm fucking your brains out. Maybe I want them to hear you come."

Her cheeks flushed prettily, and she didn't argue further as she pulled the shirt over her head. Though her movements were quick, each article of clothing she dropped got him harder, until the press of his cock against his pants felt like torture. *Worth it.* Especially when he put her back in position against the door.

"I want to touch you too." She squirmed a little against his hold, so he tightened it.

"Not now. You're being punished."

The spike in her breathing turned him on even more. "I am?"

"Definitely. The penalty for dereliction of duty and

worrying me is..." He set his mouth on her neck and bit until she moaned. Her skin filled with heat, her pulse racing beneath his tongue. Afterward, he licked the spot tenderly, feeling the shivers that worked through her. Her nipples puckered when he kissed her shoulders, rubbing his open mouth over her collarbone. Testing his hold, Pru squirmed, but he held her still, completely open to him. Dom teased her with his lips and fingertips, so that she shifted against him feverishly. Her heat might burn him alive before he gave her more.

"Please," she whispered, eyes hot and bright.

"What?"

"I want your teeth."

Yes.

He grazed her nipples with them, just enough pressure that she arched and cried out. Alternating teeth and tongue, he controlled her body so that she couldn't get the friction she wanted against her shifting hips. A sound of pure frustration broke out of her, low and throaty. Slowly, gradually, he nibbled downward, but he couldn't keep hold of her wrists.

"I'm letting you go. But if you lower your arms, I'm stopping. Understand?"

"Got it," she muttered.

Such a sexy, petulant tone.

Dom dropped to his knees before her and parted her thighs. For a while, he nuzzled her there, back and forth; she shivered from the ripple of his breath. Already soft and slick, her pussy demanded immediate attention, and he gave it with long, lavish licks, avoiding her clit until her legs quivered. She groaned a protest, and then he went in, savoring her wild reaction. His heart hammered in his ears—to the point that he couldn't hear—and Pru hooked a thigh over his shoulder, bucking against his face. He didn't mean to let her come this way, but she was almost there, so he pressed just so.

Her juices sweetened his mouth, but he didn't give her a chance to calm down. With one hand, he opened his pants, and then he lifted her. "Hang on to me now."

She needed no further instructions. Pru wrapped her legs around his hips, arms about his shoulders, and then he took her. *Mine. You're here. You're safe. You're mine.* Each thrust pounded her against the door. Impossible to pull back completely, but she drove him wild by grinding in slow, tight circles in a controlled but demanding fuck. He pushed deep and held so she could feel him throbbing. At one point, he heard footsteps pause outside, and by Pru's fevered expression, she did too.

He pushed. Arched.

She panted. Moaned.

Feels so good.

"Yes. Fuck me. *Please*. Harder. Dom, please."

For some reason, the words hit him like a sex typhoon, the hottest thing he'd ever heard. *My name, sweet kitten, you said my name. Begging me for it.* His cock swelled inside her, and she rolled her hips faster, thighs squeezing, sex tightening on him until he couldn't do anything but take more of her, all of her. Her hands kneaded at his arms, his shoulders, clumsy and frantic.

Her audible grunts as her back slammed the door were too guttural to be sexy, yet they got at him until he might lose his mind. *She's coming again.*

Dom didn't even try to hold on; orgasm swept him like him a tidal wave. The strength went out of his arms and legs. Somehow he switched off the manual lock and staggered with her to the bedroom because it would be beyond awkward for her father to catch them naked in the foyer. Collapsing with her on the bed, he closed his eyes for a few seconds, pretending there was no big picture, no problems looming.

Just Pru.

"Consider me chastened," she said with a sleepy satiation that sent residual heat spiraling through him.

They were still joined, and he flinched when she slid away, because the loss of her heat registered like pain. His softening cock gleamed with her wetness, and he throbbed, already hungry for round two. *What the hell's wrong with me?* Without volition, Dom rubbed a hand over her shoulder, down her arm, marveling at her silky skin. His heart calmed a little too at having her close enough to touch.

"You said—"

Before he could finish, she shook her head silently, then said aloud, "You want a shower? I'll scrub your back."

She must have a good reason for this. I'll play along.

"Give me a minute. That's too good an offer to refuse."

Pru pretended to watch the clock as she teased, "Time's up."

But her eyes were sober, sending their own message. She kept up the banter until they got in the bathroom, where she turned the pressure to high. With the water for white noise, she rose up to whisper dangerous secrets in his ear.

They were worse than he'd imagined.

12.

EARLY THE NEXT morning, Pru asked Magda to bring scanners over. She hoped the team didn't find anything, but everybody went into silent frantic mode when they picked up an audio bug, hidden in a vent. As the security chief crushed it, Pru tried to remember what they'd talked about here. *How long has this been here?* Dom swore beneath his breath, but even if there was other spyware, the sound of her mate cursing wouldn't raise any alarms.

Is it safe to talk? she wrote.

Magda shook her head and gestured for the team to finish the sweep. Ten minutes later, they didn't find more, so the security chief dismissed them.

All clear? she mouthed at Magda.

"Go for it."

First, she glanced at Dom for confirmation that she should share what she'd learned the night before, and he nodded without hesitation, so she went for it. Gavriel had said she wasn't to tell anyone else, but there was no way the two of them could manage a crisis this size. She had no doubts about the security chief—or Slay, for that matter— but right now he was taking the Eldritch entourage on a winery tour.

Once Pru finished, she thought aloud. "We did the briefing here with you and Slay. If that was already in place, then Talfayen knows about the attack, but he doesn't know it was a warning that went wrong. So he probably thinks he has a rival?"

"Or an overzealous supporter," Magda suggested. "If his endgame is Dom's demise, maybe he'll suspect somebody tried to hand him a surprise success to kick off the conclave."

Dom wore a speculative look. "But since they failed, they probably wouldn't rush to admit it. So Talfayen might be scrutinizing his followers right now."

"That's not bad for us," Pru said.

Scowling, Magda pounded a fist against her knee. "I wish we had a timeline. Did they get someone in here before their group arrived? And if so, how long have they been recording?"

"I'm guessing it's fresh." Apparently agitated, Dom rose and paced, covering the distance wall to wall in six strides.

"Why?" Magda arched a brow.

"I don't say they *couldn't* get someone in before." The twist of his mouth told Pru he was thinking about Dalena. "They did. But prior to our return, there was no reason to spy on Pru."

He's right. Before, I was just a Latent schoolteacher, and it's impossible that they'd be interested in Dad's business.

Dom stopped at the window, staring out over the courtyard. In winter there was precious little to see, but she suspected him of internal gazing anyway. Today, he wore black trousers and a pale blue shirt, loose on his lean back. His rigid shoulders spoke of some fresh pain, and her hands itched to knead it away. Yet she only sat and watched from a distance, unwilling to be rebuffed in front of Magda. In some ways, she was dead sure of her role, but in others, she couldn't be certain if she would be treading solid ground or eggshells.

The security chief didn't need everything spelled out. "I'll take the team and sweep the other key sites, including the lounges, changing area, and conference rooms. You never know."

"Keep me posted," Dom said.

Once Magda left, Pru mustered her courage and went to the window, hesitating only a moment before setting a hand on his shoulder. At her touch, he sighed softly, not in a way that made her want to withdraw. In fact, he seemed to lean into her palm a little.

How did he live alone for so long? He's starved for comfort.

"What's wrong?"

"With this new information, I'm wondering…"

"Tell me." She wrapped her arms around him from behind and leaned her head against back. Guilt pricked her, along with awareness of how often Dalena must have done this. It was almost enough to make her let go, except that his hands covered hers, linking past and present.

"Does this shit with Talfayen cast such a long shadow? Just a theory, but… in collusion with the Golgoth, the Eldritch murdered Dalena to destabilize Ash Valley, and I…I did exactly as they expected. Broke and ran and damn near left my people open to their machinations."

"Even if that's true, it's not a fault to love your wife."

"No, but if I was stronger, I wouldn't have run. We'd be better situated to deal with the fallout instead of perched on the brink of some true fuckery, right before the conclave."

For a moment, Pru had no idea what to say, because he wasn't wrong. "What does regret change?" she asked finally. "I have to live with the fact that I ended somebody who was trying to save you, and now his brother wants me dead."

Dom made a sound somewhere between a laugh and a groan. "That was a shitshow. They did say something like, *calm down, we're not here to harm you*, but when the person claiming that comes at you with a knife, I don't take it at face value."

"If they'd tried talking first... but from what Gavriel said, they were afraid you'd be executed before they could explain, so they rushed and used force. It went bad. But that's my point. They screwed up, we reacted, and nothing will change any of it. Being *too* sorry could keep us from moving forward, so all we can do is learn from our mistakes."

He turned in her arms and gathered her into a reciprocal hug. Startling how good that felt; it seemed to Pru that she'd spent most of her time giving with so few people ever glancing around to offer something back. For years Slay had worn her heart on a chain while keeping his safe. She'd been startled by his reaction to the loss of her, expecting a shrug, a smile, and an indifferent, *Well, we were just killing time anyway*. In her wildest dreams, she never could've imagined breaking Slay's heart.

I hardly knew he had one.

Dom dropped a kiss onto her forehead. "That... was a surprisingly effective pep talk. Message received, kitten."

Startled, Pru stared up at him, but he didn't seem to realize he'd used a pet name. It felt a little strange, yet she didn't entirely hate it. As far as she knew at least, he'd never said it to Dalena. Good thing, as a recycled endearment would start an argument, and they had more important shit to consider. Come to think of it, he'd called her a clever kitten before, so she didn't make a thing out of it.

"I'm glad I could help."

"More than I can say. Until you came, I was rudderless and nothing mattered." Dom hesitated, citrine eyes bright and soft at once.

"You can tell me, whatever it is."

"Devotion to Slay is what drove you to me, and that's why you wouldn't relent, no matter what I said or did. But nobody else could've reached me, and it's sure as shit, they wouldn't have gone as far as you did. So sometimes I don't know how to feel." He cupped her cheek in his big hand, visibly conflicted. "Because... the four of us..."

Dalena, Dom, Pru, and Slay. She understood his confusion, but she couldn't guarantee how Dalena would feel; Slay had made it damn clear that he disapproved.

"Maybe... we should just focus on doing what we must," she said softly.

"An excellent idea." Dom framed her face in his hands, searching her gaze for a few seconds and then he seemed satisfied by whatever he found. His mouth took hers, first in a teasing touch, then in deepening glides. Pru dug her fingers into his shoulders, unable to think for the unexpected sweetness of this demand.

"We promised to meet our visitors at the winery," she reminded him, breathless.

"Let's go before Slay does something regrettable. He's never patient, and his mood isn't the best right now."

Understatement, Pru thought. But his temper wasn't her problem; his mother could talk him down and soothe him with whispers of how he'd had a lucky escape. In a few days, the woman would be showing him pictures and nudging Slay toward her top choices for his mate. Eventually he would take it seriously and pick someone to make his mom happy. Pru wasn't even angry or hurt anymore, likely a good sign.

THE WHOLE DAY was fucking exhausting.

Dom seethed as he made nice with Talfayen and company. He also had to mediate between Eldritch, bear, and wolf, not easy when Raff seemed committed to causing the war-holes some grievous offense by day's end. Fortunately, Pru was good at defusing bombs as they dropped, and Slay was behaving well. Best he could reckon, the Eldritch had come early to keep the allied Animari from finishing whatever hurried strategy they could concoct.

He suffered through two meals and a lengthy after-dinner drink before Talfayen elected to retire. The effort to be polite irked him because you'd think someone who had turned traitor would exude a bit more charm, if only to put others off the scent. Yet from what his father had said, the Eldritch leader had been about this querulous the last time the accords were drafted. The lounge seemed incredibly quiet without Talfayen, and the others relaxed a trifle.

"I miss war," Beren said with a sad droop to his weathered features. "Sure, a bunch of us died, but at least there was an end to it, unlike all this talking."

"That's what we call a filibuster," Raff admitted.

Dom stretched and popped his neck. He hadn't shared everything with the other two, though not from a lack of trust. Mostly, it was his responsibility to manage the situation, and it might make things worse if the wolf and bear lords knew a silent Eldritch civil war was raging beneath his roof. Added to the complication of the mysterious Golgoth troop movements Beren had reported before, he had headaches to last for a month of Mondays. So instead of briefing them, he made his excuses and went to look for Magda.

Her words echoed in his head. *Feel bad? Do better.* She'd also suggested he revert to his old self as soon as possible, but thinking back, Dom recalled an artesian well of confidence that never seemed to run dry, but then, abruptly, he fell into that bubbling water and nearly drowned. Now he couldn't factor why he'd reckoned himself so wise, so infallible, so fucking indestructible. These days he felt like he'd been walking a tightrope above a chasm for a thousand years.

Until Pru threw me a lifeline.

On the way to confer with the security chief, he spotted Slay stepping out of the private quarters they'd assigned to the Eldritch. Even Dom hadn't been invited inside, so he slowed, watching as a cold smile crooked Slay's mouth. When his second turned, he seemed startled, but he sauntered toward Dom with no hesitation.

What's he up to?

"Productive visit?" he asked.

"Just a little private meet and greet. I brought over a few vintages that I promised from the winery tour."

Definitely not like Slay.

He loathed the awkwardness that stood between them now like a wall, but one punch hadn't made things right, not by a long stretch. Though he'd meant to meet with Magda, he offered, "Want to go a few rounds?"

Slay laughed, the sound quiet and caustic. "You're in no

condition to square off against me, and I'm in no mood to go easy on you, either."

"So don't."

The other man spoke through a clenched jaw. "Sounds like you understand that I owe you a beating."

"You're welcome to give it a shot."

"Big talk. Let's go, then."

Back in the day, even at Dom's peak, Slay beat him about half the time. Jaguars tended toward a heavier build than leopards, along with great strength, and Slay brought that to his human form too. So his second might be right, especially since he'd spent three years dwindling. Yet he had to do something; it wasn't like he could spend the rest of his life in an armed truce with his former friend.

In silence they went to the training center, dark and deserted this time of night. Slay threw down the mats. "Cat or hand-to-hand?"

Dom shrugged. "You choose."

"Cat. That way your bruises won't show and Pru won't come crying to me over how bad I fucked you up."

Though Slay talked a big game, Dom half-suspected he was being kind since a bout in feline form would make up for some of his muscle loss. But he didn't say anything as he shucked his clothes and shifted. Slay cut the lights and did the same. Even in the dark, he was an impressive beast, larger than Dom, heavier, with a round head and a wide jaw. If Slay got his fangs sunk in, Dom might lose an arm.

For a few seconds, they just circled, and then Slay lunged. The leap knocked Dom back, and he scrambled, tail lashing, for a better angle. His ears went back as he analyzed Slay's posture. *Too pissed to think, he just wants a piece of me.* The next time Slay leapt, Dom bounded over the top and pounced hard enough to knock him down. He'd already noticed that Slay wasn't using his teeth or claws. But even a kick from his powerful back legs felt like taking a Rover door in the ribs.

He lost track of how long they tussled and rolled. Eventually Slay did bite him, but not hard enough to break the layers of fur, muscle, and skin. Dom rolled over and went belly up; he could've fought on, but Pru must be wondering where the hell he was. If she came looking, she wouldn't be amused to find them squabbling like kits over a dead bird.

At last he shifted back and got as far as putting his pants on when Slay tackled him and drove a fist into the mat beside his head. "Fucking bastard."

He stared up at Slay's angry face. "I'm sorry."

"Don't lie, brother. I've had her with me, and I've watched her with you, and I know damn well which is better."

Since Dom had a vivid recollection of how hellish life had been before Pru, he had no rebuttal. "I can be sorry for hurting you without regretting her," he said quietly.

"I guess that's true." A hard breath slid out of his second, and suddenly all the bravado went too. "I love her… and I hate you, and this is killing me."

In all the years he'd known him, he'd never seen Slay cry, but his shoulders crumpled and the tears just came. It was awful and absurd that he'd be the one stuck trying to comfort him, but there was nobody else. Pru was the one who had always taken care of Slay, stroked his head, and looked at him like he was all the light in the world. So Dom wrapped an arm around his sweaty shoulders and held on while Slay screamed, over and over, bursts too wild and angry to be sobs, but they held raw grief at the heart of all that fury.

Dom's whole body hurt, and now his spirit did as well. He could only say, "You're crap at communication. Use your words."

"It wasn't even me," Slay said in a broken voice. "I didn't give two shits whether Pru could shift. My mother just gave me so much grief when I mentioned a permanent bond... *think of our bloodline* and *what about your status as second* that I figured it wasn't worth the drama. She can't live forever, right? And that's a fucking weak path to happiness, I know."

"Pru thought you were playing with her," he said.

Slay made a strangled sound. "I get that now, asshole. But... I wasn't. There's never been anyone else. I always planned to make her mine."

"You can't expect a woman to wait forever."

"True. But... you and Pru, instead? You know that's wrong. You fucking do know." Some of Slay's anger seemed to fade, leaving him weary-faced and with eyes full of despair.

Yeah. I know. But he wouldn't acknowledge it aloud. He already felt enough like a thief, stealing happiness from someone who deserved it more. *I had my shot. Now I've got his.*

"Night, Slay."

His second didn't answer, so Dom left him in the darkened sparring room. He lacked the energy to check in with Magda tonight, but he took a quick look at the preparations on his way to their flat. The decorations were nearly done, wreaths hung, and the wintry air rippled with the sweetness of hothouse flowers. *Hope those demonic bastards appreciate my people working all night.*

But probably not. Because that was life, where selfish assholes thrived, beautiful women died in their living rooms, and Slay was weeping alone in the dark.

Meanwhile, Pru is waiting at home... for me.

Sometimes the world made no damn sense at all.

13.

THE GOLGOTH PRINCE had arrived at last.

As his convoy halted outside the gates, Pru smoothed her black dress. This time, the welcome party wasn't hastily assembled, and the plaza by the gate shone with the preparations. At some point, they'd even laid down a red carpet, and the wreaths on the walls were woven carefully of basil, lavender, and violets chosen for their message of peace. Beside her, Dom waited with expectant tension. In addition to the official members of other factions, most of the pride had turned out to spectate. While Pru understood their interest, it was also nerve-wracking. The more bodies in this area, the more potential something could go wrong.

If she'd thought the Eldritch party was impressive, the Golgoth group put them to shame. Six vehicles parked outside the gate, larger than a Rover, and when the gate swung open, the Golgoth marched in formation, dark green uniforms contrasting to the snow-white suit their leader wore. Stories always painted the Golgoth as brutish and monstrous, but Prince Alastor was slight and angular with a mane of raven hair that he wore long and braided on the sides. Though his features lacked Eldritch sharpness, he was more delicate than the average Animari male.

Dom stepped forward, likely to keep Lord Talfayen from upstaging him. "Welcome to Ash Valley. You must be tired."

"Only of traveling," the Golgoth prince said. "It is good to have arrived."

He exchanged greetings with Beren and Raff while Lord Talfayen seemed amused by something he didn't share. That roused Pru to greater awareness, but despite the crowd, she spotted no trouble in the plaza. Everyone looked faintly disappointed that the Golgoth didn't have horns or cranial ridges, but otherwise, the pride members present showed no signs of alarm.

Once the first wave of welcome passed, Pru offered a simple bow as she hadn't found much on Golgoth customs, unlike the multiple volumes on Eldritch ways. "We have a number of activities planned later, but for now, I expect you'd like to freshen up and rest."

"We would appreciate that." The so-called demon prince promised to be much more affable than anyone had predicted, though it could be pretense.

"This way, please."

The onlookers parted in an ocean of humanity, so Pru and Dom could guide the Golgoth visitors to the floor of the residential annex that had been cleared for their use. A number of families were now staying with relatives, and they'd also conscripted the empty flat where Dom used to live. That space, they offered to Prince Alastor, who made sure his men were all settled comfortably before heading to his own apartment. But it didn't escape Pru that his face was wan and drawn, like his skin was too small for his bones.

"I hope this is sufficient," Pru said, demonstrating the numeric pin.

Stepping inside, the prince took a cursory look around. A tremor quivered through one of his long fingers, which he swiftly hid by curling it into a fist. "Very spacious. Thank you."

"There are no retainers staying with you?" Dom asked.

"I prefer my privacy when I'm afforded the opportunity." A flicker of something in the prince's gaze whispered of sadness.

"It sounds as if you don't get much of it ordinarily," Pru observed.

"Already trying to unravel my secrets?" With an inscrutable smile, the young Golgoth deflected with as much grace as she'd witnessed earlier. Yet he clearly wanted them gone. Soon she'd see a more tangible sign.

"Please don't hesitate to ask if you need something. We've stocked the fridge with the necessities, but anything you desire will be made available," Dom said.

"Anything?" For a moment, eyes like chips of ancient jade lingered on her, skimming down in a mockery of a compliment. "How generous."

When Dom stirred, she put her hand on his arm and tugged him toward the door. Pru smiled over one shoulder as she opened it. "Rest well."

"That bastard might be a little more civilized, but he's still terrible," Dominic snarled once they left the apartment.

Pru shook her head and hurried him out of the residential annex. "He was taking your measure, gauging your temper. And I admit, I'm startled by how quick you took the bait. He doesn't actually want to fuck me as part of a feudal *droit du seigneur*."

"That look was a bucket of disrespect."

"No, it was desperation."

"What do you mean?"

She wasn't ready to put her suspicions into words yet. At the moment, she had only intuition, no evidence. "I'll tell you more after the banquet. You just stay calm. That's your specialty, remember?"

"I got it." Dom dropped a kiss on her temple. "Now I'm off to entertain the rest of this diplomatic zoo. Any chance you'll go with me?"

"Later. I should've checked on Eamon days ago."

He inclined his head. "As pride matron or his friend?"

"Both. I try to stop in once a week."

"Then don't let me keep you. I'm sure Lord Talfayen desperately needs to complain about his mattress by now."

Smiling, Pru headed off to the commissary to fill a basket with Eamon's favorite snacks. He had been part of Ash Valley for almost five years, a recovered hostage who never healed enough to rejoin the pride fully. Sometimes she ached to ask what he'd seen and suffered in Golgoth hands, but he clammed up tighter than an oyster anytime she even skirted the subject. If he realized who had just arrived, he would probably be panicked.

She quickened her step, reaching the apartment a few minutes later. After she rang the bell, it took a couple of minutes for her to hear movement within. He'd look out the peephole first, then confirm it was safe to open the door via chain. Once Eamon completed that ritual, Pru heard him unbolting the seven locks that kept him safe. Inside, his flat was like a darkened lair with fabric on the walls and windows. Fortunately, shifting had enhanced her vision in the dark, and she was used to navigating the maze of furniture he'd built. Eamon was always thin, and he liked the dark to hide his scars. Sometimes she tried to imagine what he must have been like before he was taken: young, confident, and unbroken.

"I wondered when you'd come again," he said, taking the goodies she offered.

"It's been busy. I'm sure you noticed some of the preparations."

"How many strangers are in the hold?"

Though she hated the prospect of alarming him, lying would serve no purpose. "Around a hundred, all told."

"The Golgoth arrived today." It wasn't a question. Eamon sank to the carpet, arms wound around the basket like it offered some protection.

"They're not in the building with you," she said.

"No, I know. You wouldn't do that to me."

"Neither would Dom."

"He's back, I hear?"

Curious, Pru cocked her head. "How did you know?"

"You're not my only friend," he chided. "Your cousin visits, and she couldn't wait to tell me about your new role as pride matron. Is she still basking in your importance?"

Laughing, she shook her head. "Probably. I'm glad school is on winter break or I wouldn't have enough hours in the day."

"Will you keep teaching?"

"Definitely. I'd miss the kids if I gave it up."

Pru told a few anecdotes about the students who had become Eamon's favorites over the years, and by the third story, she had him laughing. Since he didn't always, she counted the days he did a quiet victory. The pride counselor had come twice a week for a year until Eamon asked her to stop. He was working through it at his own pace, he said, and words had never been a friend to him. Over the next hour, she drank a cup of tea while he told her about a painting he was working on. In the time she had been visiting, Pru had never seen anything he'd created.

Eventually, like always, he said, "You must be busy."

That had become a code between them. It wasn't that Pru had other matters to attend, more that Eamon wanted her to go, but he didn't wish to be rude.

So she always agreed. "It's a circus out there. You wouldn't believe how the work piles up. Do you feel like a hug?"

"Pass. I'm a little spidery. But thanks for the offer."

And as always, sadness swept her when she stepped out of his domain and heard the repeated clicks that meant he had locked the world out. Again.

DOM COULDN'T REMEMBER if he'd ever consciously thought this before, but his mate was beautiful. No, not just beautiful. Breathtaking. When she stepped out of the bedroom in a bronze and black dress, his heartbeat notched up. She'd pinned her hair up to show the graceful line of her neck, and he immediately wanted to kiss that soft skin. Her lips were frosted like a caramel cupcake, and she'd dusted on some kind of glittering powder, so her skin looked sun-kissed, and her eyes, *oh damn*. He'd seen mountain streams that sparkled less.

"Should I change?" With a quiet frown, she tugged at her dress.

Hell. She thinks silence means disapproval.

"You look phenomenal."

"Really?" Seeming pleased, Pru twirled, so that the skirt belled about her thighs.

"I'm a little worried about taking you out of the apartment," he teased. "Rioting will start, and I'll have to duel villains who want to steal you."

"Idiot." But from the flush rising in her cheeks, she didn't mind.

"Ready to head to the hall? We shouldn't keep our guests waiting."

"I'm set."

"No jacket?"

"I don't have one that goes with this dress, so I'd rather suffer."

Dom gave her a look, but Pru wouldn't budge. He hadn't realized she had even a narrow streak of vanity, so this was unexpected and adorable. As they stepped out, her arm brushed his, and it took a second for him to grasp that there was no problem that required his attention; she just wanted to hold hands. The sweet simplicity of it arrowed straight to his heart as he laced their fingers together. Immediately, the nerves that the stress of the day had rubbed raw smoothed out, leaving him calm and focused.

The bond's set. It would be hard to send her to Slay now, even if I wanted to. And I don't.

"I won't let you," he said.

"What?"

"Suffer."

With that, he wrapped an arm around her shoulders. It was cold enough he could see their breath coming in white puffs as they hurried across the plaza to the hall, where pride staffers were finishing up the arrangements. White fabric banners draped the beams overhead, red flowers on each table, candles—this wasn't his forte, but from his mate's approving inspection, he guessed that the decorators had hit the mark.

"We're early." Pru beamed up at him, appearing to guess he hadn't tampered with her clock settings.

As quirks went, it was a harmless one. So if she preferred to live ten minutes ahead of schedule, he could adapt. "It's served me well before. Everything seems to be in order?"

She glanced around once more. "It looks fantastic. Let me check with the musicians and make sure they're all set."

Pru spent the last few minutes rushing around while Dom watched in baffled admiration.

"She's a manager," said Slay.

Before Dom could respond, the first guests arrived. Predictably, it was the Eldritch entourage. The red-eyed Noxblade caught his gaze long enough to convey that he wanted to talk, but this wasn't the time or place. Dom lifted his chin faintly in acknowledgment. With any luck, the assassin could read a room and deduce that there would be a better opportunity.

For the first hour, he greeted the arriving guests in a formal reception line, along with Magda, Caio, and Slay. Pru played her role to perfection, offering a smile or a friendly word, even for the visiting guards stationed along the walls in an impressive display of martial prowess. Since they weren't allowed to drink on duty, Pru kept them supplied with a steady stream of sparkling water and fresh juice. More than once, he noticed an overly interested gaze following her movements around the room.

Dinner can't be served soon enough.

At least when everyone took their assigned seats, Pru

was next to Dom as a matter of course, but she had Prince Alastor on her other side. The Golgoth asshole touched her five times—arm, hand, shoulder, hand, arm—Dom knew, because he was counting. None of it was brazen enough to constitute an offense, but he still felt like taking Alastor's head off. Beneath the table, he curled his left hand into a fist as Pru's cousin, Joss, took the stage, a gilded lily in a gold dress. Her performance wasn't meant to inhibit conversation, but when she started the song, competing voices fell silent one by one.

Dom flashed a startled look at Pru, who offered a smug smile. "Told you she's good."

"A mere word like 'good' does her a disservice," the Golgoth prince whispered.

Though he didn't know much about music, Dom had to agree with him. Joss had a mournful, sultry sound that riveted pretty much every listener in the hall. When she finished, thunderous applause rang out. Her smile flirted with the whole room as she began the next number, this one more upbeat and joyous.

He leaned over to ask Pru softly, "Did you arrange this?"

"Of course. You put me in charge of entertainment, and Joss thrives in the spotlight. The orchestra will play after her set. Dinner should be done by then, and there will be dancing."

"I hope you'll honor me," Alastor said.

Pru accepted the offer before Dom could shut that shit down. Diplomacy was *not* supposed to include watching other men handle his woman. To keep from objecting, he clenched his jaw so hard he could barely eat any of the food on his plate. Halfway through the meal, Beren managed to

start a conversation that didn't make him want to crawl out
of his skin. With liberal applications of wine, he thought he
might survive.

Until the dancing started.

Prince Alastor rose with a flourish and offered his hand
to Pru. Watching her go off with the pride's greatest enemy,
Dom felt ten kinds of complicated. In his head, he heard
battle cries, a thousand dead warriors protesting that pale
hand on the curve of her waist.

Slay came up behind him to snarl, "You're letting that
happen?"

"Keep smiling. Ask one of the Golgoth ladies to dance."

His second showed teeth but did as he was told. Likewise, Dom made nice, circulating to partner pride mates and
visitors alike. Pru proved popular, and he barely saw her for
the next hour as she circled the floor multiple times with
Alastor, Beren, Raff, and even Talfayen himself. If that red-
eyed Noxblade made a move, Dom would probably start a
brawl.

"You're staring a strip off her," Magda muttered as they
twirled. "Relax, she knows what she's doing. And everything's proceeding well so far. She's gathering good intel."

Apart from minor dustups between guard forces, the
banquet *had* gone better than expected. Pru had worked
wonders on the seating chart, lacing pride members and
esteemed guests, separating those who were likely to
conflict. And now everyone had drunk enough to find each
other amusing. Over the security chief's shoulder, he saw
the Noxblade—Gavriel, he thought Pru had said—dancing
with Joss.

Under the best of circumstances, he didn't enjoy formal
events. Tonight resonated with a special sort of torture,

however, because he kept waiting for someone to keel over with poison in their drink. *I'm looking at you, Eldritch.* Historically, the Golgoth tended to be brutal, so he was also alert for the shimmer of a blade. Everyone had been scanned for weapons as they entered the hold, but there were always methods to smuggle them inside.

Or they could be ceramic or composite—

No, it's going well.

Several hours in, Dom settled at a table with Beren and Raff, letting people come to him. Pru was still dancing, and it rankled that he hadn't partnered her even once. *You assholes know she's mine, right?* Trying not to look as pissed as he felt, he started a card game, dealing in the wolf and bear lords. Eventually Magda joined, along with two Golgoth, and an Eldritch guard.

Two hands, three. He won one, lost two. It seemed like forever before his mate came to check on him. With her, she brought a whisper of sweat, other males, and a dying echo of her goat milk soap. It took all his control to focus on his hand instead of dragging her off to scrub her down, so she only smelled of him.

Smiling, she leaned in to inspect his cards. "Discard that one."

And then she dragged her nails down his back.

14.

A T FIRST PRU feared she'd gone too far. Too bold, too wicked, and in front of all these people too. Dom had been glaring like a thundercloud all night, and gambling didn't seem to have cheered him any.

Maybe I can pretend I forgot what that signal means.

But then he rose from the table in a smooth motion, his face artfully blank, yet she read the lambent shine of his eyes. "I fold," he said, tossing his cards.

In a casual motion, he leaned down and kissed her neck. *That's a definite yes.* A covert thrill spiraled through her. *Nobody suspects a thing.*

"Now I'll never know if you were bluffing," Raff mumbled.

His cheeks held a high color, perceptible even above his well-groomed beard. Normally, the wolf lord could hold his drink, but Pru had no clue how much he'd already imbibed. Beren threw down his hand with a disgusted grumble while an Eldritch raised and Slay took more cards. It seemed that the game would continue without Dom.

He wrapped an arm about her waist, distracting her from anything besides his touch. "If you gentlemen don't mind, and even if you do, I'm dancing with my beautiful wife."

Wife. He'd never said that word before, at least not in conjunction with her, and a pit that was equal measure dread and yearning opened in her stomach. They hadn't spoken formal vows, only made a desperate deal on the mountain. Yet she took his hand when he offered, and the dancers actually made room for them on the floor, as if together, they radiated some kind of undeniable magic. *Like Dalena and Dom.*

"I hope you don't mind," he said. "I'm probably rusty."

"I'm sure it'll be fine."

Around them, the music swelled, and none of it felt quite real when he drew her in. Though she'd danced with so many partners she'd lost count tonight, somehow this was the only song that mattered. His hand glowed with pure heat when it settled on her waist, and when he swung her into the first turn, Pru let out a little gasp. Her feet nearly left the floor.

"Warned you," he whispered.

She couldn't take her eyes off his face. This party weighed with every bit as much importance as it ever had, but the nuances faded until she couldn't read them. If someone was plotting on the perimeter, they would succeed with their clandestine agenda. In this moment, there were only his eyes, his hands, and his mouth. Pru had never known the world to disappear... until right then.

As if the musicians sensed what was unfolding, they changed the tempo for the next number, slow and sultry with the sweet wail of horns. He drew her even closer, so each step felt like foreplay. His thighs brushed hers, his chest, and then he tilted his head to hers. Ostensibly they were dancing cheek to cheek, but the rasp of his breath and the scrape of his whiskers against her jaw felt wicked as sin. She had never been more conscious of the heat and strength of him, and she couldn't resist the urge to wrap her arms fully about his neck.

"I'm one heartbeat away from taking you on a table. Do you think we can slip away?" His tone was so matter of fact that Pru couldn't believe she'd heard him right, but the simmer in his gaze confirmed the question.

She cleared her throat. "We should say our farewells to our guests of honor—"

"Fuck that," he growled. "Talfayen is gone already, Alastor is dancing with Joss, both Raff and Beren are dead drunk."

"Then let's sneak off." For once, she'd throw caution to the wind. What were the chances that anything awful would happen, just because she pretended her name wasn't Prudence?

"Finally some good news. You know how tired I am of watching other men touch you?"

"Is this a trick question?" she teased, towing him toward the exit.

They almost made it all the way out of the building, but Magda stopped them in the corridor. "Is this wise?"

Dom shrugged. "Don't care. I feel like we've given fair entertainment value. You and Slay take over."

The security chief sighed, but she didn't argue. "Understood."

After that, he pulled Pru away from the event hall, out into the chilly night air. She half-expected him to toss her over one shoulder—and she wouldn't have minded—but instead he spun her to him, cupped her face in his hands, and went for her mouth like her kiss could keep him from dying of thirst. With his whole body, he backed her up, until she hit the chilly stone wall, and Dom kept coming, sealing them together like missing pieces of a puzzle.

Moaning softly, she parted her lips, and the minute their tongues touched, he made such a hungry sound that her toes curled in her fancy shoes. Dom stole her breath again and again, his mouth wild on hers, her cheeks, jaw, throat, back and forth. Countless moments later, she realized they were rocking together, his hands on her ass, skirt rucked up so anyone could see.

"Dom," she panted.

"That's good." He seemed one kiss away from opening his pants.

"N-not here." The caress nearly stole the last of her common sense, as he delved between them, into her panties.

"You're so wet. Driving me crazy."

Two or three strokes from coming, Pru whimpered as she tore away. *We can't do this here.* But a good portion of her wanted to, and she didn't care who might be watching or listening. Calling on the last of her discretion, she quelled those urges, broke free, and stumbled a few steps away. Her mouth felt soft and swollen, and Dom's gaze scorched like lightning raking over her. Tousled hair, rumpled dress, kiss-stung lips—she'd never felt so sexy in her life.

"Don't run," he warned.

On wobbly knees, she did exactly that.

From behind, he let out a growl that might have worried her, if she hadn't been so busy giggling and dodging him. He nearly caught her in the stairwell, but she took off her heels and chucked them at him, and then she raced him to the apartment, wildly positive this was only making him hotter. It wasn't that she actually wanted to escape, just delay long enough that they wouldn't ruin the conclave with a mating-frenzy scandal.

She made it all the way to the bedroom, and then he was on her, hand on her neck, pressing her into the mattress. Dom came down on top of her from behind, his breath coming in great gasps. Her heart thundered with excitement that was minutely spiced with alarm. Pru had never guessed he could get so out of control, never imagined it was even possible. He yanked her skirt up and tore her panties clean off; the ferocity sent a shiver through her, and she lifted her ass, just a little, sending the silent message that it wasn't too much or too far. That earned a grunt of pleasure and two hard thrusts, his hard cock gliding between her slick lips. Then he added fingers as he circled his hips, fucking into her harder with each touch.

"You…" Stroke. "Are…" Stroke. "Mine. Say it."

It was all she could do to get a breath for the wrenching pleasure, let alone speak. But she got, "Yours. Only yours," out around a guttural cry.

"Pru… Don't run, understand? I can't—" But whatever he might've said was lost in a shudder and a moan.

Driving into her from behind, Dom fastened his teeth on her shoulder, hard enough to bruise. The slight pain didn't hinder the spikes of sensation from his cock working inside her and the fingertips strumming her clit. She rocked back on him, not thinking of anything but the perfect angle. Pru huffed out an incoherent demand when she found it, and he steadied her hips with one hand.

"I'm coming." Not that she needed to tell him.

From the frantic increase of his thrusts, he felt it, and he held her down until his hands hurt her a little, and his teeth sank in. Dom shook and pushed and came, all liquid heat inside her. Pru felt it on her ass, on her thighs, and her entire body went boneless. Afterward Dom's breaths sounded almost like sobs, and when she tried to turn over, he held her closer and wouldn't let go. If she hadn't been so physically blasted, she would've pushed for a kiss.

"You okay?" she asked dreamily. "I've never seen you like that."

In answer, he grazed her jaw with his lips. He didn't roll over. He didn't pull away.

In the morning, she woke early and found him already gone.

LAST NIGHT, WHAT *the hell was that?* Dom wouldn't have said he had a plan for his relationship with Pru, but it shook him when he realized how *much* he wanted her, how crazy she could make him. He'd never chased a woman down and fucked her like some nonverbal sex beast. Sick to his stomach, he wasn't entirely sure he would've heard or stopped even if she'd asked him to, and that was so far past okay—and well into terrifying—that he didn't know if he could find his way back with a map and compass.

For a long moment, he saw again the imprint of his hands and teeth on her body, marks and bruises he'd left. It wasn't supposed to be that intense. If he could've predicted, he would have guessed that their relationship would be warm and comfortable, like a pair of cozy slippers. Not... this, whatever it was. Wanting her this much bothered him on multiple levels.

He was far too rattled to face their guests, and it was too

early besides. At first he didn't know where he was going until his steps turned toward the greenhouse. Inside, the hot, humid air came as a shock after the crisp cold outdoors. Arran was working with the orchids, and though Dom didn't really want to make small talk, it would be rude to bypass the pride seer without a word. Plus, Arran always saw too much, so he shouldn't give him a reason to analyze.

"Morning," he said.

"You look rough."

Exactly what I'm talking about.

Dodging that question, he noted, "I didn't see you or Hugh at the banquet last night."

The seer shrugged. "He hates that sort of thing, and I'm not likely to force him to attend. It's not like I love formal events either."

"But you both shine in tailored suits." Though Dom was teasing, the statement held more than a grain of truth. The pride seer and his mate were handsome, and they cleaned up well.

"I'd rather talk about you and whatever put that look on your face."

With a faint sigh, he waved away the concern. Arran took him at his word and left him to collect a handful of flowers; he didn't pick the rare ones, though nobody would chide him if he did. His intention coalesced as he gathered the simple bouquet. At the center of Ash Valley, he found the columbarium with a niche set aside for each member of the pride that had passed, along with pictures left by loved ones, small offerings beside their urns of ash. This was why there were no dead buried in what the others called the city of bone.

First he made his bows to his parents and greeted them.

"It's been too long. I wish I had a better excuse, but I can see someone's been taking care of you."

Their space was clean and polished with fresh flowers in a vase, but Dom added a couple of his own blooms to show proper regard. He touched the last picture they'd taken together. *Eighteen. I was eighteen.* When he thought back, it had been a hell of a decade. Just before his nineteenth birthday, his mother died of a virus she'd contracted on vacation in the south, and six years later, his father fell to a Golgoth guerrilla squad in the north. *It was supposed to be a routine visit to the bear hold, no complications.* And three years ago, he lost Dalena too.

Maybe it's no surprise I fell apart. Maybe the shocking bit is that it took so long.

"I hope you're both well." Even at his lowest, he liked picturing his parents together. "Things are kind of a mess, here..." For the next ten minutes, he told them about the state of affairs in Ash Valley, and he felt a little lighter when he finished.

But now, a more difficult visit lay ahead. Dalena's memorial wasn't far, only three steps to the right. As ever, her beauty took his breath away, but as he studied her familiar features, he realized he'd *forgotten*—that she had a divot in her chin and no dimples, that her cheekbones were so lovely and sharp, that her eyes were so thick-lashed, and her nose was longer than he'd remembered. Fresh pain broke over him in a drowning wave, and he went to his knees, hands shaking too hard to present the bouquet to the one person who had been his since the first moment he saw her.

Dalena hadn't been born in Ash Valley. She came from one of the satellite settlements in the east, near the wolf border. But when that small township burned, the refugees came in fives and tens, her family among them. Even at nine, he had been riveted. She was even smaller still, and for years, he had no name for the feelings that kindled at the sight of her. Yet they were always inseparable, along with Pru and Slay who made up the other sides of the square.

"I'm sorry," he whispered.

There was no stopping the tears. *It's too early for anyone to see.* They burned his cheeks like acid, dripping salt over his mouth. The worst part was that he could still taste Pru's skin as he made this apology to her best friend. *What am I doing? The fuck am I doing?*

Slay was right to object.

"Are we hurting you? I wish you could tell me. But if you could..." His words stalled, and he bowed his head, hands clenched on the shelf that housed such scant evidence that such an amazing person ever lived. "You might even say, *Why does it have to be Pru? I could understand anyone else.* And I'm sorry, I don't know. You must be wondering why... and what about Slay. Everything is just so fucked up."

Dom couldn't quite bring himself to whisper that he'd been ready to die. Surely Dalena wouldn't wish to hear that. If he knew her, she'd want him to live on and be as happy as he could without her. Shivering and swallowing a sob, he hauled himself upright and laid her flowers on the shelf, next to the smiling portrait.

"I miss you. Since I came back, since I stopped drinking, I haven't seen you even once."

He'd lived for the rare nights that she came to him, healthy and whole instead of wheezing and bloody. But since the first time he took Pru, he didn't dream at all, or if he did, they were so innocuous that he didn't recall. At first

that peace seemed like a good thing, but now he wondered
if it meant Dalena had gone away, driven off by the
conviction that he didn't love her anymore.

"I'm not replacing you," he said then. "I'm not. Just…
this is for the pride. I have to—"

The quiet scrape of soles on the tile startled him, and he
turned to find Pru there, so pale that each freckle looked like
a copper dot. Her hand clenched until her knuckles went
white on the flowers she held. With some dim, horrified
part of his mind, he realized her bouquet matched the ones
in his family vase. It was so Pru. Before they were mated,
she must've been tending to the courtesies for him. A few
days back, Caio had even mentioned that she was the one
who had taken care of his apartment after it became a crime
scene. When he imagined her on her hands and knees,
scrubbing up her friend's blood, he couldn't breathe.

He already owed her so much, and now he'd stolen her
chance at happiness too, tying her to him with a deal she
hadn't needed to make. Aching, he couldn't meet her gaze.
How much did she hear? How much did I hurt her? While the
marks might not be physical, like last night, they probably
cut deeper.

For an endless moment, only the rasp of her breath
broke that awful silence. He feared she might cry, but then
she lifted her chin and forced a smile. "It's all right," she said
softly. "I was… these are for your parents, and I'm visiting
my mother too, but you were here first. I'll come back. Go
ahead."

He would've felt better if she shouted at him or sobbed.
Inexplicably he felt as if she'd caught him doing something
awful. *Those wounded eyes.* But he couldn't chase her as he
had last night; his shoes felt as if they were filled with lead.

Somehow, it seemed best to let her go.

15.

THERE'S NO REASON I should feel like this.

When Pru found Dom talking to the love he lost, it shouldn't rip her chest open. *He never promised his heart. Friendship. Respect. I knew what he could offer when I went into this, and I'm lucky overall.* The silent pep talk didn't help much. Her sternum still hurt, and the tears simmering in the back of her throat wouldn't go away.

She couldn't go home because that would be the first place he'd check. Either way, Pru wasn't ready to talk to Dom. The flowers she'd collected were already wilting in the cold, so she waited, hidden, for Dom to leave the columbarium. It took nearly fifteen minutes, and she wondered what more he had to say. Finally, she got the chance to slip in and leave her forlorn floral offering, splitting the bouquet between her mother and his parents. Since she'd been back, she hadn't visited Dalena, but today was definitely not the time, given that she felt equal measures of sorrowful and apologetic.

Afterward, she stepped into the icy air and pulled her coat collar up. In better weather, the park would be full of families, laughing children, and pride warriors engaging in friendly competition. The sky above reflected her mood—heavy and leaden—and it spat intermittent snow, mixed with freeing rain, so her hair was damp when she reached the uncertain shelter of the gazebo. Summertime would find musicians gathered here, but winter brought only silence, exactly what she had in mind.

The ashes were cold in the fire pit with enough wood stockpiled that Pru busied herself lighting it. Warmth would be nice, plus she hoped focusing on a task might calm her down. But when she finished, she only had a fire going and no greater sense of calm. With a quiet cry, she collapsed onto the stone bench nearby and buried her face in her hands. No amount of looking on the bright side could stop the pain, so she let it come.

I'm not replacing you, Dom had assured Dalena.

For some reason she'd forgotten—and she shouldn't have—that he'd said, *You will never fill her shoes. You're not even her shadow anymore.*

Not even her shadow.

In school it didn't bother her to be called Dalena's sidekick. None of this was fresh or new, so why did she feel so raw? At first she tried holding her breath, but that only set her head throbbing like it might explode. At last Pru gave in and cried until she couldn't breathe. Afterward, her eyes stung. Just as she was winding down, the last person she wanted to see strode up the path toward her. Not Dom.

Slay.

He perched beside her, wrapped in a leather jacket with a wooly lining. Before she could retreat, he touched her cheek. "You're fucking frozen, and your face is chapped."

That was to be expected. She leaned closer to the fire and wished she could blame her tears on the smoke blowing into her face. Slay shrugged out of his coat and wrapped it around her, hovering with an uncertainty that might have been touching if she hadn't closed the door on him so firmly. Before, he never seemed interested in her wounds, preferring to disengage before they talked about anything important. But she had followed him long enough to find his smell comforting, even now.

"Thanks, I guess."

"What's wrong?"

"Don't worry about it." Though Pru didn't say, *I'm not your business,* she tried to make it clear from her tone.

Slay flinched. "It was bad enough when I thought you were happy. But this is worse. What happened exactly?"

"Go away." When he didn't, she stood up. "Or not. Put out the fire when you leave."

"You said we could be friends. The way you're acting now proves that's bullshit."

As she turned, he caught her wrist. Pru shook him off, quietly grateful that he was so good at making her mad. "How did *you* see this going? You give me your coat, I weep in your arms and... what? Fill in the rest because I don't know what you're trying to achieve."

"Never mind."

"Here." She stripped out of his jacket and handed it back. "I'm going."

If nothing else, fighting with Slay had restored her equilibrium enough for her to carry on. Weeks ago, she'd promised to stop by the training center, as most of her class would be playing there today, and she liked her students enough to spend time with them even during winter break. Before she headed in for a rowdy morning, she paused in the public restroom to put a cold, wet towel on her eyes. A few minutes later, Pru decided she looked passable for sweating with small children. When she arrived, Hugh— Arran's husband and the pride athletic director—had the kids lined up in preparation for a round of Red Rover.

"Sorry I'm late," she called. "Who's ready for a history lesson?"

A chorus of young voices rang out in protest, and Hugh grinned; he was short and fit with light brown skin and freckles that made Pru like him in solidarity. She joined the opposing team and linked hands, so the fun could begin. Emptying her brain, she fixed all her efforts on preventing the runners from breaking through... because with so much running and screaming, it was impossible to focus on being sad. The first small body hit her arms, and she locked on with fresh shifter strength.

A black-haired boy named Felix sprang back and tumbled onto his bum with a betrayed expression. "You don't *look* that strong."

"I heard Miss finally changed," a girl whispered.

"Isn't she Matron Asher now?"

Oh, shit. I didn't think of any of that.

Thankfully Hugh blew his whistle. "Less chatter, more running!"

He guided them through a series of challenges after Red Rover ended, and Pru appreciated her new level of endurance, a free gift from the Animari gods. Her class was too young or he'd add some shifting practice, as he did with the older students. She recollected sharply how humiliating it had been to be one of three Latent pupils exiled to the library while the others did wilderness training.

"Did everyone have fun?" Hugh called, as parents came to claim their offspring.

Pru smiled and blotted the sweat from her forehead. "*I did.*"

"You've got about two weeks left on break, right?" He worked closely with the pride school, scheduling activities when classes weren't in session.

"Yep. I hope you'll wear them out proper for me so they're docile enough to learn when they come back."

For a moment, he watched the kids rush from the room as if they'd been shot from a cannon, then gave a rueful grin. "Tall order, but I'll do my best."

This was a crucial break from life-or-death issues.

"I'm off. Hug Arran for me."

"Does it still count if I do it for me instead?"

Pru laughed. "Definitely. I spy your next group queuing in the hall, so I'm escaping before you talk me into another round."

"Coward."

She waved in acknowledgment and headed for the exit. Past the cluster of training rooms, a well-lit tunnel led from the sports complex to the adjacent spa, complete with steam rooms, bubbling hot baths, and dry heat sauna. Private apartments had at least one shower stall, but for a long scrub and soak, nothing beat the pride tubs. Screens separated small male and female bathing areas for those who preferred privacy, but the biggest pool was communal. Pru stripped off, stowed her belongings in a cubby, and slipped into the water. This time of day, nobody else was around, just what she needed to finish getting her head in order.

Steam rose from the bath in contrast to the relative chill of the room. For a bit, she paddled and splashed in the hot water before getting down to the business of a proper scrub.

It would be better if someone was around to wash her back, and she could've called Joss, who was always up for a gossip and soak, but her cousin would know something was up, and she had nothing to say about what happened that morning.

From across the path, she heard a quiet splash. *Odd. I didn't see anyone come in.* All the water dimmed her ability to scent intruders, but a chill rolled over her anyway. Suddenly Pru felt more than naked, and she thought of Dalena, what her last moments must've been like.

When the corpse floated past her, she couldn't even scream.

As Dom settled at the conference table with Magda on his right and Slay on his left, he noted that his second smelled faintly of Pru. His first impulse was to punch some answers out of Slay, but that was wildly inappropriate for multiple reasons. First, he was the one who'd hurt her, so if she'd gone to Slay for consolation, while that left him feeling shitty, he couldn't complain. Second, with the conclave about to begin, there was no room for personal issues. Finally, the last thing he needed was for Talfayen or Alastor to get a glimpse of inner turmoil and try to wedge a knife into those cracks.

The accords were piled at the center of the table, a boggling hundred and seven pages in small print, with codicils so outdated and obscure that it addressed the jurisdiction of someone else's sheep encroaching on your property. Dom hoped the document could be updated this time since nobody was raising sheep these days. Well, he couldn't speak for the Golgoth, actually, but from the terrifying glimmers he'd gotten from Eamon on his return, it didn't seem probable. For all he knew, the demon kin feasted on the flesh of fallen enemies.

"Everyone has gathered. Do you plan to keep us waiting?" Talfayen asked sharply.

With perfect timing, a guard burst into the room without knocking. She rushed over to whisper, "Murder, sir. One of the Eldritch entourage has been found in the baths."

The wolf and bear lords certainly had hearing keen enough to catch that revelation. Talfayen proved he did too by lurching to his feet. "Who? What's happened?"

No hope of keeping this quiet.

"Peace talks will have to wait," he said. "This is urgent. Come with me if you wish."

He hoped the other leaders would opt out, but all of them followed him out of the admin center, across the plaza to the spa. Ash Valley was a sizable settlement but still small enough to be traversed on foot, part of why he insisted all vehicles remain on the other side of the gate. For once, Talfayen had no complaints, only maintained a grim silence that worried Dom more.

When they arrived, he found Pru giving an account to two pride guards. A body had been covered nearby. He didn't smell even a trace of blood, so the Eldritch probably hadn't been killed here. The bath was the perfect place to dump a body, the hot water scouring away any evidence that might be left behind. Talfayen knelt and uncovered the man's head, revealing an ivory mask. Dead eyes stared up at nothing, and the Eldritch leader's face sort of... crumpled. He went to his knees and with shaking hands touched the waxen features.

"This is Iolas, my sister's son. You offered hospitality, I

accepted, and now a member of my family has been struck down." Shaking with rage, Talfayen rose, seeming as if he would challenge Dom right then.

We won't even make it to talking about the accords.

"This isn't the first security issue they've had." That sly observation came from Prince Alastor, who regarded the dead Eldritch with an indifferent tilt of his head.

Before things could escalate, he nodded at Magda, who went to work in soothing mode. While she preferred physical challenges, she was better at calming troubled waters than Slay, who would take affront and fight somebody, left unchecked. *This is exactly why I came back.* He dragged his second over to the guards recording Pru's statement.

"Do you know what killed him?"

"Garrote," she said.

"Is that your professional opinion?" Dom should have smiled at her or something, but between their exchange earlier and the corpse on the ground, his face wouldn't shift from sad and somber lines.

Just as well, for Talfayen would've taken it the wrong way, and he joined the group a few seconds later. "I demand answers."

Wish I had some.

"Perhaps we should remove ourselves before the Animari pick us off one by one," Alastor suggested.

Beren seemed to have had enough. "Look here, there's a whole mess of possible culprits gathered. You have some nerve blaming *us*. Let's see some evidence."

"I'm neither judge nor juror," the Golgoth prince said, smiling.

Is he behind this? But to what end...? It wouldn't benefit anyone if the peace talks dissolved so early. Hurriedly, he stepped in before the irascible bear lord could come to blows with the bereaved Eldritch leader. His heart dropped when Slay went to Pru immediately and touched her shoulder.

Dom clearly heard him murmur, "You all right?"

I should've done that first. But today seemed determined to test how many things he could get wrong.

"Fine." Pru stepped away and folded her arms in a defensive gesture.

He shouldn't be glad over her putting distance between them, but a tiny part of him eased a bit at seeing he still had her loyalty. Somehow. Things were still beyond fucked up, but maybe they weren't irretrievable. Talfayen's grim aspect told him it wouldn't be easy to keep him from packing up. The Noxblade had claimed the Eldritch leader was a traitor, so maybe this murder related to his secret Golgoth alliance.

Assuming that's even true.

Mustering his courage, he strode over to Pru and wrapped an arm around her shoulders. She tensed. There were a thousand ways she could reject him, shame him, or send a message. He wished there weren't so many witnesses, because he owed her an apology for hurting her. *Not the time. I'm sure she knows that.* But he didn't relax until her hand settled on his back; it felt like silent reassurance.

"We'll put all the personnel we can spare to finding answers," Dom said. "I recommend forming a task force with members of each faction."

Raff nodded. "I'll send the captain of my guard. That way everyone can be assured the same access to information."

The bear lord added, "Likewise. Until we get to the

bottom of this, nobody is safe."

"You have my deepest condolences and profuse apologies." He bowed to each member of the Eldritch party in turn and waited for acknowledgment from Talfayen before straightening.

"It's sickening. And so strange that your mate happened to find him."

Dom's blood chilled, and his skin crawled with the desire to shift. With every fiber of his being, he wanted to teach Talfayen a lesson with fangs and claws. He resisted; the conclave wasn't completely a lost cause yet, but the prospects of getting all factions to sign off on new agreements seemed unlikely. If he mauled Talfayen over his bad attitude, he might as well sign and stamp a declaration of war.

Easy. He's grieving and has the right to blow off some steam.

"I hope you're not insinuating she had anything to do with this. Ash Valley gains nothing and loses much with your nephew's death."

"Please forgive Lord Talfayen," a Noxblade said. "He's distraught."

"You're all beasts. If I could, I would cut all ties with your kind," the Eldritch leader spat.

Raff's lips curled back in a snarl, but Dom motioned him to silence as the pride physician arrived. They didn't have enough foul play to warrant someone dedicated to full-time forensic science, but Sheyla should be up to the task, though she usually treated illness. The onlookers fell quiet as she studied the body.

"He wasn't killed here. Someone surprised him from behind. Based on the angle, they were of a similar height. For what it's worth, it was quick." She bowed to the

Eldritch leader as well, and he seemed more amenable to receiving condolences from her.

"That rules out your mate," said Talfayen in a grudging tone.

Dom reckoned that was as close to an apology as the Eldritch would offer, so he inclined his head and turned his attention to the crisis. "Assemble the task force and interview anyone who used the baths this morning. Magda, you take a look at surveillance footage. This conclave will be postponed until we solve this."

"Then there's no point to my being here," Prince Alastor said.

"Nobody leaves." That came from Slay, but he agreed with that judgment, so he didn't cut in. "Apologies to Your Royalness, but we can't risk the culprit slipping away."

He nodded. "As of now, Ash Valley is in lockdown. Until we clear up who's responsible, nobody will be allowed in or out of the hold."

16.

GAVRIEL WAS THE last person Pru expected to find at her door so late at night.

It had taken hours to conclude the preliminary murder investigation, and as the closest thing to a witness, she had repeated her story multiple times to a plethora of questioners. Now it was nearly midnight, and Dom was still dealing with the damage. Ignoring her shock, the Noxblade slipped past her and closed the door.

He carried a small black box, and he used it to check every inch of the flat. Apparently satisfied with his inspection, he sat on the sofa without waiting for an invitation. "How long before your mate returns?"

"I'm not sure," she answered. "It would've been better if you'd made an appointment."

"Try not to be stupider than you can help."

"Pardon me?"

"If I have business that requires I ensure that we're not overheard, do you think I can put it on a schedule?" His voice contained enough blistering scorn to strip the paint from the walls.

I'm too tired for this shit. Only the fact that she'd killed his brother kept her from kicking him out. With effort, she held on to her composure. *For once, I hope Dad comes back late, if at all. He'll be safer that way.*

"That's true enough. Do you want something to drink?"

"You'd probably poison me."

"Only on Tuesdays."

In the end, she made tea, which he pretended to drink and so did she. They stared at one another for an awkward half hour before Dom keyed the pin and shambled in, seeming truly wrecked. The dark circles were back, along with fresh lines, and his hair was badly rumpled by endless rakes of restless fingers. He drew up short just inside the door and stared at Gavriel.

"This must be important." Dom dropped into an armchair and offered an expectant look.

"First, a confession. But it won't help you. I need you to promise to hear everything before you react. Can you do that?" Gavriel glanced between them, evidently seeking agreement.

Pru nodded as Dom said, "I'm listening."

"I killed Iolas."

At first Pru thought she must've imagined that, but based on Dom's expression, he'd heard it too. So she had to ask, "Why?"

"I was searching Talfayen's quarters... and Iolas returned unexpectedly." From his expression, Gavriel bitterly regretted that failure. "It was him or me."

"We've seen no proof, none whatsoever, that Talfayen is in league with the Golgoth. I'm half-inclined to turn you over as the traitor." Dom sounded dead serious too.

"That would be extremely ill-advised. I didn't find what I was looking for, but what I did carry away will suffice. I'll warn you, this won't be easy to hear." Serious red eyes studied her mate's face, and ice formed in Pru's stomach.

Dom rapped his knuckles against the side table as a sign of readiness. "Let's have it."

"I pulled this audio file from Iolas's phone. You'll probably understand why he was keeping it once you listen to it."

"Stop talking and hit play," Pru said.

But how bad is this that a trained assassin feels so uncomfortable revealing it?

An unknown male spoke as soon as Gavriel tapped his screen. "Are you certain this is necessary? It seems... extreme."

But the man who replied, Pru would recognize his voice anywhere. Lord Talfayen sounded brusque but also hushed. "You lack the experience to understand, but trust me, it's for the greater good. I'm starting us on the road to reclaiming lost glory. The endgame will unfold over a measure of years, not months, but we are a patient people, and you will appreciate my brilliance in due time."

"Understood. The pride bitch will be dead by nightfall."

Dalena. They can only be talking about her. There had been accidents among other settlements, deaths by natural causes, but *only* Dalena had been murdered in recent years. *So Iolas did the killing... on his uncle's orders?*

Dom was so pale that she feared he might pass out. For a long, agonizing moment, he said nothing. Then, "Can you show me when that file was created?"

"I copied it from Iolas's phone, so it says today. For obvious reasons, I couldn't risk being caught with his property. You will have to take my word that in his directory, it was dated the morning of your first wife's death."

First wife. That makes me second. Funny how the Noxblade twisted the knife, even when he was trying to be delicate. Apparently they just had that sort of bad, bloody fate between them.

"I have to ask, did you dump Iolas with me on purpose?"

Gavriel chuckled with every evidence of delight. "That was just fate being whimsical and kind. The baths were the obvious place to dispose of him, and you happened to be there. I couldn't have planned it better."

Asshole.

"Did anyone see you move the body? What about our cameras?" Dom cut in, impatient.

Gavriel sighed and curled his lip. "Do you think this was my first sanitation?"

She'd just been curious if he meant her to find the victim, but if he said it was a coincidence, there was no reason to mistrust him, not that it mattered anymore.

Lacing his fingers together, Dom studied the assassin so intently that Pru would've fidgeted. "You told my mate you didn't know of her arrival, but I came across some footage that made me think you were surveilling her. Explain."

The Noxblade lifted a shoulder with careless disinterest. "I have no way to prove it wasn't me, but things would've gone better if I had been. This is the only truth I can offer— someone *else* was watching her."

A chill prickled her nape, creeping over her shoulders to her lower back, where the ice settled. "But we don't know who?"

With her eyes, she asked Dom why he never mentioned this. He only shook his head, and she gathered from his expression that he hadn't wanted to worry her. Pru filed that away under questions that needed answering; she had a bunch of those, including one about the conversation they'd just heard.

"Why would Iolas keep that recording?" she wondered aloud.

Gavriel glared like the answer should be obvious. Maybe, if it hadn't been such a long, dreadful day, she could've come up with a clever theory, or even the correct one. But her head ached, full of the dead Eldritch's face floating past her and the excruciating snapshot of Dom weeping before her best friend's memorial.

"Leverage." Dom's voice came out harsh and raw. "In case he needed it against his uncle. Or if we ever tracked him down, he could claim he was only following orders."

"The worst crimes are often committed by those 'following orders'," Gavriel snapped.

"It appears I'm in your debt," Dom said. "Today you answered the question that has been tormenting me for the last three years *and* you dispatched the murderer."

Pru tilted her head, thoughtful. "This doesn't tell us what Talfayen is planning with the Golgoth, but it does bear out your report of collusion."

The Noxblade nodded. "I'm glad you've surmised as much. I was hoping to uncover some correspondence or hint of their intentions, but…" He shrugged.

"Talfayen hasn't come this far without being careful." If she didn't know Dom so well, she would miss the way the fingers of his left hand dug into the arm of the chair, nearly rending the fabric. "What is it that you want from me? I'll cooperate."

"Make a show of investigating. Invent leads if you have

to. I just need more time. If I can find a hint of their plan, we can stop it and I can send word to..." Gavriel hesitated and then appeared to come to some conclusion. "My lady, Princess Thalia."

That shocked Pru more than anything he'd said so far. She couldn't help but whisper the question. "Talfayen's daughter?"

"And Iolas's cousin. Her father keeps her imprisoned on their estate, but she is not without resources." Unmistakable pride colored Gavriel's voice. "I am not the only Noxblade sworn to her service. We act as her agents until such time we can free her and take the crown."

"So you want me to stall," Dom concluded.

"With every gram of your skill. I realize I'm asking a great deal since you must want to tear out Talfayen's throat and have done with all this."

When Dom smiled, all empty eyes and chilling menace, Pru's blood iced over. "It's a viable solution. He can't do shit bleeding out on my floor."

Gavriel seemed ready to kneel, out of keeping with his usual attitude. "You've acknowledged there is a debt between us. To repay me, you must aid the Eldritch. We need to root out those loyal to Talfayen, or my lady's regime will never be secure. I'm sure she will be generous in her gratitude."

"Plus, they're still plotting to kill you," Pru added.

"Fine. In the morning, I'll spin all our wheels pretending to hunt you down. It'll be a great show. Now if you don't mind, I need to get to bed."

"Of course." Gavriel executed a formal bow, somehow managing to make it clear that courtesy was for Dom alone.

Pru didn't bother to see him out.

RED-HOT RAGE CHOKED Dom until he could hardly breathe.

Now I know who held the knife, and the bastard who ordered it done has been eating my food for how long? He flattened his palms on the cool wood of the door, struggling to get a handle on the rising fury. Biding his time seemed impossible. He needed to shift. The roaring in his head demanded that he find Talfayen, drag him out of his warm bed, and—

"Dom." Pru called him back from the brink like that was her prime directive.

He took a long breath, let it out. Another. "How am I supposed to do nothing? Pretend it's all the same when everything has changed?"

"It's for the pride," she said.

That was always her answer. Didn't she *ever* get tired of setting aside her own wants and desires? But before he could ask, she went on, "If it falls apart too soon, we go to war. Right now, there's a chance we can resolve it peacefully. If that happens, we save a lot of lives and you get justice for Dalena."

"I want to kill Talfayen with my bare hands."

"That's murder, and without sufficient proof of his misdeeds, it draws down the wrath of all Eldritch. They come after Ash Valley, and maybe the other Animari in retaliation. In conjunction with the Golgoth, that could mean the end of everything we are. I know you won't choose that path."

"Why do you have to be so fucking sensible? You won't let me rage or bleed." He hauled his arm back to punch the wall.

Pru caught it, and she was strong enough to twist it behind his back. "That's wrong. You can rage. Not bleed. Let's take this conversation to the bedroom."

"I'm not in the mood." He shouldn't be snarling at her. Damn, he *knew* that. In fact, he should be on his knees begging her forgiveness.

"My dad will probably be in soon. Do you want him seeing you like this? Would you care to explain what it's about?"

That penetrated his fury fog, so he let her lead him into the room they shared. Her timing was uncanny because only a couple of minutes after she squirted toothpaste on her brush, he heard the click of the door. Pru flashed him a look that conveyed *I told you so* pretty clearly.

With a breath that was more of a soft groan, he sank to the floor beside the bed. "It doesn't help. I thought finding out who did it would change something. But it doesn't. She's still gone, and I'm still the asshole who didn't save her."

"That's not fair."

Dom closed his eyes. "Bullshit. I don't even know what I was *doing* that day, and if I'd come home ten minutes earlier or called to check in—"

"You had no reason to suspect she wasn't safe," Pru cut in. "So stop blaming yourself. If I'd knocked off work early or invited her to lunch, she wouldn't have been home. Iolas would've missed his window. But then, maybe he'd have tried again. When someone is determined to do an awful thing, the timing doesn't matter, only their intent to do wrong."

Her logic was insidious, permeating his wild thoughts like soothing smoke. Everything she said sounded true, but it didn't touch the pain excavating his gut. Dom buried his face in the covers dangling over the side of the bed. The fabric felt cool and comforting on his skin, and he couldn't stand for Pru to watch him fall apart. It seemed like she hadn't seen anything good from him in years.

Warmth startled him.

He'd expected to hear the sounds of her completing her nightly rituals and then the soft creak of her getting into bed. Instead, she seemed to be leaning against his side. Dom couldn't make heads or tails of her behavior; she should be exhausted, furious, or both. Yet when she touched him, the hurricane in his head receded. She rubbed his shoulders and back with perfect pressure, digging deep enough to ease the fiercest knots.

"Please don't be good to me," he whispered.

But he didn't have the fortitude to stop her. That became evident when she wrapped herself around him, and he turned into her arms with a shudder rooted in requirement and relief. In his entire life, he'd never cried so hard; the effort to keep quiet nearly strangled him. *Can't let her dad hear.* Pru held him and whispered nonsense until the shaking stopped. Her body felt incredibly soft, and the curve of her neck tasted of salt from his tears. As he nuzzled her throat, his cock sprang awake. In the wake of the emotional storm, he had the furious urge to fuck, but when he lifted his lips to hers, she only gave him a soft peck.

"Not tonight. It'll make you feel better for a while, but I don't want us to get sucked into a loop, where you use sex to forget and then when the endorphins drop, you feel worse again."

"A sex loop, huh?"

"Let's go to bed," she said.

"Are you sure this has nothing to do what happened this morning?"

Her eyes dropped, so he lifted her chin to search her

gaze with his.

"No. And it's not that I don't want you. But it would be awful if you started feeling guilty... about us."

Without meaning to, he flinched and pulled his hand back. "That's pretty—"

"On the mark? Everything happened so fast. It's natural that you need some time to adjust and process what we learned today."

"I wish you'd just yell at me and call me an asshole," he said softly.

"But you're not. You're pretty fantastic, and I'm lucky—"

"No," he cut in. "That's me. I'm so sorry, Pru. You're all the sweetness in the world, and this morning, I had no idea you were around."

Dom didn't miss the way her hand curled up on her knee, as if to battle a bad memory. Yet she still excused him. "You didn't do anything wrong. It was just bad timing, that's all."

"If you say so." While he didn't feel good about leaving it there, he'd apologized. If she wanted to sidestep the issue and move on, how could he argue? "Well, then. Am I allowed a good-night kiss?"

She smiled. "If you want one."

"Always."

The ache in his chest lessened as Pru offered her mouth. Since he understood this wasn't going anywhere tonight, he took his time, teasing her lips with his. He spent forever nibbling her lower lip, licking the upper, until she made a sweet sound in her throat and tried to take his tongue. Instant heat blossomed, but he tamped it down in favor of kissing her more, deeper, sweeter, until she trembled in his arms and her breath came in delicious puffs. When he finally pulled back, she grabbed his head and pulled him back in. Eventually, he realized he had Pru flat on her back beneath him, and his cock was so hard it hurt. She didn't help matters by rubbing against him as if she'd forgotten her sexual proscription. A groan escaped him.

"You said no sex. Not no orgasms." While he respected her reasons for drawing a line, their hormones wouldn't simply evaporate.

"I like the way you think."

"I'm offering for your sake. Who knew you'd get so turned on from a little kissing?"

Her smug look sent a clear danger signal. "Who says I plan to stay frustrated? I know my body. I can take care of it."

"What?" She couldn't mean what he suspected.

When she slipped a hand into her panties, Dom couldn't look away. The soft, slick sound of her stroking herself stole every word from his head. Pru kept her eyes fixed on him as she did it; a sexy flush started at her shoulders, worked up her neck, and into her cheeks. As she rubbed, her lips parted, breath coming faster.

"Feels good," she whispered. "Want to see more?"

Wordless, he nodded.

She paused long enough to slip out of her panties and settle on the edge of the bed, above him. That move left him feeling like a worshipper at the feet of a goddess. The irresistible smell of her sex went straight to his head. Dom didn't realize he was squeezing his cock through his pants until he caught her gaze on his fingers. He should probably stop, but it was impossible. To stifle a groan, he bit down hard on his lower lip.

A few seconds later, when she came, he did too.

17.

I N THE WAKE of an intense orgasm, Pru jerked with the aftershocks.

She expected Dom to withdraw. Most likely, they shouldn't have done this much. He needed time to accept his new reality, and this probably just muddied the waters. But instead of locking down emotionally, he seemed shy and shaken, more than a little off balance. Then he went up on his knees and wrapped his arms about her waist, burying his face in her belly.

The position should have felt all kinds of strange and awkward, but it didn't. Of their own volition, her fingers sifted through his hair as he shivered beneath her hands. Moments like these gave her this awful, blighted hope that maybe someday, he could be a little bit... hers. Not borrowed, not stolen. But Pru couldn't even imagine what that would look like.

With all her heart, she wished she could reassure him, yet in all likelihood, tomorrow would be worse, as Dom would have a hell of a time keeping his cool the first time he saw Talfayen. The Eldritch traitor would be lucky if Dom didn't rip his throat out, no matter how many logical arguments she presented. There was a savage side to her that would rejoice in that because with one flick of his blade, Iolas had stolen her best friend.

Forever. On Talfayen's orders.

Dom cleared his throat a couple of times before he finally got some words out. "We should shower."

"Together?" Surprise flared up; this was the first time he'd suggested that.

"Unless you don't want to."

"It's more efficient," she said. "And we'll be done faster, but it'll be a tight squeeze."

"I'm good with that."

He got up with a minor grimace, she assumed because of the mess in his briefs, and went to start the hot water. She joined him a moment later, which gave him time to strip down and get in the stall. There was barely enough room for her to step in and shut the door, so for a few seconds, they wriggled, figuring out the best way to stand. The mood turned sensual when he spun her so he could wash her back. This wasn't about sex; she recognized the intimacy of his touch and his silent, unacknowledged need to take care of her. So she leaned forward and gave herself into his hands—and they went everywhere. With each swipe of the sponge, he apologized more profusely than he ever could in words. Afterward, she lathered him the same way, rinsed, and her heart didn't ache as much by the time he shut the water off.

His hands were clumsy as he dried her, and Dom offered a crooked smile. "Sorry. I'm just so fucking tired."

"Me too. Bed?"

"Not yet."

With gentle hands, he pressed her to the edge the mattress and got her brush from the dresser. Long, soothing strokes coaxed the tangles from her wet hair. She'd never even dreamed that she'd be lucky enough to have a mate who cared this much. *Imagine how it would be if he loved me.* Pru flinched away mentally from the question.

"That's good," she said softly.

In answer, he crawled under the covers naked, and it seemed wrong to get her pajamas, like if she did, she was the one putting barriers between them. Dom snuggled into her at once, but even as he did, she couldn't rid herself of the truth that she was—and always would be—a poor substitute. At last exhaustion dragged her under, freeing her from such dark thoughts.

When she roused, it was barely pushing daylight, and he was still sound asleep. It didn't take much to extricate herself from his loose hold; in fact, he curled up around her pillow as she slid from the bed. Pru got dressed quickly, trying to outrun the implications, and then hurried from the room with a quiet snick of the door.

She found her dad nursing coffee, despite the fact that he'd come in late. His tired face told her he still found it tough to sleep, though it had been a year since her mother passed. Pru accepted the mug he slid her, and she gulped half of it, reaching for normalcy. *I can't fall into Dom like this. He's my mate, not a black hole.*

"Heard about what happened yesterday. You all right?" That was her dad, gruff and laconic, even with serious issues.

"It was pretty awful. And now that we're in lockdown, things will only get worse."

"They wouldn't let me out to prowl last night," he complained.

"So that's why you came home."

He skirted that with an invitation. "You want to go for a run?"

"Right now?" Actually, it didn't sound bad.

There was a track through the park, where the wind might blow away doubts and mental cobwebs alike. Since her father rarely asked for anything, she guessed he must really be feeling the sting of being cooped up. *And it's only been a few hours. What will the pride be like when it's been days?* For a while, they might enjoy the break from patrols and recon, but sooner or later, tensions would rise—

And I'm not worrying about it right now.

Since her ability to fret was practically a superpower, she slammed a mental gate in front of all the ways this situation could go horribly wrong. Then she downed the rest of her coffee. "Let's go."

A real smile creased the tired lines of her dad's face. He got to his feet immediately. "Don't worry about gearing up. We can shift at the pavilion."

"That sounds fantastic."

At this hour, they only passed a few guards, and the park was empty, apart from Hugh and Arran. She recognized them straightaway, serval and wildcat roughhousing in a patch of snow. For a moment, she just let their joy soak in—two beautiful pride mates in love—and then she hustled after her father, who was almost to the changing area. Pru stripped quickly, put away her belongings, and then shifted; the pavilion was open on one side so the pride didn't have to worry about dealing with doors in cat form.

In lynx form, her father was impressive: amber-eyed, big and rangy, with white fluff on cheeks and chin. He bounded toward her and knocked her down with an exuberance she never saw in his human aspect. Pru lashed her tail, sprang over the top of him, and pushed herself at top speed toward the track. Hugh snarled a greeting, but she didn't pause. Today, she'd just suck in the crisp air, savor the wind in her fur, and run until she fell over. Soon, her dad caught up because he spent his nights building stamina while she was curled up in a cozy bed.

They ran three laps before more family showed up. Pru had no idea how they'd heard, but she spotted Joss, two younger cousins, along with her favorite uncle. They waved madly on the way to the pavilion, and her heart went buoyant. *Why did I think nobody cares?* Somebody had clearly spread the word about her ordeal yesterday, and now the family was out in force. It was impossible to laugh as an ocelot, but she hoped the loud purring sent a clear message.

For at least an hour, she *ran*, didn't think, didn't fear, and it was glorious. Other pride mates had experienced this as kits, but she'd never known how it felt to frolic with her family as a cat. Eventually Joss tackled her, so they went sideways into the snow, and they wrestled until Pru's muscles felt like jelly. Then she just rolled around in the icy white, kicking up a huge mess, much to her younger cousins' delight. Eventually her dad signaled toward the changing area with a jerk of his head, and everyone headed that way.

As she shifted back, a pleasant exhaustion suffused her. Joss waited until she got a shirt on to hug her tight. "I bet it was awful."

Pru held on, letting the familiar scent wash over her. "I've had better days."

Briefly, she wished she could confide in her family, but there was too much at stake to be careless with these secrets. So she pretended she only had the trauma of a dead body weighing on her. Another cousin, Naveen, came over and joined the group hug for a moment, but her grumbling stomach ruined the moment.

Naveen grinned. "You're coming for breakfast, right? Ma's been cooking for two hours."

"Wouldn't miss it," she said, smiling.

FROM A DISTANCE, Dom watched as Pru came out of the pavilion surrounded by her family. Though he wasn't sure of her intentions, it had straight up sucked waking to a silent apartment and an empty bed. Concerned, he had gone looking, and he half-wished he hadn't found her, as he felt more alone now than he had on the mountain. Before he hurt her, she had shown him that life could be sweet again.

He shouldn't be loitering in the park, quasi-stalking his mate. There was no time to join her family for a long breakfast. Not now. But he wished she'd asked if he wanted to come. Because now, it felt like a party he hadn't been invited to, so he could only stand in the cold, listening to the laughter and music.

Enough of that. At least she isn't with Slay. Seeing that first thing would've been creamy shit frosting on a turd cake of a day.

The day had started out overcast, but a chill wind blew away the clouds, leaving a pale, clear sky. Even in winter, Ash Valley held glimmers of loveliness; Dom couldn't appreciate any of it. A dark mood gripped him when he wheeled and headed off to find Magda. Talfayen would want a report on their progress first thing, so he had to make the pretense convincing.

As expected, he found her in the hub, hunched over the

screen. From the look of her, she had been up all night scrutinizing footage. Guilt settled on his shoulder, hard. *I should tell her not to bother and get some sleep.* But that would open the door to questions, and she was too canny to be fooled by random excuses.

Magda had cared for Dalena too, and if she knew, everything would escalate. There was a saying that two people could keep a secret if one of them was dead, and as of now, they had three in the loop. He didn't entirely trust the Noxblade, but so far, it seemed like Gavriel had been dealing straight with them. *He has a lot to lose if this goes sideways.*

"What have you found?" he asked.

She growled deep in her throat. "A whole lot of nothing. It's like the attack on the retreat. The culprit knows all about our security, even where we've hidden cameras. Two of the units went down yesterday too."

"That can't be a coincidence."

"I'm trying to recover footage, but..." She sighed. "This asshole is seriously pissing me off. Not only is he a ghost, he's a gifted fucking murderer."

"Strange compliment."

"I can respect somebody's skills while still fantasizing about how satisfying it will be to disembowel him."

"Don't prejudge your enemy. It could be a woman. After all, you're one of the most dangerous people here."

Magda brightened at the compliment, which was no more than the truth. "I've missed your sweet talk. But seriously, I'm sorry I don't have any news. Talfayen is going to lose his mind over our 'incompetence'."

"I'll talk him down."

A muscle ticked in his jaw just from thinking about it. But he wrapped himself in Pru's cautionary words, using them as ropes to bind his darker impulses. With a nod for Magda, he strode through the admin center and reached the conference room as Beren arrived.

The bear lord wore a grim expression. "Bad business. Have you turned up any leads?"

"Not more than we knew yesterday. We're looking for an assailant around the victim's own height, strength enough to overpower him from behind."

"Most likely a man," Beren said.

Magda could pull it off.

For obvious reasons, he didn't say that aloud. "Have you seen any of the Eldritch today?"

"Not a single flowing lock or a chin hair. Not that they have whiskers." Beren rubbed his jaw and muttered, "Hairless bastards."

"Raff?" Dom asked.

Beren smirked. "Last I saw, he had a bag of sticky buns and a carafe of coffee. Think he meant to deliver breakfast to your security chief. How would a wolf and cat crossbreed work out, I wonder?"

"It's not unheard of," Dom pointed out. "And from what I recall, the children are one or the other, not mythic creatures."

"Next thing I know, you'll be telling me you're fine with mixing across Eldritch and Golgoth lines."

In all honesty, Dom had never given it any thought. "It would be hard for whoever gave up home and family to follow their mate to a strange land."

"Fool cub. Some barriers even love can't conquer. This nonsense almost makes me glad my heir has taken a vow of celibacy."

The seeds of an idea took root. If words on a page

weren't enough to keep the peace, maybe... well, Dom didn't have all the particulars in place, so he'd let it germinate for a while. The bear lord scowled, probably over his lack of response, and peered into the conference room. He came up behind Beren to scope things out. *Empty.* It had been optimistic to entertain the possibility that talks could commence with the shadow of murder looming over the table.

"Looks like I need to pay a consolation visit."

"Better you than me."

That seemed to end the conversation, so he left the grouchy bear to his own devices. Dom definitely dragged his feet on the way to see the Eldritch leader, but when he got there, he found a notice on the door that read IN LAMEN-TATION, DO NOT DISTURB. Though Gavriel hadn't mentioned anything about such a cultural observation, that didn't mean anything.

"I wouldn't knock," Prince Alastor said from behind him. "They don't take kindly to having their rituals interrupted."

Something about the Golgoth royal rubbed him the wrong way. Maybe it was how he always looked like he was about to laugh at somebody else's expense.

With effort, Dom kept his expression neutral. "Noted. I hope you can entertain yourself. Seems we have an unexpected day of leisure."

"I'm on my way to meet the fair Jocelyn. She's prom-ised a riveting inspection of your greenhouse. *I'd* prefer to drink myself into a stupor, but I haven't given up all hope for later."

It was impossible for him to tell if that was supposed to be funny, so he offered a polite smile. "Let me know if you need anything."

"What I need, pride master, neither you nor anybody in the waking world can provide." With that quietly caustic rejoinder, the prince sauntered away.

Dom sighed, wondering how long the Eldritch would be in seclusion. *Pru would probably know.* After a moment's consideration, he decided it would be odd *not* to ask her. Rather than interrupt her breakfast with a voice call, he sent a message.

Apparently Talfayen is incommunicado, some kind of mourning ritual?

She replied fast enough to make him smile. *Sorry, I completely forgot. Right now, they're fasting, painting each other in ash, and rending their garments. Tomorrow, they'll probably want to discuss funeral arrangements.*

Then I guess I have nothing to do today. He didn't intend that message as a hint, but she evidently took it as one.

Did you eat yet? If not, come to building four, unit 16. There's a ton of food left, and I promised you a boisterous family gathering.

Suddenly the world seemed five shades brighter. *Be right there.*

Dom set off at a brisk walk that became a run halfway through the admin center. A few people raised their hands in greeting, but nobody tried to stop him. They probably thought he had urgent pride business, considering how fucked up the situation had become. For the moment, however, there were no fires to put out and he'd savor the eye of the storm.

He didn't slow until he reached the third floor, where laughter drifted toward him like a kindly will-o'-the-wisp that could lead him out of darkness, if he was brave enough to follow. Breathing deep, he inhaled the scents of cooked apples, cinnamon and vanilla, warm coffee and buttery pastries. For some reason, the simple act of eating breakfast with Pru's family gained gargantuan significance. A strange insecurity took hold as he reached the door.

All I have to do is knock.

18.

WHEN PRU'S COUSIN Naveen opened the door, Pru was startled to see Dom. Though he'd said he would be right over, she'd suspected he was being polite and that she'd have to make excuses to her family. Yet he swept in with a smile, as if they didn't have a hundred problems boiling beneath the surface. If he was here, however, he must have time for a break, as he wasn't the sort to shirk responsibility.

A few more relatives had gathered, so her aunt and uncle had a full house. She spent a few minutes reminding Dom who everyone was, and he frowned. "Why do you seem so convinced I won't remember their names?"

Smiling, she whispered a reminder of who everybody was. Uncle Chaz and Aunt Glynnis were Pru's favorites among many relations; Glynnis was her mother's younger sister, so when she looked at her aunt, if she half-closed her eyes, she could pretend her mom was still around. Glynnis was more exuberant than her mother had been, but there was a definite resemblance. The best thing about her big extended family was that they didn't draw lines. Joss was a cousin from her dad's side, but she was still at this impromptu celebratory feast, filling her cheeks with hothouse strawberries and homemade yogurt.

"I remember that stage," Aunt Glynnis said fondly. "Everything seemed like a sweet little secret, didn't it, Chaz?"

Pru smiled at her aunt. "I'm just filling him in how everyone's related to him."

"Oh, good thinking," her uncle said. "It's a bit complicated at first, but you'll sort us out in no time as you're used to managing much more complicated pride business."

"Did you tell him I'm the best cousin?" Naveen asked.

Joss threw a wadded up napkin at her. "As if. What's the judgment criteria? Are you rating yourself in decibels?"

"Pot, kettle," Naveen said, catching the serviette and blotting her mouth with it daintily.

Laughing, Pru fixed a plate with pastries, fruit, eggs, and crispy bacon and offered it to Dom with a flourish. "Now, now, you're both pretty."

Her aunt circled Dom until he seemed faintly alarmed. "Are you sure you're feeding him enough? He's all gristle and teeth."

"I'm a good eater," he said defensively.

With fixed determination, he devoured all the food she'd given him. Since he'd said bring on the big domestic gathering, Pru didn't try to shield him from familial interest. Soon he had two small second cousins on his lap, rumpling his hair, while her uncle hovered. Her aunt was watching these two for their mother, her oldest daughter Caroleth, who was currently working in the admin center with Caio.

"Are you planning to save him?" Joss whispered.

Pru shook her head. "Dom's the pride leader. He can extricate himself from Jilly and Jase if he puts his mind to it."

"I'm more concerned about Chaz, to be honest." But when Joss grinned, she seemed more amused than troubled.

"I have a genealogy chart if you'd like to see it," Uncle Chaz said.

As Dom nodded and answered, "Yes, please," Pru swapped a look with Naveen, who didn't bother covering up her giggles.

"Your man's done for," the younger girl murmured. "Once Dad drags out all his lineage papers, there's no shutting him up for hours."

To Pru's vast amusement, Uncle Chaz *did* haul out all his notes, including a family tree painstakingly charted for five generations, and he explained it all in exhaustive detail with a number of historical anecdotes, some of which dated back to the Great War. As ever, that got Jilly and Jase's attention, and they paused in harrying Dom to listen to an account of how the Animari won their territory. Since she was a teacher at heart, she seized the moment.

"What year did we gain our independence? I forget…"

"1887," Jilly shouted.

"Close. It was 1888." She looked at Jase. "How long was the Great War?"

He sighed with all the boredom a nine-year-old could project. "We *just* learned this. In 1876, humans discovered our existence. War broke out in 1880 across two international borders, and we fought hard for our freedom. We allied with Eldritch and Golgoth in 1884. In 1888, the war ended with the signing of the Allegheny Accords. We were awarded territory to govern in the north, humans emigrated voluntarily, and our borders were declared in-in…" As Jase struggled with the word, Pru mouthed it, until he took the cue. "Inviolable. In 1890, we divided our homeland among the victors: Golgoth in the far north, the Eldritch got the far east, and we split the southern remainder, east to west, among the Animari."

"Wow," Naveen said. "He got all the dates right and everything."

"Good job." Uncle Chaz ruffled Jase's hair, or tried to, but the boy ducked away and put out his tongue.

"I know things too." Jilly's sulky face said she would be wailing soon if she didn't garner some of the attention.

"Tell us, please." Dom bounced his knee once, making the child giggle and earning Pru's gratitude, as Jilly's tantrums could be legendary.

"We got the south, wolves are east, and bears took the north, closest to the Golgoth. But since we were allies in the Great War, we didn't sign peace agreements until 1907, after the Golgoth started attacking us." Her recitation lacked the confidence of her twin's, and she glanced at Dom for confirmation when she paused.

"You're on the right track. Do you remember what the 1907 meeting was called?"

"The conclave," she answered, beaming.

"That's happening now," Jase said. "We review the terms every hundred years."

Pru got back in on the teaching action. "The papers we sign at the conclave, cementing the peace between our three factions, can anyone tell me the formal name?"

Uncle Chaz raised his hand, and Aunt Glynnis elbowed him. Pru noticed that her father had filled his belly and nodded off in an armchair, as ever bored by such discussions. His consistency was endearing. Jilly and Jase collaborated on the answer, whispering back and forth, and then Jilly said, "The Pax Protocols."

She gave them both a thumbs-up. "Excellent. That's enough history review for today. I'll be sure to mention how clever you both are when I see your teacher at school."

"Not school." Jilly moaned and collapsed in Dom's arms as if she were dying at the very mention of the word.

To Pru's delight, Dom played along. "Stay with us, you have so much to live for. If I survived grade four, you can too."

Jilly cracked an eye open to ask, "Did you hate it too?"

"Sitting still is the worst," Dom said. "But it's also good to learn things, otherwise your head will float away because it's too empty."

The little girl scowled at him. "That's a lie. Right?"

But everyone else was laughing too hard to answer her properly. In the confusion, Pru's dad woke up and randomly demanded to know who'd stolen his hat. That was funnier than it should've been too because she couldn't ever recollect him wearing one. Joss hugged him and patted his back as she giggled.

Amid the merriment, Aunt Glynnis drew her aside. "At first, I wasn't sure what to make of your news because I thought, under the circumstances, that he'd be all somber shadows, but he's quite a sunny person, isn't he?" With a pat, she added, "I like him. You chose well."

Presently, Dom was all smiles, tickling the crap out of Jilly, who might never leave his lap. There was no way she could disillusion her aunt with the truth. So she smiled and accepted the praise with a quiet face that hid her byzantine reaction. Her mate grabbed Jase then and dragged him into the tussle, so he was covered in shrieking, laughing children.

Maybe someday, they'll be ours. The sweetness of that possibility made her want to go over to him and kiss his head. But a thunderous pounding on the door prevented her from making that public claim.

DOM USED THE visitor as an excuse to stop wrestling. Waving the others off, he answered with an inquiring look and found Beren, red-faced and short of breath. "Sorry to interrupt but I have urgent news."

"Let's talk privately."

In short order, he said farewell and thanked the family for their hospitality, and then he followed the bear lord to his quarters. The fact that Beren didn't want to talk in the conference room spoke volumes. Dom expected to find Raff waiting, but not only was the wolf lord absent, even the clan guards had been dismissed.

"I received this ten minutes ago," Beren said.

He handed his phone over with a video file queued up. The sound and picture quality was shit, and it was obviously shot raw, but the content chilled Dom's blood—only thirteen seconds of footage, men in fatigues, shouting, cries of pain, a kaleidoscopic glimpse of live combat—and then static. No attached message, text or voice.

"From who?"

"One of my scouts. I can't raise him. His unit is comm-dead too. As I see it, the Golgoth have already broken the Pax Protocols, and they're massacring my people. I'm telling you in private as a courtesy... I'm done with this farce. First thing tomorrow, I'm going home."

Dom tried to sort bad from worse. "Are you sure it's the Golgoth?"

"Who else? I showed you the troop movement reports before. You think humans bypassed you and went straight for bear territory? Offer some bullshit that at least makes sense."

"I'm not arguing. Just fact-finding. Why strike now?"

"Element of surprise, fool cub. We're all away with unproven people left in charge of our demesnes. Lockdown or no, don't try to stop me."

"I'm not giving you an answer right this second. You do what you must in the morning, and I'll do the same. Because you know as well as I do that if you bail out on these talks, I lose all authority and the others will follow suit."

"I give no fucks about your authority. The only reason I'm not moving right now is the fact that half of my guards are hungover. It wouldn't serve me to drag them into combat at half efficiency. They're under orders to eat well, sleep it off, and be ready to move at six sharp."

"Calm down—"

"Are you trying to piss me off? If not, let's shorthand the rest. I have more important things to do." With that, Beren went to the door and gestured, clearly wanting Dom to get out.

"Why don't you contact another unit to investigate? I don't underestimate the danger to your people, but if things fall apart here, the consequences—"

"Good day, pride master."

Beren grabbed Dom by the shoulders and shoved him so hard that he slammed into the opposite wall. As the door closed, Dom balled up a fist and contemplated breaking it down. *No, that will only escalate. Maybe I can talk some sense into him in the morning.* If he couldn't, then he'd have two bad choices: either let Beren break lockdown, setting precedent for everyone else, or take up arms against an allied Animari. Under the circumstances, it wouldn't surprise him if Raff sided with Beren, and he definitely couldn't count on support from the Eldritch whereas Prince Alastor struck him as the sort to play the fiddle while the city burned.

Knowing the problem didn't bring him any closer to solving it, of course. With a muttered curse, he sent messages to Magda and Slay. Unlike Gavriel's request to stall Talfayen, he couldn't keep this development under wraps. Surprisingly enough, breakfast had relaxed him somewhat and taken his mind off his troubles, but the throb in his head came back with a vengeance. By the time he got to the ops center, his second and security chief were waiting.

"You said it was crucial," Magda said. "And your timing couldn't be better. I was about to pull that wolf's head off."

"Listen up," he barked.

Dom didn't mince words, and when he finished, both Magda and Slay were staring at him like he'd kicked them in the face. Understandable. The situation sucked in every conceivable way. For obvious reasons, he didn't want to be the one on record when the Pax Protocols collapsed like a badly designed bridge in earthquake territory. The humans had been watchful and cautious on their side of the border since the Allegheny Accords, and they limited travel like their neighbors to the north carried a host of infectious diseases. If the conclave failed, it would be as good as admitting humans were right about how warlike and dangerous the Animari, Eldritch, and Golgoth were. Shit, a full-scale conflict might even draw an attempt at human intervention since they were fond of imposing their will for the "greater good".

"Where are we on the spectrum of fucked, so fucked, and completely fucked?" Slay asked finally.

Dom shrugged. "Depends on how it goes with Beren in the morning."

"Any chance we can talk sense into him?"

"He's been grumbling about the talks since the beginning. To be honest, I think he *wants* a chance to kill some Golgoth. I'd hoped he was just venting, but…" Dom trailed off, as there wasn't a whole lot more to say.

"You want to greenlight a lockdown in the bear section of residential?"

That was one option. But with enough rage and sheer brute strength, electronic locks probably wouldn't keep Beren and his clan pinned long. Then they'd rampage through the hold on the way to the gate. One way or another, it would most likely get ugly tomorrow, and he had to figure out how to best minimize collateral damage.

"That's a temporary solution," Magda objected.

Slay cut her a dark look. "I don't hear anything better coming out of your mouth."

"Well, think about it, both of you, and get back to me. Before I take off, do you have anything to report?"

"Talfayen sent me a message," Slay said. "Wants to talk to me alone in the morning."

"Not the first time," Dom noted.

Magda wanted to know, "What's that about?"

Slay shrugged. "I'll tell you when I know. But I figure I need to put it on the table because I might be occupied when the shit goes down with Beren, unless you want me to postpone the meeting."

"No, go ahead. Inform me as soon as you know anything about what's up with the Eldritch. Whatever you learn will help us."

"Wonder why Talfayen's targeting Slay," Magda said softly.

Dom had that question too, and he had suspicions, none of which he'd speak aloud when circumstances were already so tenuous. They talked a while longer, but nothing concrete could be accomplished via conversation. Then a thought occurred to him, something useful at last.

"Mags, do we still have an operational drone?"

"Just one. Why?"

"Send it north. It's a long shot, but maybe it will deliver additional intel, something we can use to reassure Beren and buy a little more time."

"You have coordinates for me?"

Closing his eyes, Dom wracked his brain to remember the scouting reports he'd read when he first arrived back at the hold. "Close enough."

Leaning over the console, he tapped the screen and highlighted a zone for her. "For now, aim for this area. Stream the footage live. If we lose the drone, it's fine. We can buy another from Raff. The important thing is to get all the info we can, as soon as possible."

"I'm on it," the security chief said.

A few minutes later, the drone was online and zooming north. At its current airspeed, if it didn't encounter hostiles, it would reach bear territory in six hours. Dom glanced at the clock. *That'll be almost five in the afternoon. Damn. I wish we had more time to search.* After a moment's contemplation, he rang up the bear lord.

"I need coordinates on the last-known location for your unit."

"What for?" Beren demanded.

"I'll have eyes on site in five hours and forty-two minutes."

"What about your fucking lockdown?"

"Drone bypass," Dom said. "I'm pretty sure I said nobody in or out. Not no machines."

"Maybe you're not as dumb as I thought. I'm texting you longitude and latitude. Are you in the ops center?"

"Yes."

"Let me know when the infernal gizmo gets close. I'll head over. But won't this take a lot of time, keeping track?"

Dom offered a weary smile to Magda and Slay, who were unabashedly eavesdropping. "I'll do it. All things considered, I wouldn't be sleeping much tonight anyway."

19.

"WHERE ARE YOU?" Pru practiced the question in the mirror.

No, too confrontational. She paced in the bedroom, fretting over whether she should call Dom, but it was past midnight. Really, he should've messaged her if he didn't plan to come back, and she had no idea where the lines were drawn. *Am I supposed to worry... or not?*

Finally, she took a breath and dialed. "Is everything all right?"

"Oh, shit. Pru." From his tone, he'd completely forgotten that she existed.

Awesome.

"I'm so sorry. I'm tied up in the ops center and won't be back tonight."

This time, she didn't swallow her ire. "Next time, message me. Or call. I'd like to know whether you're coming home or not."

"It's my fault. I won't do it again. I'm sorry, but I have to get back to it. Things are a mess. I'll tell you more later." With that, he disconnected.

Her dad had gone to bed an hour ago, disgruntled with

the lockdown. Still, it was good to see him eating well and sleeping enough, even under these circumstances. Pru could've retired without guilt, but when she thought of Dom's dinner in the fridge, it didn't seem right; he probably hadn't eaten yet. Plus, she admitted to a certain curiosity about Beren's visit and what new catastrophe it portended.

I won't sleep without checking in anyway. Thus decided, she warmed his food and packed it up, along with a thermos of strong tea. He'd need the boost to stay alert through the night. She slipped out of the apartment with his lunchbox and navigated the silent residential building.

Outside, a light snow was falling, dusting her hair with dainty ice crystals. The night seemed to hide all kinds of secrets, and she shivered a bit as she hurried down the walkways that crisscrossed Ash Valley. A few times, she thought she glimpsed a shadow in her peripheral vision, but possibly it was just her nerves. Normally Pru didn't roam around so late. Of course, the hold was also lousy with Noxblades, one of whom had reason to want her dead.

The admin building was locked at this hour, but Pru entered her personal security code, hoping Caio had upgraded her status. Sure enough, he was as efficient as he was old school, and the door clicked open. She pulled it firmly shut behind her and hurried through the eerily silent halls toward the ops center. Through the frosted glass, she made out Dom hunched over the console, chin propped on his hand.

Well, he's certainly not living it up without me.

Quietly, she rapped on the door. He jolted in his chair and swiveled to stare at her. But he quickly motioned her in and turned back to the screen. As Pru came in, the image resolved to a low-resolution live feed being shot by what she guessed was a drone. Setting his meal on the table, she leaned in for a better look.

"What's going on?"

In a few words, Dom summarized the issues. "So that's where we are. Beren was here earlier, but so far, the drone hasn't spotted combat or corpses."

"That's good, right?"

"Not necessarily. If the Golgoth slaughtered the bear's scouts, they might have also concealed the bodies, so it'll take more than a hovering camera to spot them."

"Then what're you trying to accomplish here?"

Dom groaned, but he didn't look away from the monitor. "I thought I might learn that the situation isn't as bad as Beren thinks... that maybe I can still save the conclave."

"All right," Pru said. "If you're looking for combat or corpses, I can take over while you have a dinner break."

"Dinner... did I have lunch?" Since he didn't seem to remember, she shooed him out of the seat and took his spot.

"Just eat. I've got this."

"I can't believe you came over. You should be in bed."

"Why?" Pru asked.

But Dom was too busy shoveling food to respond. He scraped all the containers clean and guzzled half the tea before he seemed ready to focus on words again. Though she studied the screen that whole time, the drone didn't show her anything but darkness, trees, and bushes. It was probably a long shot that they'd learn anything this way, yet she understood why her mate would be clutching at straws.

"Actually... I'm glad you're here," Dom said, once he finished.

"Tired of watching? If you want to rest—"

"I'd be lying if I said there wasn't a whisper of that, but

more importantly, there are a couple of things we should discuss."

That conversational gambit struck Pru as a gentler version of *We need to talk,* and that never went anywhere good. But... he wasn't wrong. So without taking her eyes off the shifting landscape, she said, "I agree. Is it all right if I go first?"

"Of course."

"I know you apologized over what happened at the columbarium, and my gut reaction was to wave it away and smile and act like it didn't bother me. But... I've been thinking about how I said we need to be honest and... well, I *was* hurt. I'm not saying you did anything wrong. I meant that. But it wasn't right for me to act like something was nothing. If that makes sense."

"I guessed that." Since she wasn't looking at him, she didn't see him move, but suddenly his chair was close, and he wrapped his arms about her from behind, resting his chin on her shoulder. "But it's good to hear you confirm it. I've been worried since then that things were not okay between us. Which brings me to my next point."

Pru raised a hand to stroke his cheek. Until this moment, she hadn't realized the core of dread that had settled inside her or how much she feared the threat of emotional distance. "You have my full attention. Let's clear the air."

"I'd rather have you chew me out than hide it when I hurt you. The best thing about us is the fact that we're friends first, and we've always been straight with each other. Over time, petty shit could poison what we've built. I hate wondering how you feel. I hate suspecting you planned a party and chose not to invite me."

That almost made her turn around; only recollecting

how critical this could be to the fate of the conclave and the Animari overall kept her watching this damned monotonous drone feed. Covering his hand with hers, she explained how the breakfast came about.

"That's just how my family is. My dad wanted to go for a run, and it spiraled from there."

"Can we both promise to do better and call it even?"

Pru smiled. "That sounds fair. It's inevitable that we'll rub each other wrong. The important part is how we deal with the aftermath."

"I really like it when you come across so levelheaded and wise."

"Yeah?"

"Most definitely. Hang on a sec, I have an idea."

Letting go of her, Dom got up and dragged one of the armchairs from the meeting room and deposited it in front of the terminal. He dropped into it with a weary sigh and opened his arms. There was no reason to feel shy, but she did a little, as she slipped from her seat into his arms. She'd never been cuddled on somebody's lap before, but it felt fantastic. His arms encircled her with a palpable tenderness, then Dom kissed her temple.

"You feel good. Smell better. I've been cooped up with Beren and Slay all evening."

"Seems like an apt penalty for neglecting your wife. Can you see the screen?"

"Does it matter? You're watching for me, right?"

"If you'd filled me in sooner, I would've been here hours ago."

"At first, I didn't want to worry you until I knew more, and then I just got wrapped up in this. After you do it for a while, it becomes strangely hypnotic."

Given how the drone cam swayed and buzzed, she could see falling into a fugue state. "I'll let it go this time. Just don't forget what I said about halving your burdens."

He let out a soft sigh, tickling the hair near her ear. "I'm afraid that by morning, they'll be too heavy for even the two of us together to lift."

"OH SHIT," PRU muttered.

Dom jerked awake, slightly disoriented, but gratified to find his mate still curled up in his arms. "What's wrong?"

"Combat. These are definitely Beren's men, and I'm not positive, but those look like Golgoth on the attack."

"Where is this?" Gently, he shifted her off his lap and got his phone, sending messages to Slay, Magda, and Beren at once.

This won't help the conclave. But it's proof. I can't carry on with the lockdown. It's time to admit that the conclave has failed.

Fate forgive me.

Pru rattled off the coordinates, her gaze locked with abject horror on the violence unfolding. It was hard to make out numbers, but this didn't seem to be a limited engagement. Someone was shouting orders as the scouts went bear, and the enemy responded with the most horrific shift Dom had ever seen. No one creature was the same, and they were easily twice the size of the largest grizzly, like reptile demons, or shit, he didn't even know what: thick scales, horns and tusks, grotesque plates and protrusions. A bear went down beneath the heavy onslaught, and blood spattered the drone.

Pru shuddered. "This can't be happening."

"Stay focused. Are you recording?"

She checked the equipment and nodded quickly. "We have hours of boring shit. But this is all that matters, and I've got it."

Nodding, he picked up Slay's call. "Yeah, it's certain. Round up all the key players. No honor guards. I don't care if you have to drag Talfayen here by his hair."

Something boomed off camera, and then the drone went dark, nothing but gray snow shimmering on screen. As Dom swore, Pru queued up the footage, then rearranged the room to hide the fact that they'd spent most of the night curled up together. He didn't give two shits if someone saw, but she seemed to think it would detract somehow.

Raff arrived first, but Dom wouldn't give any information. He waited until Beren, Alastor, and finally Talfayen assembled in the ops center. His heart thundered in his ears, but this was the only move left. There was no way he could deceive the bear lord, and the rest of the leaders had to know too.

"What's this about?" Talfayen demanded. "You have some fucking nerve dragging us out of our beds—"

"Enough." The word carried substantial bite, so that the Eldritch bastard actually shut up. "Just watch this. I don't think I'll need to explain."

Pru took the cue and played the two minutes they'd collected before the drone went dead. The room got ominously quiet, and then everyone got a visual lock on Alastor, who put up his hands with a convincing aspect of innocence. "I don't know anything about that. I have no idea why there are troops moving on bear territory. I was tasked with handling our role in the peace talks. If we intended to abandon the Pax Protocols, why would they bother sending me at all?"

"To waste our time," Raff snarled, lunging at the Golgoth prince.

Magda grabbed his arm, and the wolf lord cared enough about her opinion that he stood down with another menacing snap of his teeth. The security chief pointed to the frozen image on screen. "Explain that, Your Highness. We saw the change. You want to claim those are men in costume or something?"

The Golgoth royal squared his shoulders as if bracing for an attack. "I never said I could elucidate. I have *no more* information than you."

Uncharacteristically quiet, Beren was still staring at the carnage on screen, just a few seconds before that vicious blood spatter. "Get that bastard out of here or I'll kill him with my bare hands."

Slay evidently took this at face value. "You should go."

"I'll escort him back to his quarters," Magda offered.

But Prince Alastor pulled away from her firm hold and faced off against Beren. "If you wish to challenge me, go ahead. Otherwise, I have the same right to attend this meeting as the rest of you."

A duel would just make things worse, so Dom headed this off. "I have a couple of things to say first. Then we can all go our separate ways." He glanced between Beren and Alastor. "Is that all right with both of you?"

They nodded grudgingly.

"Fine. At this point, there's no reason for me to pretend the conclave can go forward. Fact: Lord Talfayen's nephew died on my watch. Fact: the Golgoth attacked the bear clan. That means the Pax Protocols are irreparably broken, and we're living in lawless times, the like of which nobody here can even remember."

"Tell us something we don't know," Raff muttered.

"I'm done trying to sort this shit out. Lockdown is over. It's four in the morning, and you can leave as soon as you get ready. I'll make it clear to the guards on the gate that we won't interfere. Just know this... I don't warranty your safety once you leave these walls. If Prince Alastor doesn't know what his people are doing, who does? We haven't been patrolling the last few days, so I can't say how it is out there."

"Are you trying to frighten me, cub?" Beren's scowl didn't even faze him.

I'm so tired of this crap.

Dom went on like the old bear hadn't spoken. "Understand that we will defend our territory, and we'll be assessing economic agreements on an individual basis. We *will* embargo all trade with hostile states. That means no wine, no produce, and definitely none of our proprietary technology, so I hope your systems are in good repair."

The wolf lord smirked. "Yeah? How's your drone inventory holding up?"

For a moment, he wondered why the other Animari seemed determined to fuck with him at such a critical time. "Finally, if you leave the hold and encounter trouble, we will not send aid. We will not undertake rescue missions. Even if we've been on good terms prior, if you leave without renewing peace agreements, then go to hell your own way because I'm done."

Prince Alastor startled him by breaking into delighted laughter. "Diplomacy has failed, but I think I prefer brutal honesty. Before, you said the Pax Protocols have imploded, but if I'm interpreting your farewell speech correctly, it seems as if you have something else in mind."

That was exactly the opening he needed. He had been germinating this idea for a while. "Words can only take us so far. Obviously it's time to change it up, or we wouldn't have such problems trying to get the treaties signed again. I propose a more intimate solution."

Talfayen had been silent this whole time, and his mouth curled in a scornful smile. "This should be rich."

"In the old days, they sent emissaries to each demesne, not hostages exactly, but more pledges of good faith. If we continued that tradition and added in a marital alliance, it could foster greater trust among our people."

"I... what?" For once, Raff seemed at a loss for words.

"You want me to send a bear princess to the Eldritch or something and expect she'd survive in their court?" The old bear practically snarled the question.

"I haven't worked out all the details," he said.

But it was no use. The room devolved into chaos even worse than it had when Pru first played the footage of the Golgoth attack. Raff and Talfayen nearly came to blows while the Golgoth prince seemed thoughtful. *Maybe they don't all hate the idea.* Finally, his mate put two fingers in her mouth and let out a whistle so shrill that half the room's occupants flinched and rubbed their ears.

When she seemed satisfied she had their full attention, she spoke. "It's been a long night. There will be nothing gained by further discord. I humbly request you return to your quarters to take in the implications of what you've heard. If you feel it's best to leave at first light, we'll send supplies. But as my husband said, that's the last help or support you'll receive from Ash Valley. I'm sorry for everything that's gone wrong and greatly regret that the conclave seems to be ending before it's begun—and on such a sour note. Please, get some rest, all of you."

"The pride master's idea might not be so bad," Alastor mused quietly on his way out. "Perhaps marriage could cement the alliances like nothing else."

With a dark look, Beren snapped, "Who exactly do you think you're fooling, treacherous scum? *We* are at war."

20.

A T 5:37 A.M., a series of explosions rocked the hold.
Jolted from sleep, Pru dove out of bed toward the
doorway as part of the ceiling collapsed; plaster and scraps
of metal rained down where she had been lying a few
seconds before. Smoke and dust clouded the air, so thick she
could scarcely breathe. As far as she knew, Dom wasn't
home as he'd stayed to talk more with Magda and Slay.

Dad... where is he?

On her hands and knees, she scrambled through the
wreckage, cutting herself on broken glass from where the
kitchen cupboards had collapsed in a shower of plate and
mug shrapnel. If nothing else, the pain sharpened her focus
and firmed her resolve. *At least I've shifted and have accelerated
healing.* Fear took hold when she thought of all the children
in the hold, those who hadn't changed yet. Taking a deep
breath to steady herself, she crawled over the mound of
rubble in what used to be her living room.

Part of the wall had given way, creating a partial barricade. From inside her dad's bedroom, she heard muffled
cursing, thanks to her enhanced senses. With her bare
hands, she yanked at the debris, flinging chunks of cement

and broken furniture over her shoulder. From the sound of it, her father was doing the same on his side. Her urgency increased until she was working flat out, shredding her palms faster than they could heal.

Finally, together, they cleared an opening large enough for him to crawl out. Pru grabbed her dad by the shoulders and inspected him head to toe. With an annoyed grunt, he jerked away, but not before she spotted the shard of metal jutting from his side. A shuddering breath escaped her, but she knew enough of emergency first aid not to yank it out. *He could bleed out before he's treated.* Though it had to hurt like a bitch, she got on his good side and draped his arm over her shoulder. If he didn't get help soon, the wound would heal around the metal, and it would require surgery to remove it.

"I'm fine," he muttered.

"You're partially impaled. This is no time to be stoic."

As she stepped toward the door, he flinched and shuddered. "You might be right. Take it slow. That shard's... scraping something fierce."

"Sorry."

There was no need to open the door, as it was broken in three places and they had to tromp over it to leave the apartment. In the hallway, visibility was no better. Pru pulled her shirt up to cover her nose and mouth, but her eyes stung as she guided her father toward the stairs. Some neighbors stumbled out of their apartments, dazed and dripping blood. Mindful of her role as pride matron, she couldn't just ignore them.

"What's going on?"

"Are we under attack?"

The questions multiplied, and she had no answers. Her

father's brow beaded with sweat from the effort of remaining upright. Really, he should be on a gurney with doctors and nurses ready to take care of him. But two of this group seemed almost as badly hurt, and one of them was a little boy who couldn't shift yet.

"Stick with me. We'll get out together."

Their progress through the murky building was glacial, and more than once they had to stop and rest. When they reached the nearest stairs at last, Pru almost wept. The outer wall had caved in, blocking all but the most precarious path. If she shifted, she could run down with no problem, but that was out of the question for her father and the wee one. *I'm leading this group. I won't abandon them.* In the distance, she detected sirens, which signaled that this constituted a true emergency. Guards and rescue personnel would be searching, but from the delayed pattern of detonations, she suspected multiple strikes had been unleashed all over the hold.

There were four stairwells, one at each corner, and they couldn't *all* be blocked. Yet it made no sense to drag injured people all over the place, draining energy they likely didn't have. Swiftly she made a decision.

"Stay here," she said. "I'm going cat to scout, and when I find a clear exit, I'll head straight back. Try not to worry in the meantime."

"I'll keep everyone calm," her dad said.

Nodding her thanks, she whirled and shucked out of her clothes in record time. When she shifted, it only shocked her, like a mild current, no pain at all, and soon, she was loping along the hallways, searching for a way out. Along the way, she ran into more survivors, and she signaled with a swipe of a paw that they could find more pride mates in the direction she'd come from.

Low to the ground, she could see better, less dust and better vision. The air reeked with blood and terror, some fading chemical that was probably tied to the explosion. No time to track the bomb origin. For the first time ever, Pru had people's lives hanging on her every move. The next nearest exits were compromised too, the first with a slow-burning fire and the other was missing six steps, too far for her dad and the little boy to leap without shifting.

This can't be happening. I hope Dom's all right, wherever he is.

No, can't think about anyone else.

She ran on, and the final possibility proved to be golden. Though it was smoky and damaged, the stairs diagonal from where she'd left the survivors were passable. With a silent thank-you to her mother, who was surely watching over them, she raced back to the group. The little boy's sobs were audible even from five hundred meters away, and as she drew closer, it sounded like the newcomers were arguing with her dad about the wisdom of standing around.

"She's not coming back, I tell you. I saw her running like the devil was after her, and that's been a good ten minutes ago—"

Pru shifted and grabbed her clothes from the floor. Normally, she might've minded a little, getting dressed in front of so many strangers. But today there was no time for modesty. As soon as she got her head through the shirt, she snapped, "Shut up and follow me. I've found a way out of here."

To her astonishment, as nobody ever claimed she had an air of command, the complaints quieted, and everyone fell in behind her without protest. *Is it because I'm pride matron now? Because of Dom? Or have I changed a little too?* The questions had to remain rhetorical, as she focused on guiding the group to safety. Perforce, they moved slow, and by the time they reached the diagonal stairwell, she was trembling in reaction—from multiple shifts, nerves, fear, and low blood sugar.

Thankfully, the stairs, though still chipped and crumbling, held together long enough for most everyone to get down. She sent the most injured first, some borne on the backs of relatives, and as they reached the ground floor, two weakened stairs collapsed. Everyone still upstairs was hale enough to shift, so they stripped and went for it, one by one. Conscious of her role as leader, Pru made sure everyone else was out of the building before she changed.

For the first time, going cat made her dizzy instead of hurting. Backing up, she made the leap and landed unsteadily below the gap. She ran down the rest of the steps and out into a frigid dawn. Her survivors gathered around with incoherent thanks, patting her back and promising future favors.

The scene struck her as surreal, like something she'd watched in an old film. People with bloody faces and wild eyes clustered around fires burning in metal trash barrels while three different tents had been set up in the park. She also scented cats, wolves, and bears, plus more mysterious and arcane aromas that probably came from the Eldritch and Golgoth. *Sensory overload.* Smoke rose from multiple points in the hold. Her ears swiveled. Sobs, cries of pain and bereavement, wails of fear and devastation—the noise blended together into a cacophony of grief, so she couldn't sort it out.

"The medical tent is that way," her dad said.

Someone handed her a basic bundle of clothes, and she ducked around the corner to change. This time, she staggered and had to hold on to the wall for almost a minute until the sparkle-confetti left her field of vision. Stubbornly she rounded the corner and reached for her father.

I have to be strong.

DOM HAD TWENTY fires to put out—literally—and he couldn't stop asking this one question. "Has anyone seen my wife?"

Most of the building had been deemed inaccessible, but low risk. With the sprinkler system malfunctioning and flames smoldering all over the hold, he shouldn't fixate on one person's fate. *I'm responsible for everyone, not just Pru.* But he wouldn't be able to focus until he found her. *She's alive, she has to be. I'd know if she wasn't, right?* Possibly their mate bond was too nascent and fragile, so maybe—

No.

Slay went by at a run, and Dom grabbed him with both hands. "Did you *find her*?"

"Sorry, not yet. I've asked all the guards to keep an eye out. You have other things to worry about. Let me take care of Pru."

"Fucking never," he snarled, and let go of his second so hard it was nearly a shove.

But come to it, Slay wasn't wrong. *I have to focus.* His people were well trained, and they were already executing emergency procedures. Medical tent, temporary shelter for those displaced—quickly he ran down the list of things they should be doing. The rescue brigade was working on the pocket fires, but it looked like somebody had tampered with the dampening system, so it required time and manual intervention.

Magda ran up before he could complete the mental inventory, panting. "Mob. They're trying to execute Prince Alastor."

Shit.

With the Golgoth attacking the bear clan in the north, it made sense to blame their royal emissary, but what kind of an idiot would detonate multiple explosives while he—and his people—were still in the city? Dom nodded and followed her at top speed, shouldering through the crowd milling between park and plaza. It was a mix of Animari in humanoid and animal forms, so he had to wade through wolf, cat, and bear to get to where Raff was holding the prince by the scruff of his neck, forced to kneel amid threats of a public execution. Honestly, it was hard not to wonder if things could've gone worse, left in Slay's hands.

"Golgoth scum," someone called. "They stuck around to watch us suffer."

"Stand down," Dom growled at the wolf lord.

"Like hell. This bastard killed Beren."

Not the old bear. Beren's passing marked the end of an era. Then a troublesome thought surfaced, circling like a shark.

Don't tell me those assholes went at it as soon as my back was turned.

"In a duel?" So galling to ask questions when he wanted to snarl and keep snarling and claw people until they left him the fuck alone.

The wolf lord snarled, "No, you stupid shit. When that bastard prince detonated half the hold."

"Did you see him do it? Did you witness his people

planting explosives?"

Raff's gaze shifted away just for a second. "Who else could it be?"

"I don't know, but I promised this man my protection until he leaves the walls of my city. If you try to make a liar of me, we'll go. You want that? Now?" Dom popped his neck and said with a look that he'd fight.

There had been no battles between wolf and cat for as long as he could remember; he couldn't even think of any stories where it had happened. For a long moment, Raff stared him down, and then he flung Alastor free as Dom had Slay, in a fit of impotent fury. Letting out a slow breath, Dom helped the prince to his feet. Based on the footage he'd watched, if the royal had gone brute, he could've slaughtered a good portion of this mob by himself.

"My apologies," he said. "Everyone's on edge."

"It's understandable."

"Golgoth sympathizer!" a bear clan warrior shouted.

"We should go."

Nodding, the prince followed him out of the throng. It still hadn't sunk in. *Beren's dead?* Dom didn't even know who would rule in his place; the old bear had said something about his heir taking a vow of celibacy. *I guess I need to talk to his second, assuming he survived.* Once they got some distance away, the royal paused.

"I lost two men in this attack, and it's on my head. You see, I wasn't entirely honest with you this morning. Though I have no concrete information about what's happening, I have a guess. And I should have shared my speculation with you earlier. The fact that you saved me—for no tangible gain—entitles you to my candor and loyalty."

There was no safe spot where he could hold a conference, but he found an out-of-the-way corner near the wall, beyond the range of interested ears. If this turned out to be nothing, Dom would be pissed at the waste of time, as he had so much shit to do. Yet from Alastor's sober mien, he wasn't messing about.

"Speak."

"I'm unsure how much you know about Golgoth internal politics?"

"Not much. Can you give me the short version? It's not that I'm disinterested in your culture, but..." He gestured at the weeping wounded in the park and the columns of smoke.

"Yes, quite. Well, it tends to be vicious and competitive. Birth order doesn't determine who will rule. My older brother has already done away with three of our siblings, and I rather suspect I was meant to die here as well. I wondered why he entrusted me with this... and now I have an answer. As he also thinks the Pax Protocols are a waste of paper, I suspect he's also responsible for the raids in the north."

"What's the asshole's name?" Dom demanded.

"Tycho. There were five of us, once. I'm the last. Two of my sisters and one brother have died on his road to the throne. He left me for last because he thought I'd be the easiest to defeat."

There was an element of pathos in this honesty. As Prince Alastor held Dom's gaze, he realized he didn't have a single doubt about what he was hearing. He made a snap judgment. "If you agree to tell me everything you know about your brother—assets, strategy, potential targets—I'll offer you asylum until the war ends, one way or another."

"Many of my people will consider me a traitor if I ally

with you," Alastor said.

"You think Tycho will let you live if you go back?"

"Definitely not. I never wanted the throne, but it seems as if my only shot at survival is directly linked to taking it."

"Then gather your people. Send some discreet messages, and summon any soldiers loyal to you. This will be our staging ground."

"Your other allies probably won't take this well."

"I'll make it right with Raff and..." Hell, he didn't even know the name of Beren's heir. "Right now I need to find Lord Talfayen."

And Gavriel, he added silently. *So help me, if the Eldritch had anything to do with this...*

"Understood." Prince Alastor swept a regal bow, somehow elegant despite his torn, stained clothes and filthy face, which looked like Raff had rubbed it in the dirt.

"Please excuse me, we'll talk more later."

As he turned, the Noxblade he'd just been thinking about melted out of the crowd and tapped his arm. "This way. We don't have long."

"Until what?"

But Gavriel was running, weaving through the crowd with an adroitness Dom would be hard-pressed to match as a leopard. On human feet, it took all his endurance and speed to keep the Noxblade in sight. This wild chase led through the hold to a pile of rubble, and he pictured what used to be here. *One of the lounges?* But when he spotted Slay kneeling beside Lord Talfayen, half-buried in broken stones, it drove all other thoughts from his head.

"Too soon... it was too soon," the Eldritch leader wheezed. "Remember your promise."

Rage drowned all the questions as blood trickled from

the Eldritch lord's mouth. His torso was crushed. All Dom could think about was that this asshole was about to pass of his injuries, despite ordering Dalena's death. *It'll take too long to change. I have to be the one to kill him, or this will never be over.*

There was no thought of mercy in him as he grabbed Gavriel and shook him hard. "Your blade, I know you have one. Give it to me. *Now.*"

Once he had it, he blasted past Slay and stared down at Talfayen's broken form with as much hate as he'd felt in his life. In one vicious slash, he opened the bastard's throat and watched as he bled out.

Finally, Dalena can rest. And I can let her go.

21.

THE RESCUE EFFORT went on for hours.

Pru paced the medical tent as the team removed the metal spear in her dad's side. With proper treatment, he recovered quickly, and soon he just had bloody clothes as a terrible souvenir of their ordeal. Young pride mates weren't so lucky, and two Latents had been killed in the explosion. Heavy-hearted, she aided where she could, but somewhere around noon, she staggered. Lightheaded, she finally yielded to her body's demands for food and a moment of rest. The pride had a camp kitchen open by then with vast pots of soup bubbling away to ward off the bitter chill. She drank hers in three gulps and then hurried off to continue working.

But she paused when she spotted her father lending a hand despite his healing injury. "Have you eaten, Dad?"

"I have more sense than you," her father muttered.

Just then, Magda called her name from across the park, so Pru waved to him and moved to join the security chief. It was a relief to find her hale and whole. "You need me?"

"Has Dom found you yet? He's half-crazed at this point."

She shook her head. "I haven't seen him, but somebody told me he was all right. If you run into him before I do, let him know I'm hanging in there."

"No problem," the security chief said. "But that's not why I flagged you down."

"What's up? Apart from the obvious."

"I'm sorry," was all the other woman said.

Since Magda wasn't known for screwing around, Pru followed her without question. Most of the health center was still intact, and Sheyla was doing the best she could, along with half the nursing staff and a room full of volunteers. The only other physician was stationed at the medical tent, taking care of triage.

But Mags didn't turn toward the ward. Instead, she led Pru to rooms that were ominously drafty and cold. Here, part of the wall had collapsed, letting in the winter air, but when she saw the rows on rows of bodies covered in white sheets, she understood that the temperature didn't matter. Actually the cold was probably for the best.

"How many have we lost so far?"

"I don't have a number. You can count the victims here, but there are a great many more waiting to be dug out of the rubble. We may lose others to hypothermia as night falls."

"Are any of the visiting dignitaries willing to pitch in?"

Magda nodded. "There's a Noxblade already leading a rescue crew."

"Gavriel?" she guessed.

"How'd you know?" The other woman cocked a brow in surprise.

"Just a hunch. Anything else?"

"Most of the bears are grieving hard, but I'm working

on them. Raff's got his men helping, but many of them want to march out and cut their losses."

"I can understand that. Update on the rest of the Eldritch?"

"Bad rumors afoot. I caught a whisper that their leader died in the attack, but so far his body hasn't turned up. It's also strange that their group seems to have split into two factions, the one helping us on recovery and the one trying to locate Talfayen."

Thanks. You made it easy for us to ID the traitors.

"If there's nothing else," she started to say, but the cloud in Magda's expression stopped her. "What?"

The security chief walked over to the nearest body. "I wish there was something I could say to make this easier. Just know that I'm very sorry for your loss."

Then she unveiled the familiar faces one by one. *Cousin Naveen. Uncle Chaz. Cousin Caroleth and her mate, Perry. No. This isn't possible.* They couldn't all be lying so pale and still, the wounds still fresh on their stiffening bodies. They were all shifters—with accelerated healing—so none of them died easy. They'd all suffered sudden, catastrophic injuries, too severe for their metabolisms to save them. The Animari weren't invincible, just tougher than most.

Pru dropped to her knees as the strength drained from her legs. Thoughts whirled so fast they made her sick, and the questions tried to fight free of her mouth like word vomit, until she choked on it. Magda touched her shoulder, and it took all her self-control not to savage the woman's hand with her teeth. Not because it was her fault, because she was *here*.

Fucking unfair, yeah.

Somehow she got out, "Aunt Glynnis? What about Joss?

My cousins, Jilly and Jase?"

They're orphans now.

"Your aunt was injured, but she came through surgery and she's healing well. I haven't heard anything of Joss. Jilly is fine, but Jase..."

"Just tell me."

"He was pinned beneath some fallen wreckage. It seems probable that if he survives, there will be permanent spinal damage."

That news shattered her determination to be strong. In that freezing makeshift morgue, Pru drew her knees to her chest and sobbed. She had no idea how long she cried, but eventually, a warm hand settled on her shoulder. Dom's smell roused her first, as she'd recognize her mate anywhere. He hauled her upright and into his arms, a hold so tight it hurt in all the best ways. Over and over, he ran his hands down her body as if conducting a tactile inspection because his eyes couldn't be trusted.

"You're all right," he whispered. "You're safe."

It took forever to gasp an answer. "But... so many people aren't."

Belatedly, he seemed to recognize the family members she was mourning, and he cupped her face in his hands. "What can I do?"

"Just find the bastard who did this."

"It's definitely at the top of my list." Dom lifted her face and kissed her tears away, each brush of his lips exquisitely tender.

Pru didn't even notice when Magda slipped off, and she let Dom guide her away from the dead with minimal protest. It wasn't like her presence would bring them back again. Pain washed over her in waves, striking hard so that she couldn't breathe. At those moments, Dom half-supported her, like he had nowhere more important to be.

"Sorry," she mumbled.

"Don't be. I need to thank you."

"For what?"

"Keeping a level head. Staying safe. If I lost you…"

You'd replace me, she thought. *Anyone who isn't Dalena is interchangeable, as long as it's for the good of the pride.* The bitterness of that thought surprised her, and Pru did her best to quell it. *It's not his fault. That's grief talking.*

When she didn't respond, he appeared to gather himself enough to continue. "Well, let's just say you're my whole world, now."

Wistful, she lifted her gaze to his and wished that were true and he wasn't just saying it because he'd caught her weeping like a lost soul. At this point he'd probably say anything to cheer her up.

"How's Slay?" Immediately after, she wished she hadn't asked, because his citrine eyes wavered and dropped away from hers.

"Fine." Dom's tone became brusque. "You just saw Mags. I don't know if you heard, but we lost Beren and Talfayen today. I also learned something critical from Prince Alastor."

Reeling from all that info, Pru tried to process the fact that the old bear was gone. "Oh no. Have you spoken with his second?"

"So far, nobody's located him. We don't know if he survived the attack or left the hold in the confusion."

"Talfayen?"

"Fatally wounded." Her mate's eyes gleamed with an icy light as he added softly, "Some might even call what I did a mercy killing."

Her heart skipped. "You…"

Then she remembered. *Because of Dalena.* Gavriel had sworn that Talfayen put his nephew up to the murder and he'd brought the audio file as proof. Pru hesitated, trying not to shiver over the idea of murdering Talfayen in cold blood. Part of her understood and rejoiced that it was over. Next time she went to the columbarium, she could give her best friend answers and light some candles in hopes her spirit found peace.

Shit. If the memorial center is still standing.

But she also feared for Dom's soul, the cost of such a merciless retaliation.

Her silence seemed to put him on edge. His words tumbled out fast, one after another. "There never would have been a trial. What court would even have jurisdiction?"

For a moment, she imagined the Eldritch lying helpless, and she couldn't find it in her heart to agree, so she asked, "What did you learn from the prince?"

"That we must fight his brother, Tycho."

HOURS AFTER DOM found Pru, he couldn't stop thinking of how broken she'd seemed, couldn't stop wondering if there was a path he could've taken that wouldn't have ended with her family decimated. *I just had breakfast with them. Just spent an hour with her uncle telling me about their ancestry.*

But he didn't have the leisure to obsess over personal matters, not when there were actual holes in the walls his grandfather had built to keep the pride safe, and he couldn't see to shoring them up until the last victim was pulled from the wreckage. *Still such a long way to go.* As the bodies piled up, he had people matching faces with names, but some of the victims were unrecognizable. Eventually they might be reduced to DNA testing, but he didn't have the equipment for that in the hold.

"Sir, we have vehicles at a thousand meters and closing fast." The sentry who made the report looked like he hadn't eaten or slept in days.

Dom didn't show even a fraction of the alarm flickering through him. "I'll take care of it. Take a break now, that's an order."

As he ran for the gate, he got on the radio and barked orders. "Get eyes on the breach points, however you can manage it. We may be looking at an incursion."

They didn't have men to spare for guarding all the gaps, but everyone should be on high alert until he figured out who these new arrivals were. Dom went up onto the wall for a better view, and he watched the snow flying from the rapid approach of seven vehicles running in a tight, armed convoy. The way things had been going, it wouldn't surprise him if they rammed the gates, but as they drew closer, he recognized the build: square lines, matte camo paint job.

"Those look like bear clan reinforcements," he called to the sentry. "But let's wait for confirmation, just to be certain."

The fleet parked outside, sending a message about the group's intentions, then a mountain of a man clambered out of the lead Rover. He wore a full beard and flowing brown locks that looked as if they had never been cut, bound away from his face in a leather tie. Even at this distance, there was enough of a resemblance to the old bear that Dom tentatively identified him as Beren's heir. At a gesture, the rest of the men fell in behind him. None of them dressed like the other bear guards in the hold, however. Instead of uniforms, they wore heavy gray greatcoats of leather and sheepskin and leggings tucked into heavy boots.

"Open the gates," he shouted.

Running the stairs at top speed, he managed to get there in time to greet the new arrivals. *At least the fires are out.* But he didn't look forward to giving this man the bad news. As the bear party arrived, Dom stretched his neck to make eye contact. *That means he's two meters tall, if not more.* The width of this man's shoulders was intimidating, broad as a sequoia compared to the other bear warriors, and Beren hadn't been small.

"I received a distress call from my uncle's second," the great bear rumbled.

When he put out a hand, Dom took it, and the other man crunched his knuckles in a grip that was probably meant to be firm, not punishing. "Dominic Asher, master of Ash Valley. I wish we were meeting under better circumstances."

"Callum McRae. You didn't blow up your own hold, so I don't hold you accountable."

That's a relief.

If the old bear had been all bluster, there was an iron composure about his heir. Dom had the feeling Callum would crush anyone who wronged his people, slowly and methodically. Stepping back, he waved the group into the plaza, and once the forty men cleared the gate, he signaled for the sentries to lock it down. That might be pointless since there were so many breaches in the wall, but it wouldn't help to drop their defenses even in disarray.

"I suspect you want to see your uncle?"

"That's where we'll start," the other man said grimly.

Then Callum turned to his men. "Find the bear survivors first. Afterward, render aid wherever possible."

"To everyone?" The bear warrior who spoke sounded as if he'd been asked to complete a particularly distasteful mission.

"Yes, everyone. Our kindness and compassion must extend beyond the order, beyond our clan. We've spent too long apart, and look at the result."

That's right. Beren said something about his heir taking a vow of celibacy. So these bears are from… a monastic order?

His gaze must've contained an undeniable question because Callum sighed. "The Order of Saint Casimir, at your service."

"Thank you for coming. If things hadn't been so chaotic, I'd have notified you myself."

"I understand. Please… may I see Uncle Beren now?"

"This way."

Dom didn't bother with small talk; it seemed improbable that a monk would be uncomfortable with silence. Besides, the hold wasn't quiet. Though the first chaos had passed, there was still a lot of confusion, people running, and those who couldn't stop crying. With Animari senses, it hovered on the bearable side of overwhelming.

Callum seemed to take in everything with cool, assessing eyes, but when they stepped into the temporary morgue, he drew in a breath. Even in the cold, the smell of death permeated each inhalation, as if you were taking that loss of life into your lungs. The chill might be slowing decay, but the specter remained, grim and inexorable.

"Where is he?" The low timbre of the question could have been created by two boulders grinding together.

"Here."

With no fanfare, he pulled the sheet from the bear lord's face. But that wasn't enough for his heir. The monk removed it entirely to gaze on the magnitude of the wounds that had brought his uncle low. Beren's clothes were tattered and bloodstained, and Dom glanced away from the mangled limbs, crushed torso, and partially obliterated face.

"Would you give me a moment?"

"Of course."

No words would suffice anyway, so he stepped out and closed the door behind him. He imagined the massive bear warrior imploding in silent grief, and an agonizing ache woke like live coals in his chest. *We've lost so many. I don't know how we're going to rebuild the hold, let alone take the fight to Tycho.* Plus, he had so many doubts about that final exchange between Slay and Talfayen, and the unquestionable wrongness of it raised more questions about the secret meetings between them. *Not Slay, he wouldn't. No matter how pissed he was, he wouldn't.* Despair the like of which he hadn't known since Dalena died threatened to drown him.

A few minutes later, Pru peeked around the corner. Her small face was smudged with smoke to the point that he couldn't make out her freckles, though the dirt brightened her eyes by comparison, two beacons in a life that offered only an eternity of starless nights.

She hurried toward him as if he'd confirmed a suspicion. "What happened?"

Stunned, he raised his head, unable to believe that she knew. "How…?"

Sometimes, through a powerful mate bond, couples came to share each other's emotions. Dom would've sworn it was too soon yet she was here in response to his mood.

Pru lifted a shoulder in helpless confusion. "I'm not sure. I just... my chest is really tight. I mean, it has been for a while. How could it *not* be? But this feeling seems like it's yours, not mine. But if I'm wrong, if—"

"No." Quietly he elaborated on recent events, including the arrival of the Order of Saint Casimir, and closed with, "No matter why you came, I'm glad you're here."

With a tentative smile, she went into his arms and held him without asking anything else. At the moment, she might be the only person who didn't want his head on a pike. Even if they didn't admit it, most of the pride probably blamed him for letting the Golgoth execute this attack. They also wouldn't understand why he'd chosen to shelter Prince Alastor, which was why he'd asked the royal to keep a low profile.

"We'll get through this," she said.

If anyone else had said it, he would have dismissed it as empty reassurance. Somehow, when Pru spoke those words, they metamorphosed into liquid titanium, infusing his spine with the necessary fortitude to keep going. Breathing deep, he pulled the comforting scent of her into his lungs and held her so tight, he half-expected her to complain. But she only held on harder, until the tears receded from his throat and eyes.

"Thanks for your understanding," Callum said from behind them. "Now you've only to point me at the enemy, and they *will* fall."

22.

PRU WISHED IT were that simple.

But a week later, they were still putting the pieces back together. They'd set up a dormitory for those rendered homeless in the bombing, and the lack of privacy, even among allies, was starting to wear thin. Conditions were worse for the Golgoth because they were squatting in a damaged building, well apart from the others. While Pru understood the reason for the segregation, sadness also overwhelmed her whenever she delivered supplies.

"You grace us again with your presence, dear lady." Prince Alastor was visibly thinner, yet he still swept an elegant bow as her party came in with boxes.

"I'm sorry, Your Majesty. Conditions should improve soon... and I see you've been working independently on repairs. Thank you for that."

"Let's not pretend I'm a valued heir any longer. The pretext is wearisome. I trust we both know that my brother sees me as a stain he'd prefer to scrub away."

Pru didn't know what to say to that, but she soon rallied. "He feels that way about a number of us, I gather."

"Well said." Despite his smile, there was a core of sorrow, laced with bitterness, that no light banter could touch.

"Everyone is tightening their belts at the moment. Our hothouses were damaged, reducing our available food stores. We're hunting as we can, however, so we should be able to offer more fresh meat soon."

"Whoever planted the charges knew a great deal about Ash Valley resources."

"Yes," Pru said, sighing.

That was one of the issues hindering the reconstruction. There was division among the Animari, as the bear clan didn't care about Ash Valley and wanted to go Golgoth hunting. Raff had chosen to stay momentarily, mostly because they hadn't done a complete recon mission yet. He didn't want to lead his surviving soldiers into an ambush. These days, Dom hardly slept, and she could tell he felt like he was failing on all levels, but with massive damage to infrastructure and serious casualties, it would be irresponsible to commit to an external offensive without seeing to his own first. Pru had said, *What's the point of fighting a war when our warriors won't even have a safe place to return to afterward?* Eventually, he'd listened to her, but his caution didn't impress Raff or the new bear leader, Callum.

"You look pensive. I'd offer you a coin for your thoughts, but I fear our currency is soon to be worthless."

"Not if your brother has anything to say about it," a Golgoth soldier muttered.

Pru paused in the midst of starting a pot of soup for the hungry men. "What did you say?"

A few others tried to shush him, but the young Golgoth shrugged their hands away. "It isn't like Tycho's drive to conquest is some big secret. If he has his way, he'll crush all resistance and become the sovereign ruler of all Numina."

That was a very old word, one they had chosen to describe themselves, entirely different from pejoratives like "freak", "beast" and "monster" that humans had preferred during the Great War. To the best of Pru's recollection, it meant a sort of divine will, or an energy that pervaded them, which clay men lacked. Some humans had taken umbrage over the term, asserting that the Numina thought humanity lacked a spiritual element they called the soul. But she wasn't a philosopher or a theologian, even if she knew more history than most.

With a crooked smile that didn't touch his eyes, Alastor said, "I stand corrected. It's not our currency that'll be devalued but everyone else's, should my brother's plan come to fruition."

"I know you don't want to the throne," the young soldier went on. "But if you don't fight for it, so many will suffer."

Given the stories about the Golgoth, faint surprise kindled in her. But of course it made sense that they couldn't *all* be heartless monsters. Not all Animari were feral beasts, after all. Along with everyone else, she waited for the prince's response.

"I'm not meant to be king," he said softly.

Pru spoke without thinking. "For every born leader, there are a hundred normal folks who stood up and tried their best because it was all they could do."

Prince Alastor let out a caustic laugh. "I do believe you're trying to *rally* me. How novel. Do you imagine history gives a gold star to well-meant failures?"

"I know history books better than you, I'll bet. And you shouldn't be thinking about that before the first battle is fought." She kept her answer calm and quiet as she put the finishing touches on their soup.

Though they had to be tired of eating the same thing, day after day, the Golgoth didn't complain. The strange loyalty these soldiers showed to a capricious prince who—by his own admission—was no leader puzzled her; their culture prized strength above all else, but he didn't fit the ideal of the Golgoth brute, eager to grind others beneath his heel. If she could do it, solving that mystery might prove useful.

Something icy and sharp flashed in Alastor's gaze. "You used to be Latent, didn't you, pride matron?"

Since that was no secret, she merely nodded. It wouldn't be the first time someone had mocked her for it.

"I commend you for overcoming that handicap." To her surprise, he sounded sincere. She couldn't get a handle on his character at all. "I'm sure nobody's ever used that word with you before. They might even have said it's not a big deal—to your face—nothing to be ashamed of, yes? But I'm equally certain they made you *feel* lesser, as if being locked to one form is the worst crime you could commit, and it wasn't like you chose to be that way. It just happened."

"Yes." Pru bit her lip and breathed through her nose. There could've been no bracing for the verbal barrage that fell on her like napalm truth.

"Then you're uniquely qualified to understand me. Come."

It didn't occur to Pru to question the command. Quickly she handed the spoon to the nearest soldier and ran after Prince Alastor. He took her to the far corner of the room, where he'd clearly made camp. A battered trunk with brass fittings looked as if it had survived multiple explosions, and he opened it without hesitation, removed everything inside, and pulled out a false bottom. At the very base sat a small case; he drew it out and showed her the contents: six slender vials filled with pale blue liquid.

"I'm showing you my weakness," he said in conversational tone.

"Excuse me?"

"This is why I can't fight my brother. I'm addicted to this stuff, and I'll die without it. I was born with a genetic condition, and my mother... well. She implored the doctors to find some way to save her defective runt. My father would've bashed my head in with a rock and left me to rot on a hillside, as in days of yore."

"You need it to live. That's not what I'd call addiction."

The prince shrugged. "My point is, I have six days left, pride matron. Do you think I can conquer the Golgoth in that time?"

Taking her silence for agreement, he put away the case and sealed it up in the trunk. Then he sauntered away with a bright smile affixed in place. Her heart ached, watching him. Now that she understood him a bit more, she wanted desperately to help. But she had no idea what he took to keep his condition at bay, and analysis would take a while, even if they had equipment on site.

As she stepped into the hall, the young Golgoth who had spoken before hurried after her. He caught her arm and let go when she flinched. Immediately he dropped to his knees before her. "Please, save him."

"I wish I could."

"You know all of us who follow him? We're all wrong in some way—culled, cast off—and if he hadn't taken us into his service, we'd have been put down."

Pru stared, unable to credit what she was hearing. "You

mean—"

"They say we'd be better off. Only Prince Alastor offered us a place, and he took responsibility for us. Please,
pride matron. Find a way. There are many more who would
follow him, given half a chance. I will do anything for you,
anything at all, if you promise to try."

"All right," she said, heart aching. "Get me a used vial,
and I'll do my best."

As usual, Dom spent the night in the temporary ops center,
not as well equipped as the old one, but the room had four
walls and a ceiling, along with minimal fire damage. They'd
salvaged what gear they could, and people ran in and out
with varying degrees of urgency. The way his eyelids felt,
they must be full of sandpaper. Just then, he was listening to
a scouting report.

"The bears are slowing the Golgoth in the north, but
they have forces on the move in the east as well."

"How long before they reach our borders?" Dom asked.

It's not a question of if we go to war. It's when. With the
hold weakened, their position wasn't good. He didn't feel
prepared to send out the call to the other settlements, but
they had to know. Most of them didn't even have broken
walls to hide behind.

"It depends on the fighting. But less than a week, I
suspect."

"Thanks. Tell Slay I'd like to see him."

The scout bowed, and as he ran out, Gavriel raced
inside, his expression grave and apologetic. *More bad news,*
he guessed.

"Let's hear it," Dom said.

The Noxblade didn't hesitate. "Talfayen's Eldritch slipped out of one of the breach points last night."

Dom nearly took the Noxblade's head off over that report. Even if there were only fifteen loyalists, they could wreak a lot of havoc, given what they knew about the state of Ash Valley.

"You had eyes on them. How did they get past you?" he demanded.

Deep down, he understood that this argument wouldn't change anything, but he'd put up with *so much* shit that he didn't know how he could let this go. His head ached like he was wearing an invisible vise as a headband. It was hard not to suspect that this asshole was screwing him around. The Noxblade drew in a deep breath and met his accusing gaze squarely.

"I let them go."

"*What* did you say?"

"Orders came in from Princess Thalia. She's offering her father's followers a chance at amnesty, so I had to."

"You had to," Dom repeated through clenched teeth.

Gavriel raised his eyes to amend his statement. "I chose to place her commands above yours. Punish me as you see fit."

"Yeah, because I have time for that."

"Your patience will be rewarded, I promise. Now that the schism has occurred, My Lady is no longer pretending to be her father's hostage. I have reliable intel that she'll be here in two days to lend her forces to the fight."

Suddenly Dom didn't feel like arguing over the fate of fifteen traitors. "How many men does she command?"

"It will take time for everyone who has sworn to her in secret to assemble, but she has at least three hundred at the estate proper."

"Can you guess at the total?

Gavriel appeared to consider for a moment. "We number in the thousands, pride master, and the remainder of the Eldritch will either acknowledge her right to rule or they will regret it."

"If they don't pledge to her, she'll hunt them down?"

"Don't worry about how we will restore order. Just trust that we'll support you against the Golgoth. A good portion of the harm to your hold can be laid at my door." Saying this, Gavriel bowed low. "I promised to disrupt Talfayen's plans, and I failed."

Until this moment, it didn't occur to Dom that someone else might be struggling with the same sense of shame. He cleared his throat. "Yeah, well. I could make a list of everything I did wrong too. At this point, there's no benefit in assigning blame."

"And it wouldn't be either of you," Pru said.

Dom turned to find her hovering in the doorway, so he beckoned her in. "If you've got some wise words, we could use them."

"If either of you feel guilty, stop. The people behind the attack are responsible, period. I refuse to let either of you stew over not preventing a crime."

That shouldn't feel like an epiphany, yet somehow it did. Pru had a way of cutting through the bullshit, a unique ability to drag him back from the brink and shove his ass down the road he needed to travel. With a wry smile, he nodded at Gavriel, who also wore a startled look.

"New mission. Whatever it takes, get the walls shored up. Salvage from fallen buildings, figure something out for mortar if we run out. If you need more bodies, ask the

Golgoth."

"Understood." For the first time, the Noxblade saluted instead of bowing, and then he raced off, evidently to execute his new orders.

"How does it look for us?" Pru asked.

Since he didn't want to analyze the odds, Dom said, "We're not out of the woods."

She laughed softly, though he hadn't meant it to be funny. "No kidding. Have you seen where we live?"

The sound startled him so much that the question slipped out. "How can you...?"

"Laugh? Do you think one bad joke means I'm not still mourning?" Her face fell into somber lines then. "Is this better? But... you should know by now that humor is how I survive, how I *always* have."

True. He'd thought before that she rarely let anyone see her cry. *Damn, why am I so clumsy where she's concerned? I didn't even mean it that way.*

So he tried to explain. "It wasn't a complaint, more like... I'm marveling. At how fucking indomitable you are. I've never known anybody so strong. Shit, you're the reason I can push on, day after day. I'm following your example."

"Oh," she said in a small voice. "Sorry. I jumped to conclusions. I guess I always think I'm being judged... in a bad way. Can I make it up to you?"

Even without hearing what she had in mind, he could think of ten things he should be doing. Yet it seemed like forever since he'd spent more than five minutes with her, and the hold wouldn't implode if he took his hand off the wheel for a little while. So he didn't even ask what she wanted, offering a nod.

"Of course."

Her smile made him feel like he'd already won the war. "Don't think I'm unaware how long it's been since you slept. I'm ordering you to bed."

He couldn't stop the slow grin. Pru sighed, but she also showed a hint of dimple.

"Not like that. I'll stand guard and make sure you get a solid hour of sleep."

"I wish I had the energy to tease you, but that sounds amazing. One condition, however."

"What's that?"

"You don't go anywhere. Having you close will do me as much good as pure rest."

She didn't argue, only led him off to the curtained alcove where they had been passing out now and then, usually at opposite intervals. The grubby pillow and blanket he'd salvaged from their disaster of an apartment were a far cry from the comfort they once enjoyed, but as he reflected on that, his mate took off *all* her clothes. His mouth went dry.

His expression apparently made her laugh. "It's not what you think. Take yours off too... we'll be more comfortable shifted."

That should have occurred to me first. I've been going cat much longer than Pru. But commonsense solutions seemed to be her superpower. In answer, he shucked his clothes, kissed her forehead, her freckled cheeks, snub nose, and finally, her lovely mouth. Unexpectedly, she deepened the kiss with a sweetness that stole his breath. She reached up to trace his features with such gentle hands that she stole his breath. Once, her eyes reminded him of winter, desolate and somehow lonesome, but now... for Dom, they held all the brightness and promise of springtime.

I used to see her and think of Slay. But now there's no question that she's mine. Dom didn't even care anymore if she should be. With a final kiss, he slid into leopard form as she went ocelot and rubbed her cheek against his, then touched their noses together. They should have done this sooner. Unlike most couples, their moments together had been driven by necessity, and the time they got to spend with each other diminished with each new disaster.

Curled up with his mate, Dom made a silent promise, then and there. *We may be backed into a corner, but this isn't the end. For you, I'll take on the world. And win.*

23.

A S PROMISED, PRU only dozed while listening for potential interruptions. She safeguarded Dom for a couple of hours, but she couldn't keep the world at bay forever. Eventually Magda came looking; she heard the security chief asking around. *In case I'm ever at risk of forgetting that he doesn't belong to me.* She shifted back and shook him awake.

"Duty calls."

A snow leopard leveled sleepy eyes on her, and then he stretched so gracefully that she couldn't resist smoothing a palm down his back. That fast, she was caressing her naked mate, who dared her with his eyes to recoil or blush. Knowing she didn't have long with him made her brave, so Pru nuzzled her face against his, much as she would if they were still in feline form.

"Morning," he purred.

"It was that already when we went to sleep."

Outside their tent-room, Magda shuffled her feet on purpose. "I realize this is probably bad timing, but..." She trailed off with more tact than usual.

Pru could finish the sentence in the security chief's

customary vernacular: *Get your asses out here anyway.* When she reached for her clothes, Dom astonished her by refusing to let go. With a muffled squeak, she toppled backward into his arms. Acutely conscious that Magda could hear everything—and everyone else probably could too—she squirmed against his hold.

He raised his voice, clearly speaking to the other woman. "Come back in five minutes, unless there's a brand-new fire."

"What are you doing?" she whispered, as Magda strode away.

"Living on borrowed time." He pulled her close and buried his face in her hair, as if she had the luxury of regular baths and smelling delicious on command.

Abashed, she tried to pull away, but he only held on tighter. "This isn't like you."

"It's *exactly* like me. You'll soon realize that I require regular fuel-ups to tolerate constant problems." Dom kissed the curve of her ear with a lazy brush of his lips.

"Please don't tell me you run on hugs," she said, stifling a laugh.

"You're cruel to mock me."

But she curled into his embrace, rubbing her cheek against his bare chest. Before, there had never been anyone in her heart but Slay, but in that moment, she had to admit that Dom had first carved out a small niche, and now he occupied *all* the space. *That wasn't part of the deal.* Though she tried to remind herself it was for the good of the pride, deep down, she didn't care about that anymore. *That's the mate bond talking, right?*

Pru sighed. "I suppose we can't hide here forever."

Trying to smile, she couldn't quite meet his gaze. All

she could think about was how much he mattered, and shit, what if he realized? It would be awful and embarrassing if he thought she expected something. *I can stand anything but him feeling sorry for me, or being pity-gentle.* The affection he'd shown already would be enough; Pru just wished making that silent resolve didn't hurt so damn much.

"I'm back," Magda called.

Thankfully, it gave her an excuse to pull away and don her clothes. Dom kissed her quickly and then scrambled to deal with whatever else had gone wrong. As she watched his back recede, a pang echoed through her, and she knew what she had to do. *It's time.* Moreover, it was too soon to check in with Sheyla, as she hadn't been working on a fix for the Golgoth prince that long when she had so much to do otherwise. The majority of the wounded were on the mend, leaving only Latents and children with extensive recoveries.

Outside, the hold looked better than it had only a week prior. Though visible damage still pocked the settlement— and Pru had to clamber over piles of rubble here and there—most of the exterior wall damage had been repaired. Gavriel was working hard on the last section, so people could sleep better from now on. She also spied Raff and his wolves clearing out the least-damaged residential building, so maybe soon people could start trickling back to their apartments instead of camping like refugees.

Waving at familiar faces here and there, Pru didn't slow until she reached the columbarium. With everything going on, she hadn't checked... and maybe on some level, she'd been avoiding this discovery. The hundreds of memorials that made up the pride's memories were gone, either buried or burned. For many families, this would be like losing their loved ones all over again. Pru staggered a little, realizing that in addition to her fresh bereavements, she also couldn't visit Dalena or her mother anymore.

But… I really need to talk to you.

Deprived of her original goal, her steps turned aimless. At the edge of winter, the weather was warm enough not to make breathing painful, but she couldn't waste time strolling. The problem was deciding what issue required her attention most urgently. Somehow her footsteps carried her to the building where Dalena had lived with Dominic. Since the columbarium was out of the question, maybe there was no better place to talk than where her best friend had died.

Entering the dusty foyer sent a chill through her. *So many people died here. It's not just Dalena anymore.* And though she hadn't seen who pulled the trigger, all those deaths had been murder too. So it was impossible not to feel that weight as she navigated the dark halls. An unnatural quiet had settled, so her breathing seemed extra loud in conjunction with the scrape of her shoes. There was no need to enter Dalena's pin because the door to their old apartment was broken. Dust motes swirled in the air as she stepped inside for the first time since she'd suggested moving to her place instead. Prince Alastor had bided here for a time, but he'd left no imprint on his surroundings. Pru's gaze locked on the wedding portrait, now smeared and hanging crooked as if it might drop off the wall at any moment.

"I'm sorry," she said softly. "It really was for the good of the pride. At first. I never meant to…" *Love him.* But if she said that aloud, then it would become inescapable fact and not the mate bond or hormones, or the sweetness of curling up with the same person night after night. "…take him from you."

That was how she finished the sentence, and it was also

true. "I never coveted him," Pru went on, trying her best to believe that. Innate honesty forced her to whisper, "I wanted what you had, I admit. Back then, I wanted it with Slay. But... not anymore."

Staring at Dalena's smiling face, Pru crossed the room and tried to straighten the picture, but she ended up yanking the nail out of the wall. With a faint sigh, she set it on the ground.

"I don't know how you feel about any of this... or how I'll face you later. Right now I'm pretending your silence means everything is all right, and that if you can't bless me, you'll eventually forgive me."

For a long moment, she hesitated, but there were only ghosts here. She turned for the door and saw Slay hovering outside, one palm flattened on the wall. *How much did he hear?* From his devastated expression, she suspected he had been there for a while.

"Were you looking for me?" she asked.

"I saw you come in, and I was worried the building might be unsafe."

She knocked lightly on the wall. "Seems solid enough."

"Yeah. Well. While I have you here... since I don't know when we'll talk next, given that shit is pretty crazy..." Such pauses weren't like Slay, and he kept fidgeting too, shuffling his feet so the movement carried his face in and out of shadow. "I just want to say that I finally understand it's over."

Pru stared at him. "You... what?"

"All this time, I've been nursing some faint hope—that maybe you were teaching me the hardest lesson ever. But considering what I just heard... well, anyway. I'm sorry. If I'd known that sending you meant losing you, I'd have gone myself. And I would've taken on my whole family for the right to stand by your side. For what it's worth, I made sure you got to the retreat safe, I even watched you mount the steps, one by one."

Once, this would've meant everything. Then it clicked. *So... Slay was watching me? That's what Dom saw?* Realizing how much Slay had cared in retrospect, it tasted bittersweet.

"All right," she said softly. "And thank you. I'm glad we can close the book now."

"I won't say it's with no regrets. But I've squared things in my head, and I don't want to strangle Dom anymore." He managed a smile that struck her as both awkward and painful.

Huh. His eyes don't do anything to me now. And while I know he's handsome, I don't feel it like I used to, down in my bones.

"Sounds like progress," she said with a shadow of her old warmth.

With that, Pru stepped past him because more talk would just open the door to pointless speculation about might-have-been. She could tell Slay wanted to ask—*what if I'd done things differently? What if—*

But that never led to anything good.

AFTER DOM CALMED a small group of pride mates who wanted to go after the Golgoth he was hiding, he joined Raff's crew because some manual labor sounded like exactly what he needed. He had limited intel about how bad it was up north, and he couldn't spare many men for multiple scouting runs. They'd lost too many already in that strike. While it probably struck the other leaders as cowardly, he couldn't react in anger, leaving his people even more vulnerable.

God, I'm tired.

The sleep he'd snatched with Pru was only a drop in the bucket, and they were working so hard to make the hold livable that they weren't remotely ready for a battle. The bright side was that Callum's war bears were standing by and Princess Thalia of the Eldritch would be arriving with her honor guard sometime tomorrow, if Gavriel could be believed. That also meant more mouths to feed on reduced available provisions. Wearily, he dragged another flatbed of rubble out of the building, exchanging nods with the wolf lord as he went by.

On the next run, he bumped Raff's shoulder. "Thanks for staying. You didn't have to."

"Your pretty mate begged," the wolf lord said. "If I'd turned her down, she'd have gotten on her knees, and that's not something I let another man's woman do for me."

Dom balled his hand up without realizing it. Because it was Raff, the info came across filthy, but as shock trickled over him, he realized he had *no* fucking idea where Pru's limits lay. She'd done so much for him—and the pride— already that he didn't know how he'd ever repay her, even with his whole lifetime. He'd been so focused on the weight on his own shoulders that it never registered that she was silently working her ass off to carry half that burden.

She even told you, more than once.

Suddenly Raff laughed. "You had no idea, huh? That woman only looks soft. She's got the Order of Saint Casimir working on the hothouses."

"Seriously?"

Eyes glinting, the wolf lord shook his head in remembered amusement. "I watched the whole thing. That war priest was all like, 'Give me battle or give me death', and Pru pats him on shoulder and says, 'You'd have more energy for combat if we had more to eat, wouldn't you?' Poor bastard turned bright red; pretty sure he's never been that close to a woman before."

"She's resourceful," was all he could manage.

"She's solid gold," Raff corrected.

"I think... I'll look for her."

"Good call. We're losing the light soon, and my boys have drinking and gambling to catch up on."

"Thanks again," Dom said.

As he headed off, the wolf warriors trickled out of the residential hall, all sweaty and exhausted. The small mountain of broken plaster and masonry attested to Pru's efficacy, and he couldn't wait to see her. Words boiled in his head, and he didn't even know which ones should take precedence. Mostly, he just had an overwhelming urge to thank her. Maybe she was sick of hearing it because he'd definitely said it before. The rest of the pride had written him off, practically rubber stamped him with NOT AS STRONG AS HE SHOULD BE, and when he first came back, he'd occasionally glimpsed surprise that he was still alive: still walking, talking, and making reasonable decisions. It sucked to know they'd considered him a lost cause.

Fairness forced him to add, *Except Slay.* Dom was here in the hold, searching for Pru, because Slay had cared enough to send the woman he loved the most to achieve the impossible. He couldn't even fathom what he could do to make things up to his second, but that quiet debt was part of why he hadn't broached the subject of Slay's entanglement with Lord Talfayen and the traitorous Eldritch.

Sooner or later, I have to ask. But not now.

Since Pru might be volunteering with the wounded, he checked out the medical center, now markedly cleaner, and the patient ward had been repaired to the point that it looked like a hospital again and less like a war camp. The staff was still overworked, however, and they rushed around him with minimal acknowledgment.

I could get used to this.

It made sense that she would be with her surviving family during her brief moments of leisure, so he peeked into the room that housed her Aunt Glynnis and her young cousin. At first glance, Jilly didn't seem too badly injured, but Dom could see that her vitality had been extinguished. For reasons she couldn't understand, she'd lost her both her parents, her uncle, and her brother still hadn't woken up. Jase must be somewhere else, hooked up to tubes and wires. He realized then that the pride prepared too little to care for Latents and kits, focusing far too much on the abilities gained after a successful shift.

I have to address that.

The older woman scented him, and her head came up, but her watchful expression melted in a sad but welcoming look. "We're not sleeping. You can come in."

"I'm sorry I didn't visit sooner."

"From what Pru tells me, you're trying to be twelve places at once as it is."

Before he could reply, Joss rushed into the room carrying a tray. "I know you're tired of soup, but you have to eat, okay, sweetheart?"

In reply, Jilly turned away from everyone else in the room, rolling to face the wall. Both her grandmother and Joss tried to get the little girl to take a few spoons, but she only shook her head and maintained an awful silence. *This is the kind of emergency I never would've seen without Pru.* It was so easy to get lost in grand gestures and the big picture, but nothing would ever be more important than the pride's smallest members.

"Let me try," he said.

The women exchanged a look, but neither objected. Rather than start with a spoon, he perched on the edge of Jilly's bed and set a hand on her back. He didn't pet her or press, just maintained that quiet contact for a good five minutes. Since this was exactly what his mother had done when he balled up in a grievous mood, he smiled when Jilly finally rolled over to give him a dirty look.

"What do you want?"

"Nothing," he said.

Since that obviously wasn't what she expected, she sat up, preparing to argue. "Liar. Everyone wants something."

"All right. I want this soup. I'm really hungry."

"That's mine," she said, outraged.

"But you're not eating it."

"I am too." She yanked it away from him and gobbled four big bites before she realized her grandmother was smiling, but hunger kicked in, and she fumed as she emptied the bowl.

Afterward, he didn't move from Jilly's bedside and smoothed the hair away from her forehead. *Her whole world went up when the bombs went off. Poor kid. No wonder she's pissed.* At first she made cranky faces at him, but he noticed when the ice of her anger melted into tears that trickled from the corner of her eyes.

"You want to tell me?" he asked.

She paused for a few seconds. "If you ask Grandy and

Joss to go first."

"Are you reporting to me as pride master and not your cousin?"

"Yes," Jilly said.

"Right then. Are you well enough to go for a walk with Joss?" he asked Glynnis.

"Of course. I'm not even getting treatment anymore." Her face said she was looking after Jilly because this kit needed her most.

The two women went out and shut the door. When Jilly seemed sure they had no witnesses, she said, "I want you to punish somebody."

"What happened?"

"When I was in the room with Jase and not Grandy, someone came and looked at him. Then he said..." her chin trembled, eyes overbright, "...that the rock should've just killed Jase, that he'll never..."

Well, shit. It was too much for a little girl to carry, but she hadn't wanted to give it to her grandmother. Like Pru, she'd probably been worried about hurting someone else. Dom gathered Jilly close as she cried, until her face was sticky and red, and tears spangled her lashes.

This is what family feels like.

"Tell me what he looks like, and I'll hunt him down," he whispered.

Jilly described the visitor to the best of her ability, and it sounded like one of the wolves, which made things a little more complicated, but he didn't doubt Raff would see the asshole disciplined. Eventually his small cousin drifted off against his chest and her kinfolk came back.

"You're good with children," Glynnis murmured.

"Since Jilly needed me, I'm glad I came, but I'm looking

for Pru. Have you seen her?"

Joss stared at him, wide-eyed. "Didn't she say good-bye?"

"What?" His blood froze solid.

24.

THIS WAS THE biggest operation Pru had ever partici-
pated in.

Since she'd been on mission precisely once, that wasn't
saying much, but when Magda asked if she wanted in on the
scouting run to make sure the road was clear for Princess
Thalia, she volunteered in a heartbeat. After being abducted
by that damn Noxblade, she was still eager to prove herself.
Nobody had questioned her status as pride matron, but she
wouldn't feel right about using the title until she returned
from a successful op like a warrior.

Probably, she should've said something to Dom first,
but she'd suspected he might object. So as a result, she told
Joss and Aunt Glynnis, then headed out to join the squad;
they were thirty strong, mostly pride mates she knew only
by sight. Hugh was the one exception, and she was surprised
to find Caio on active duty, but he was still lithe for such an
old lion.

The security chief made a tough call about traveling in
cat form, as it would leave them vulnerable if they needed
to shift later. But ambushes would also be easier, and there
was no need to haul weapons. If things turned for the

worse, they'd also be better equipped to scatter and make their way back to the hold separately. As usual, Pru was the smallest among the big cats, but it allowed her to get lost in the bodies running north. At first, it all seemed quiet. Magda took point, leading with an assurance that inspired everyone who followed.

Half of the snow had melted, leaving the ground a wet, muddy mess, and the conifer trees filled the air with a faint pine tang, much more obvious to an ocelot. Squirrels chattered overhead, tracking their incursion, and a fat one rained nuts down on them as he raced along various limbs overhead for a good five minutes. Hugh let out a warning rumble, and the squirrel thought better of provoking a big group of cats.

Despite the potential danger, it felt good to run after being in lockdown. The chill wind sang through her fur, carrying tales from other forest life. With great resolve, she ignored the interesting stories and kept pace with her squad. Three hours in, Pru heard the first rumble of what should be Princess Thalia's convoy. A glance at her pride mates' swiveling ears told her they heard it too. Magda led them off road, as there was no guarantee that this was the Eldritch royal just because it *should* be. Pru got that as she crouched in the underbrush, hoping that the vehicles would be moving slow enough to confirm their make; the first zoomed by, and she was 90% sure she recognized Eldritch colors and tech. Each seemed to be running a minute or so apart, not tightly clustered.

The security chief signaled with a jerk of her head that this was their target, but before they could put on some speed to commence escort duty, a massive boom from some distance off fractured the silence. Nobody needed the silent order to roll out, and when they reached the bend, Pru stumbled in shock and rammed into Hugh, who was the second smallest cat in the group. He bumped her upright as she took in the flipped, smoking lead vehicle.

Sniffing, she registered a cordite tang and with feline vision, she scoped out the wreckage of an IED at the edge of the road. Distance between it and the rest of the convoy had given the other vehicles time to stop, so the Eldritch only lost one instead of the whole, but there would be casualties. Magda shifted first and led the charge toward the flaming auto; the rest of the squad followed suit. Cold slammed into her as Pru joined the rescue effort, and shivers wracked her as she pulled a broken door off its hinges.

Holy shit, I'm strong.

She dragged a bleeding Eldritch out and hauled him off to the side of the road. Kneeling, she checked his pulse—weak and erratic—and that gash needed to be wrapped. *Of course I don't have bandages.* As she sealed her palms over the wound, her pride mates pulled more casualties from the wreck. A few seconds later, it went up, and the resultant blast knocked her off the road and into the ditch beside it. Pru landed with a splash in icy, brackish water. As she scrambled out, an Eldritch warrior climbed out of the second vehicle.

"I take it this isn't your doing?" he snapped at Magda.

While Mags wasn't technically the highest ranking pride member present, she *was* the squad leader, and Pru was both unimposing and sopping wet. The others had run practice missions since they were twelve, and they shrugged off the wind chill and the goose bumps through better endurance. *I'm soft,* she thought, disheartened.

Hugh whispered, "Go cat. You're not used to this."

It stung like failure when she did so, but she immediately felt better, warmer, and she could shake off the water. Magda clearly had the situation in hand.

"Not us. Golgoth," the tall woman said. "Maintain your distance as before, and follow us, slowly. We'll check the road between here and the hold to make sure it's safe."

"We're transporting Princess Thalia. You should have done that already," the guard snapped.

A slim, ethereally beautiful woman with platinum hair and elfin features alit from the fourth vehicle. "Please don't chide our allies. It's impossible to safeguard the wilderness, as we well know. Thank you for your assistance."

The Eldritch princess made it seem totally natural that she was surrounded by naked Animari. Her eyes remained on each warrior's face, touching on each gaze with sincere warmth. A collective sigh rose from the Animari, and Pru would've laughed if she could.

Magda didn't appear susceptible to anyone's charms, however. "We'll talk more at the hold, Your Highness. Let's clear the road and move."

After the rest of the squad shifted back, they moved as a unit. Pru had never sniffed for explosives before, but they found two more mines, five kilometers apart. It took time to remove them, and with each delay, the risk of an attack increased. The tension mounted the closer they got to the hold.

Golgoth hit them less than two klicks from Ash Valley, two full units—one armored and the other shifted. *Guns and foot soldiers.* It was hard not to flash on the massacre she'd watched via drone, but fear would slow her down. Yet she couldn't consider herself invincible. Consistent, sustained wounds could kill an Animari, but unless the gun delivered a burst of sudden, catastrophic damage, she had a chance to heal. Around her, pride mates shrieked in pain, and the stink of blood thickened the air, along with gunpowder, hot metal, and electricity.

The Eldritch were using explosive rounds, and each shot boomed against the armor-plated hulls of the Golgoth land behemoths, leaving their squad to take on the shifted Golgoth, and they were massive. Not just massive. *Monstrous.* Pru had no idea how she was supposed to take one out, but she raced low, dodging the spray of gunfire. Hugh snarled at her and signaled for her to stay close; since they were smallest, it made sense for them to tag team. Unlike Magda, the biggest tiger in the pride, who was squaring off against a seven-foot terror with lizard eyes, protruding fangs, and a spiny ridge crawling down its back.

No, I can't get distracted. I'm fighting as pride matron.

When Hugh leapt at a smaller Golgoth, she went with him, and there was a seamless joy in the attack. He went high; she dove low and sank her teeth into the monster's Achilles tendon. Or she would have, if it hadn't been like biting old leather. *How can such a thing exist?* Grating laughter exploded above her as the Golgoth hauled back to kick. *Too slow.* Pru bounded away and back, seeking a softer target. She circled, aware of how enormous her opponent was, how easily he could rip her apart. But he was slow, and because of some plates, he didn't seem to have great peripheral vision. Hugh went for the throat and almost got his skull cracked. The serval went flying, and she snarled her determination to draw blood, not that the brute understood her feline warning:

"I'll prove myself today or die trying."

THE SCOUT RACED up to Dom, interrupting his conference with Callum, who was surprisingly well-disposed toward his work on the greenhouse. "Multiple detonations, sir. We've got hostiles near the hold, two klicks out and holding."

That news couldn't have come at a worse time, as Dom was already worried enough about Pru. "Full report, or this info's worthless."

"Two units of Golgoth fighting Eldritch and Animari."

His attention sharpened so fast it practically became a weapon. "What did you say?"

"I think it's Magda's squad out there. Orders?"

"Rally all able-bodied warriors. Leave a skeleton crew on the walls."

"Acknowledged, sir."

Most likely this was a terrible decision, one he might even suffer for later, but he did *not* care. At the moment, he was only a man who had the power to move heaven and earth for his woman. "Anyone who's not ready in ten minutes will be left."

"Understood."

The scout raced off, and Dom ran to the staging room to wait. Thirty pride members and ten of Callum's war bears turned up, and he gave orders for the first time in forever. "We move fast, hit hard. Our objective is to wipe out the invaders and get our people to safety."

An affirmative chorus was like music to his ears. Aware that he wasn't thinking right, Dom still ran out because all his blood had turned to dread. *If she's not okay, if I don't save her*—those dark thoughts looped in his head. The distance melted beneath his feet, and he was dimly aware of growling protests at his punishing pace. *They'll keep up or catch up. Either way.*

The battlefield burst into view, a desolation of flipped vehicles, craters in the ground, bodies everywhere, and the overwhelming stench of spilled blood. Fighting still raged in sporadic pockets, but most of the Golgoth must've been defeated or driven off. His people waded in with savage joy, retaliating at last. Dom charged straight at a blood-red bastard's back; the force of his hit rocked the Golgoth forward, and Dom latched his jaws on his neck with full power. Compared to Eldritch, Golgoth blood tasted of earth and minerals, like these creatures had risen from the land itself.

Despite spinning and glancing blows from his opponent, he didn't let go until he snapped the Golgoth's spinal cord. The great brute wobbled and fell, freeing him to take on another. With the addition of their numbers, the tide turned swiftly. *But where the hell is Pru?* As he took on another, an Eldritch woman in black leather caught his eye, mostly from the silver hair, the curved blade in her left hand, and the lightning streaming from her right. Her opponent twitched, charred, and fell, then she beheaded the beast in a clean sweep.

"Mount up," she called.

This has to be the princess. Glad she's safe.

But his head wouldn't stop ticking like a bomb unless he located his mate, and Dom searched exhaustively for a small, indomitable ocelot. There were corpses everywhere, but they could be Golgoth or Animari, as both reverted after death. Dom took comfort in the fact that he didn't see her face in all this carnage. Lingering was impossible as the Eldritch loaded up their operational vehicles with wounded and resumed the trek to the hold.

In the confusion of the return, he saw so many pride

mates, but he couldn't be sure if Pru was among them. *She has to be. We're not leaving her in that clearing, no fucking way.* Yet the sickness in his stomach swelled until he could hardly see or breathe or hear. Sometimes he thought he sensed her, flickers of emotion that didn't seem to belong to him. *That means she's fine, right?* When Dalena died, he felt it, not just because she was in his arms; sudden silence dropped on him then like the veil of mortality itself. Even so, Dom blanked on the time between disengaging from battle and reaching the hold. The next thing he knew, the gates loomed before him, opening with such glacial speed that he nearly snarled.

By the time the great doors shut behind them—after a fucking argument about the princess's vehicles because they contained armaments—Dom was ready to peel his own skin off. He got changed, dressed in basic gear, and came back in time to see Magda supervising the offloading of Eldritch weapons. *That's a headache I don't fucking need.*

And he still didn't see Pru. *Enough is enough.*

"Where is my fucking wife?" he roared.

Everyone in the plaza fell silent, and eventually she pressed forward out of the crowd, so liberally smeared in blood that he couldn't tell how badly she was hurt. A shuddering breath escaped him, and he just couldn't deal with any of the other shit right then. *Slay must be around. Magda's here.* Yielding to impulse, he swept her up and carried her off.

Fuck this. Fuck all of it.

What did winning a battle matter if it meant losing her? Outrage lit him up like summer fireworks. *How—just how...?* She had the sense not to fight him at least, as he carried her away from the throng toward the residential annex. Dom swung into a building at random, the one the wolves had been clearing, and he found an apartment with a working door. They hadn't fixed the keypads, but it had a lock on the inside. The interior was fairly clean; he had no idea who lived here before and cared even less. With great self-control, he set Pru down and turned the bolt.

"I killed a Golgoth," she told him cheerfully. "More than one, if you count those I went after with Hugh. I'm blooded now. I'm proven in battle. It didn't count before since those Noxblades weren't actually trying to end us."

"Are you fucking serious?" he bit out.

Backing off a step, she seemed to register his expression for the first time. "What?"

"That's all you have to say to me? You take off without checking in, I find out from your cousin that you're gone, and you want me to praise your martial prowess?"

A tiny frown creased her brow, attesting to the fact that she had *no* idea how close he was to losing his mind. "I thought you'd tell me not to go since the last op didn't go well."

"Yes, that's my concern right now, your mission performance." If sarcasm came in a bucket, he could've painted a ballroom with that much.

"I really don't understand," Pru said in a small voice. "I just wanted to prove myself."

"Stop. You're killing me with the assumption that you have to *do* something to be worthy as pride matron or even a member of Ash Valley. Listen up, because I don't know how long I can keep it together and use my words."

Wide-eyed, she nodded. Maybe she sensed how precarious his mood was because she danced a few steps away. *Fuck. I'd never hurt you. But I might take this room apart.* And that would be a shame when Raff's wolves had worked so hard. Dom dragged in a deep breath through his nose, trying not to show how hard he was shaking, and it just sucked to scold her when all he wanted was this woman— safe and sound—in his arms.

"I'm proud of you, I am, but you left without a word, and that's not fair. I should've been given the choice to support your choice and kiss you in case shit went sideways. How could I live, knowing you didn't trust me enough to let you go?"

Her eyes filled with tears. "I didn't think of that. I just wanted—"

"I know," he snarled. "I *know*. But if you think you have to do this shit to earn me, you're out of your mind. If you never solve another problem, never again work yourself to the brink of exhaustion, never sway another leader to our side, never slay another enemy, you're still important and unspeakably precious. You were both of those things before you shifted, kitten. And you always will be."

"Dom." She breathed his name like a prayer, and he flashed on that time on the mountain when she'd made him come saying it.

Desire swamped him until it felt like he might actually die if he didn't touch her. In a flash, he had her in his arms. "That's it. I'm tapped out. No more words."

25.

STUNNED, PRU HELD still for a few seconds. "That... we can't... the princess—"

"Ask me if I care." Dom's expression made the answer clear. "Come with me."

Despite her confusion, she still took his hand when he offered it, and then he led her to the bathroom. He didn't speak as he peeled her clothes away, citrine eyes vivid and intense. She had the sudden urge to cover herself with her hands because Dom had never been like this before, as if the world could burn all around them, and he wouldn't even notice. There was no boiler, so she shivered through a bewildering shower; the combination of cold water and his hot body pressing close overloaded her senses. Afterward, he swaddled them both in a blanket, and she warmed gradually with him wrapped around her.

Just like at the retreat.

"I wish I could've taken my time, washed every inch of you, but..."

Pru smiled. "I know. The hold's not as well-equipped as it used to be. But we'll rebuild. And I get that you want a few minutes alone, but they must be searching for us by now."

"Still don't care," he whispered.

"You..." She lost her ability to speak when he twined the damp rope of her hair around his hand and used it to arch her throat. *The sex signal... he's sending it.* When his warm lips glided over her skin, Pru lost interest in responsibility, especially when he didn't just kiss her neck. He sucked, licked and bit, lingering until pleasure welled up like syrup from a notched maple tree. "So this is happening?"

"Unless you say no. I'll always respect that." But his voice sounded rough and low, like it was hard for him to speak the words. Given the fierce burn of his eyes, he'd hate that decision.

So would she. If she believed what he said about being important, even if she wasn't useful, then she could be allowed to make impulsive, irresponsible choices occasionally. It wouldn't kill Princess Thalia to talk to someone else for a while, and Pru wanted to work off the adrenaline in her blood after the battle. *No,* she amended. *Better to be honest with myself, at least. I want to love my mate.*

"I'm sure they'll be fine for an hour," she said.

When he smiled, he had never looked more beautiful to her. "Or four."

"Mmm." Pru shivered as he nibbled a path from her ear to her collarbone, paying tribute as if she were a queen deserving of such grace. Goose bumps prickled her skin, and her nipples pebbled beneath the rough drape of the blanket, just from Dom's mouth on her neck.

"Wait for me," he ordered.

Then he got up, and the cold where he had been made her teeth chatter. Soon he came back with more blankets that had been protected in their cupboards, and Dom shook them out with an impatient snap, then he layered the softest ones inside. When he came down to her, she pulled all of the covers up, and then it was delicious heat and the smoothness of his warming skin gliding against hers. She wanted him so much that she ached with it, and she couldn't sort out who was feeling what. *Mating frenzy.* Her whole body throbbed in response.

"I'm waiting."

"Best news I've had in ages."

Pru was already hot enough to get straight down to it, but Dom rolled to his side, carrying her with him. He touched her only with his lips, and in the cocooning dark, he took hers again and again, until she moaned into his mouth and urged him closer with a hand on his back. That made him gasp in turn, so she used her nails, remembering how sensitive he was. He jerked with each rake of her fingers as if she were actually pulling on his cock. But no, it pushed at her belly, hot and hard, and leaking on her skin. *If he wants to kiss, let's kiss.* They did, until her tongue tingled and her mouth felt swollen.

"Please."

"What?"

"Anything."

His soft laughter vibrated against her shoulder. "At the retreat, I noticed how pretty your tits are, and then I felt like shit."

"How about now?" Worry permeated her lust a little, just enough to take the edge off.

"I still think they're gorgeous. And I only feel bad that I haven't fucked them."

A little whimper escaped her. "You can. If you want. But I'm not really sure—"

"I don't need instructions, kitten. Only permission."

She sank back and opened her arms. "You always have that."

It took more positioning than she expected, but it was surprisingly sexy to let him *arrange* her to his liking. Once that was done, he knelt over her. "Squeeze them together for me. Play with your nipples. This has to feel good for you too."

At first, she felt self-conscious, but his avid eyes persuaded her. Soft sounds turned throaty when he slid his cock between her breasts, dizzying her with his delicious smell. For a few seconds, he held still. More pre-come leaked, but it wasn't quite enough, so as he pulled back, she reached between her thighs and stroked. *I'm so wet.*

She lingered on her lips, her clit, yielding to the impulse to hump her hand a little. Watching made him crazy; she could tell by the deep, rasping breaths, and the way his hips jerked. She brought her hand up, again and again, stroking between her breasts, until her skin was slick and glistening. Dom thrust once, and as her fingers grazed his cock, Dom let out a growl so deep that she trembled.

"How's that?"

"Filthy. Perfect. Tell me if you don't like it."

"Impossible," she breathed.

He moved, slow at first, watching her face. Heat flooded her cheeks on the first stroke, and Pru realized she was responsible for the level of pressure, of friction. Holding her breasts, she studied his expression in turn, learning what he liked. His lips parted slightly when she massaged herself against him, and when she lifted so she could lick the tip of his cock on the upstroke, he threw his head back and went faster.

"You're going to make me come," he panted.

"Like this?"

"Fuck yes."

"Then stop." Half-teasing, she pushed him away, and she was astonished when he fell back. No matter how far gone he was, he always, *always* heard her, and that lit her up as nothing else could have.

"You're vicious," he complained.

"Let's see if you're still saying that in five minutes."

Pru devoured him with her eyes. He looked healthier since they'd come back, still lean, and he'd regained some of the muscle he'd lost. With appreciative hands, she touched his arms, chest, shoulders. When her palms reached his abdomen, Dom's lashes fluttered, and his surge of pleasure zinged through her, kindling in her clit. Astonished by how keen and clear the feedback was, she stroked him again and again, and each time—

"Are you trying to drive me insane?" he got out.

"You feel that?"

"Of course, sharper each time." He had a hard time speaking. "I'm getting lightheaded, to be honest, with so much blood rushing away from my brain."

On her orders, he rolled onto his stomach, though her amusement turned breathless when she realized how tough it was for him to get comfortable. Then she made it worse by peppering kisses down his spine, his ever-so-sensitive spine. Hands and lips, teeth and tongue, she nuzzled every inch of his back, until he was practically humping the pile of blankets.

"Not vicious. Merciless."

Pru parted his thighs and licked in between, her own arousal heightening as his spiked. Her mouth grazed the back of his testicles, just another tease, not the satisfaction they both craved. Yet he still lifted his hips, letting her do whatever she wished. She couldn't quite reach, and it was all wet, messy torment as she nuzzled her face against him, and he rocked back and forth, driven by her mouth and his need. His breath became one long groan, and soon, he *was* humping the blankets as if he might come. Truthfully, she was two brisk strokes from an insane orgasm, just from feeling his reaction, and if he was getting hers too—

"Fuck me," she whispered.

YES. THANK YOU. Finally.

With absolute urgency, Dom grabbed his mate and pulled her onto his lap. She sank down on him, and her heat, her wetness, sent a sweet shock shuddering through his body. He couldn't get close enough to her, despite being inside her. He didn't question the incredible yearning, only held her closer and closer still. When her arms went around his shoulders, it was like he could breathe again.

Yes, hang on.

As the pleasure mounted to impossible levels, his head went even fuzzier. Her delight surged through him again and again, rebounding with each stroke, until it was like his mind split, and he could feel not only how good she felt to him, but also the slick, hard rub of his own cock. The sensation was so ferocious that for one long, maddening moment, he was both of them, together, separate, together, spiraling, breathing, coming, and her orgasm shivered through him a heartbeat before his own.

Too much.

Dom had no idea how much later it was, but they were

still curled together, and she looked as shocked as he felt. Weakly, he stroked her hair, still trembling, so it couldn't have been that long. *Never blacked out after sex before.*

"What was that?" she whispered.

"A spectacular cementing of the mate bond."

It hadn't been like that with Dalena, not that he should talk about it with Pru—or maybe he *should*—so hard to know what would hurt her and where the lines should be drawn. *God, it feels like I haven't eaten in a week.*

She rested her cheek against his chest, and he knew without being told that she was silently savoring each thump of his heart. *Like I'm a fucking gift and she ought to write a thank-you note.* But it was impossible not to be touched too.

"Does that mean we'll be able to communicate telepathically now?"

Amused, Dom cocked a brow at her. "Do you know anyone who can?"

"My parents used to claim they could, but I'm guessing they were just messing with me, huh?" Adorably, she looked disappointed.

I could spend quite a lot of time, happily, trying to kiss each and every freckle. In this light, she was so sweet and gorgeous and *his* that he was tempted to go for round two. But that might literally kill him, and Magda would probably obliterate the whole building if they didn't turn up soon. Between the security chief and Slay, they could only make excuses for so long. In retrospect, maybe he should've shown a little more self-control.

Or not.

He kissed Pru and said, "Let's test it out."

Quasi-serious, he set his brow against hers and thought,

You are amazing. I will spend the rest of my life treasuring you.

With a cant of her head, she tried, "You're hungry?"

"No. Not even close."

"But you are amused."

"Right now? Highly." It was so like her to want to experiment with mind-speak when they were both naked and had just fucked so hard that he'd passed out.

"So it's probably limited emotions," she mused. "How am I feeling right now?"

"Like you swallowed a ball of sunshine." Though his tone was facetious, it wasn't an inaccurate description. She radiated joy that suffused him until his whole body glowed with it.

"Correct."

"Does that mean *I'm* your sunshine?" he asked, smiling.

With a solemn nod, she avowed, "My only sunshine."

"I make you happy when skies are gray?" This was an ancient children's song; Dom was just teasing, and he couldn't remember the rest anyway.

So he didn't expect her to jolt away from him so abruptly or scramble for her clothes, muttering, "Shit. Shit, shit, shit, shit, *shit*."

"What's wrong?"

Her words tumbled out in a panicked rush, muffled by the shirt she was pulling over her head. "Eamon. I *forgot about Eamon*. He might be injured, pinned by wreckage, or out of food. There should be water in the tap at least. Shit, why am I *such* an idiot? He wouldn't come out when things were fine, and now—"

"Shit," Dom snarled.

She was right. Even if rescue workers tried, he'd probably barricade himself in his apartment rather than open for strangers like Raff's wolves. If he was sure about anything, it was that Eamon would rather starve than be taken alive. Now as worried as Pru, he threw on his trousers and tunic, and they dashed for the door together. Yet he couldn't let her carry the blame alone, for he should've remembered too.

"He has to be okay." She repeated this as a litany as he led the way to Eamon's apartment upstairs.

Damn, we were even in the building.

When they arrived, the door was still on its hinges, at least. More than could be said for many of its neighbors. That probably had to do with all of Eamon's locks and reinforcements. Dom rapped briskly, the other hand on Pru's shoulder to steady her. She seemed on the verge of a complete breakdown, and her near panic was messing with his head. Her fear had his heart racing, and he wasn't even prone to anxiety. Brooding, yes. Anxiety, no.

After what felt like an eternity, a muffled voice called, "Who's there?"

"It's me," Pru shouted. "And Dom."

"Busy day for me, it seems." Movement sounded within, and eventually the door cracked enough for Eamon to scrutinize them. "Come in, if you like."

It seemed churlish not to when they'd both been so worried. Pru was calming, and her ease settled his nerves. His breathing quieted as they stepped into Eamon's sanctuary. Compared to other units, the damage wasn't as bad as it could be. Still, he couldn't imagine hunkering down like this after the bombs went off.

"Do you need anything?" Pru asked, taking a visual inventory.

Eamon shook his head. "For the first few days, I did run

low on food, but Joss has been here twice this week with supplies. I'd offer you something, but I understand we're all on rations, so—"

"Don't worry about that," Dom cut in. "I'm just glad to know you're safe."

Eamon inclined his head with a grave expression. "Thank you for thinking of me."

Unexpectedly, Pru dropped to the floor on a shaky burst of laughter. "We are ridiculous."

Dom didn't realize she was speaking directly to him until she grabbed his arm. His brows went up. "We are?"

"Seriously. Like we're the *only* ones who ever do anything in the hold, and if we don't attend to it personally, everything will crumble. Ridiculous."

His wry smile formed slowly, but he could see her point. "We do tend to take sole responsibility for things, don't we?"

"It's a failing," Pru said, sighing. "In both of us."

"I suppose we're too much alike in that way. We'll work on it."

Eamon glanced between them with a faint smile, but his response was mild. "I *did* tell you I have other friends."

"I'm relieved. As long as Joss is checking in, I'll stop thinking I'm so irreplaceable."

"That would be a mistake. Just because Joss brings me a box of staples and sings while I paint, that doesn't mean I never want to see your face."

Dom restrained a growl at how happy that comment made Pru. If her happiness hadn't filled him up like a fizzy drink, the blush in her freckled cheeks would've given it away. Plus, he hadn't even known that Eamon was an artist, so he focused on that. "Would you let us hang some of your work in the admin center once we finish the repairs?"

Elbowing him, Pru whispered, "He never shows me anything, don't be rude."

To his mate's evident astonishment, the other man nodded. "When the work is done, ask again. I'll have a piece ready for you."

"I can't wait." Pru seemed as if she'd like to rush at the painter and hug him in a fit of enthusiasm, but Eamon might as well have posted DO NOT TOUCH THE ARTIST signs. In this hideaway, it was quiet, giving no sign of the chaos in the wider world.

"Joss told me we're up against the Golgoth. I wish I could fight them," Eamon said.

"Nobody expects you to." Dom meant his words to be comforting, but it was hard to tell if he'd succeeded.

An ocean of sadness Dom could scarcely cross in a boat flickered in Eamon's eyes. "That's exactly why I wish I could."

26.

P RU MADE HERSELF presentable as soon as possible and accompanied her mate to greet Princess Thalia. Part of her couldn't stop obsessing over exactly *why* Dom had dragged her off, another part glowed endlessly over the sweet things he'd said followed by amazing sex, and the rest knew she had to focus because with Lord Talfayen dead, if they didn't secure an alliance with Princess Thalia, relations with the Eldritch could break down completely.

Magda had the situation under control, fortunately. She'd quickly gotten the park decorated and set up portable heaters. With the band playing in the pergola and a sky full of stars overhead, the disorder of the reconstruction effort became charming rather than chaotic. Certainly the princess seemed to be having a good time when Pru made her bow beside Dom.

"Our apologies for the delay," she said.

The princess offered an amused, knowing smile. "No harm done. Though I've yet to be swept off like that, I certainly daydream about it."

"Who would dare?" Gavriel demanded.

The royal waved him to silence. "This isn't the moment

to speak of serious matters, and I thank you for welcoming me with such sincerity."

"I take it you're willing to work with us?" Dom asked.

Thalia nodded. "I've had a full report from Gavriel, and I'm sorry our alliance had such a rocky start. I take full responsibility for the tragic outcome."

"The failure is mine," the Noxblade said.

Pru couldn't help but notice the intensity with which he studied the princess, but the intimate workings of their relationship weren't her business. "This is likely to be the eye of the storm, so we should enjoy it while we can."

Thalia nodded. "That wasn't the majority of the Golgoth army, just an exploratory force. Now that we've all gathered at Ash Valley, chances are good that the bulk of the offensive will occur near here."

"An excellent analysis," Dom commended.

"Are you well situated for a siege?"

Mentally Pru took stock of the remaining supplies, factored against the influx of fresh bodies. "I don't think we could hold out long, if they disrupt shipments and highjack supplies."

"Do you have an estimate of their numbers?" Magda asked.

"I'm surprised Prince Alastor hasn't given you that already," Thalia said.

Shit. That reminds me.

She excused herself with a murmur and searched the crowd for any sign of Sheyla, but parties, even impromptu ones, weren't the doctor's thing, especially not when so many people were relying on her. Pru hurried to the med center and found it quiet compared to a week ago, but the staff seemed no less exhausted. Sheyla was visibly thinner, her face drawn and weary, when Pru found her. *She has too much to do. I wish I didn't have to add to her burdens.* But unlike Pru, Sheyla had a face that only became more beautiful when she was overworked; somehow she took that air of exhaustion and her pretty face deepened to ethereal beauty.

"Let me guess," Sheyla said with a faint sigh. "You're wondering if I've figured anything out for your fragile Golgoth friend."

"I'm sorry. I wouldn't ask if we weren't running out of time."

And we need him.

Since the conclave had failed, Prince Alastor represented their only hope at keeping the Golgoth at bay. Surely there must be some who would turn from conquest, given a more rational choice. They couldn't all follow Tycho with mindless fervor, right? Since Alastor's entourage comprised all she knew firsthand of his people, maybe she shouldn't be so quick to judgment.

"My equipment is shit, so I had to do a lot of manual analysis, and I *think* I've come up with a similar compound, but it won't do much more than buy him time if the various dosages are off, even in minuscule amounts. There may also be unforeseen side effects, as I'm nowhere near proficient in Golgoth physiology, let alone treating their ailments. Finally, and I know I sound like I'm excusing failure, but I'm not a fucking chemist. The only chemist we had died in the first blast."

"I'm sorry," Pru said softly.

"I don't feel good about this." Sheyla stared at the pale liquid in the vials on the counter. "It's like I'm setting him up for a slow poisoning. I should've run tests on him first, examined him fully, analyzed his physical condition—"

"There was no time for that. I'll ask the prince to cooperate with you in getting that done now that we have a little breathing room."

So little. We have a would-be king with an undisclosed illness who doesn't really want to wage war against his brother. But from what Alastor had said, he understood that it was the only road that led to survival. Eventually Sheyla sighed and inclined her head.

"I'm aware the circumstances aren't ideal. I guess if I accidentally kill his last rival, Tycho may be merciful when he rolls over us."

"But I doubt it," Pru muttered.

"I won't hold my breath. If you'll excuse me, I need to check on Jase."

"Can I come with you? I'll just pop in for a minute."

"Of course. Glynnis was with him while Jilly was napping, so he hasn't been alone long."

With all her heart, Pru wished she could sit by Jase's side and talk to him nonstop, but with war looming just outside the gates, she could only steal these moments. *Please don't let that inhibit his recovery.* Though Sheyla strode in boldly to check his vitals, Pru paused in the doorway, her heart wrenching for the boy who might not even know he'd lost his parents. He looked so small in the hospital bed. Once Sheyla finished, Pru sat down in the chair near Jase's bed.

"I wish I could spend more time in here. You have to wake up soon, all right? We miss you. Jilly needs you."

His fingers flickered, and she wrapped his small hand in hers. Sheyla said, "Don't read too much into that. It could be involuntary."

"But I've heard that comatose patients can sometimes

hear everything people say."

"That's not something I can validate... but just in case, try to stay cheerful."

Pru spent five minutes longer talking to Jase, but apart from that first flex of his fingers, he didn't respond to her voice. She kissed him on the forehead in farewell, and whispered, "You're a proper warrior. Thank you for surviving."

With that, she slipped out, so that the steady beeping from the machines keeping him alive faded to the quick footfalls of the medical staff hurrying to and fro. *Was Prince Alastor at the party?* She couldn't recall seeing him, but she swung by the park to check. The desperate merriment gladdened her heart, but it was a melancholy sweetness. Beneath the determined cheer lay the frantic fear that they could lose everything—not just Ash Valley—but Burnt Amber and Pine Ridge, along with the Eldritch and Golgoth territories.

We have to keep Alastor alive long enough to rally support against Tycho.

That was a shitty reason for helping someone, she knew. But her urgency didn't abate as she searched the dancers keeping warm the best way possible, hands in the air, and unlikely couples paired up in the music-rich dark. She spotted Alastor curled up near the fire, a few of his men close enough to intervene if anyone went after him, but the mood was mellow since Princess Thalia's arrival. The flickering flames painted Alastor in diabolical hues, but those colors somehow only made the prince seem more delicate.

"Have you come to deliver me from my self-imposed exile?" he asked.

"I suppose I have." She passed him the treatment Sheyla

had devised, then imparted all the caveats and warnings the doctor had shared.

"If you *wanted* me dead, there are more direct means. I've gambled my life on lesser matters, so why not?" He hefted the case and shook his head with evident bemusement.

"Something's funny?"

"You want me alive much more than my own people, that's all." By tone and expression, he tried to sell the idea that he was fine with that.

Only Pru wasn't buying it. Before she could dig into his feigned indifference, the sound of heavy weapons boomed, silencing the music. The festive scene devolved into leaders calling orders and a lightning-fast response from the warriors.

With a sardonic twist of his mouth, Alastor said, "Looks like the party's over, and I didn't even get to dance."

"THEY'RE SHELLING THE walls, and if they find the breach points we patched up, we'll have a thousand Golgoth inside our gates." Dom couldn't believe how aggressive and driven the enemy was, especially since they'd just been defeated, but he had two royals inside the hold, so that was probably why. *If they take out Thalia and Alastor, resistance among the Eldritch crumbles and the Golgoth are united.*

"Give me intel," Slay shouted.

The sentry on the wall scoped out the situation as best he could. "They're limited on heavy weapons. Right now, it's only two guys on a C-TAK firing shells, but they're working on the princess's fleet. If they get those vehicles running, I think they mean to ram the gates."

"It won't happen." Suddenly Princess Thalia was beside him, tapping away at her phone.

Thirty seconds later, a series of booms rocked the ground. With a grim look, she said, "How many did I take out in sacrificing my tech?"

Dom shouted the question, and the scout replied, "At least fifty."

"It's a start. How are we handling this, pride master? Your walls don't look sound enough for a long siege."

He practically snarled, "They were better before all the bombs went off."

To his surprise, her eyes dropped away. "My father's doing. I'm still collecting information about what went wrong, but I'll have answers soon."

"That can wait. This can't." Dom gestured at the chaos.

At the moment, each faction leader was giving his or her own instructions, but that didn't make for an organized resistance. Dom wanted that job about as much as a punch in the face, but somebody had to do it, and he had three compelling reasons to step up. One—it was his home ground to defend, and he knew the terrain best. Two—he had failed his people enough, so while he might not be the hero they deserved, he'd give his best. Three—he had to protect Pru; no way he'd leave it to anyone else.

Mind made up, he sent runners to collect the others: Raff, Callum, Alastor. Thalia stuck close to him, constantly in contact with her people via radio and phone, until the signal went out. A scout reported the enemy must be using scramblers, and Dom didn't stop cursing for like five minutes. *We can't hold out long if they keep hammering us with the C-TAK.*

"We don't have a lot of time to debate, so I just need to

ratify this with a show of hands. My realm, my rules. I'm open to suggestions, but from this point on, I'm in charge of this offensive. Any questions?" He made eye contact with the other leaders in turn.

"No objections," Raff said as a shell exploded.

The Eldritch princess shook her head. "It only makes sense."

Both Callum and Alastor kept quiet, which he took for tacit assent. He hadn't known the bear long enough to have a good handle on his personality, but he seemed slow and steady whereas the Golgoth prince was a study in contrasts, one moment flippant, somber the next. As long as they acknowledged his authority and deployed their forces accordingly, that was enough.

Callum said, "The Order of Saint Casimir stands with you. I can't call any reinforcements from the north, as they're already fighting."

Dom inclined his head. "I understand if you need to withdraw and defend your territory. We'll hold on here long enough to keep these bastards from pushing north."

"These 'bastards' are my people," Prince Alastor said in a deceptively mild tone.

The wolf lord took a step forward, one hand on the hilt of his weapon. "And they're murdering us."

Can't let that continue. But Dom decided to see how the Golgoth prince would handle the situation. *If necessary, I can always step in.*

"That's because they're raised on a cocktail of dominance and aggression. It doesn't mean they all want to ride to conquer. In our world..." A muscle ticked in Alastor's jaw, then he bit off whatever else he might have said. "It doesn't matter. Let's focus on preventing Ash Valley from being utterly destroyed."

"What's the plan?" Slay asked, snatching the segue.

Dom appreciated his friend more than ever, as the other leaders locked on to the discussion. "We send a strike force, the stealthiest bastards we've got."

"And they take out the C-TAK?" his second guessed.

There was no need to confirm the obvious. "Who do we have ready for action?"

Quickly, they assembled a team, comprised of the pride's best scouts, a few wolves, and the best of the Noxblades, including Gavriel. "Let's go."

Slay grabbed his arm. "Hold up. You can't lead this one personally."

"Bullshit I can't."

"Think for a minute. You just got everyone to acknowledge that you're running the show. In what world does it make sense for you to handle the op yourself?"

"He's right," Raff said unexpectedly. "It's worse for me, sending my men into danger, but it doesn't always make sense to lead from the front."

If he'd just scolded Pru for proving herself, he couldn't insist on doing the same out of some misguided desire to establish that he was still strong enough to head up the pride. Protecting his people didn't necessarily mean destroying enemy war machines with his bare hands, either; it counted if he made good decisions and minimized loss of life at every opportunity. *It just doesn't* feel *brave.* Recognizing that his desire to command the force personally rose from an ego in need of boosting, he conceded the point with a sigh.

"Fine, you do it, Slay. You're a better stalker than Mags. No offense," he added to the security chief, who shrugged.

Even *she* knew it was true; she was the natural choice when you wanted a target exterminated with extreme prejudice. Slay, on the other hand, excelled at the stalk and kill, maybe not quite at a Noxblade level, but he was the best the pride had on offer.

"We'll go out the side door. I need half the squad on diversion. The rest of us will take out the C-TAK."

"My crew has ordnance," Callum said. "Sounds like you could use it."

"Please," Slay answered.

An itchy feeling crawled down Dom's back, and he followed the stealth-op team to the side exit. So far, there were no hostiles here, but it wouldn't take long for Golgoth scouts to report back on all the potential entrances. The guards in the staging area were all tight and tense, waiting for that engagement. The C-TAK kept up its barrage, weakening the wall with each strike, and if they didn't get those guns shut down, there would be breach in under an hour. The war priest, Callum, met the squad with the promised firepower, but it was more than they could carry. *We'll put this to good use from the inside.* At some point, he really needed to learn more about the Order of Saint Casimir.

After the distraction team geared up, he faced the whole crew. "You don't need me to spell out what we're up against. So I'll just tell you not to be heroes and to get the job done."

The squad all saluted Dom, even the Noxblades. Gavriel met his gaze for an extended moment, and the team followed Slay out into the darkness. He partnered up with Callum to get some of that ordinance on the walls. The C-TAK was too far for traditional weapons, and he didn't want to leave his people vulnerable for long. Already heavy caliber ammo peppered the ramparts, forcing his own shooters into cover time and again.

Dom checked his watch, counting down the seconds, and the diversionary team executed right on schedule. Orange lit up the horizon, along with a series of booms. *Here we go.* From his vantage, he watched the C-TAK go up in a fireball, taking out a good number of invaders in the resultant explosion. *Yes. That's how we do it, and just in fucking time too.* The stealth crew knew to head straight back, avoiding the enemy wherever possible. *Hit and run. There's no reason to engage their main force.* Most of the stealth squad made it back, but for some reason, Gavriel was leading them.

"What happened?" he demanded.

"I don't know," the Noxblade said. "We encountered resistance near the wall and we had to cut a path." Pru appeared just in time to hear Gavriel deliver news that chilled Dom's blood. "We scoured the area, but we didn't find his body."

Slay was just fucking *gone*.

27.

FEAR HAD A hold of Pru's throat, but she couldn't sink down and cry. With Dom staring at her, that was the last thing she should do. So she fell into her role as pride matron. "You did the right thing in coming back," she told Gavriel. "Your unit wasn't designated for a full-frontal assault, and there's still a lot of Golgoth out there."

Please, let Slay be safe.

Even if she'd passed the point of wanting to build a life with him, she had sweet memories of their time together, and she wanted him home, like any pride mate. *Probably more,* she admitted silently. Fortunately Gavriel chose that moment to make a formal report on the strike they'd executed. The timing must be coincidental, but she appreciated the opportunity to collect herself.

"We lost four, counting Slay. Took out easily twice our number, more if you count the ones that died when the princess detonated her fleet. Another fifteen or so when we blew up the C-TAK. But there are hundreds of Golgoth swarming," Gavriel concluded.

"This isn't the main force," Alastor said.

"Damn. How many are there?" Raff wondered aloud.

"I told you that it's different among my people. We don't *have* soldiers. We're all warriors, so any Golgoth well enough to walk is expected to march on the king's command."

The wolf lord stared for a long moment, as if he suspected the prince of some elaborate joke. "That sounds hellish."

"Welcome to my world," Alastor said.

"Would your brother be mad enough to empty his own capital?" Callum asked.

"In a word? Yes." Alastor met the war priest's gaze squarely, evidence of his honesty.

So we might be facing that many? Damn.

"Regardless, we have to stop this from turning into a siege," Dom cut in.

"The Order of Saint Casimir is ready," said Callum.

Yeah, it's about time to deploy the war bears.

Pru squared her shoulders, amazed that she could sound so authoritative with her heart aching over Slay's vanishing act. "This isn't the time to be stingy with our resources. We need to make it clear that Ash Valley isn't a soft target."

"Some breathing room would be good," Dom said.

His gaze skittered away from hers, however, rousing a vague sense of unease. The moment passed in a flurry of strategizing. All the leaders agreed that they needed to follow the stealth strike with a ferocious offensive; otherwise the Golgoth would have the chance to regroup. If they could crush the enemy here, that would buy them some time to organize a proper resistance and get in touch with other settlements.

"We'll need to send messengers," Princess Thalia said.

"Unless we take out their jammers." But Pru had no

idea where they'd secured the tech, and they couldn't spare personnel to wander the woods with scanners.

"One thing at a time." Raff patted her on the shoulder in what was meant to be a comforting gesture, and Dom threaded between them, his arm encircling her shoulder.

"Let's finalize the battle plan," Callum said.

That took a good half an hour, but at the end of the session, Pru felt confident they could bring the fight to the Golgoth in a decisive fashion. As she moved to follow Magda, Dom's hand tightened on her shoulder. She tilted her head with an inquiring look while the others hustled to complete all the preparations.

"Are you up to this?" By the complex layers of his expression, the question wasn't as simple as it sounded.

"You don't want me fighting?"

"It's not that, exactly."

The pause told her nothing. "Then what's the issue?"

"I just... I need to be sure you're going out for the right reasons—that you're in a good place mentally."

"You think I plan to slip off and search for Slay?" Only that suspicion made sense, given Dom's awkwardness, his hesitance, and the way his eyes dropped, like he'd done something wrong by standing here while Slay was—

Missing. It hurt to breathe.

"You don't?" Dom asked.

"I'm worried. There's no point in denying it. But it won't help him or the pride if I get myself killed. If I spot him, I'll do my best to bring him back, but I won't go off target and endanger everyone else." Pru raised a brow, hoping she had set his mind at ease.

He didn't seem entirely relaxed, but he bent to kiss her and managed a smile. "In case things go sideways."

"Don't say things like that. I'm nervous enough already."

"You realize you're making it harder for me to be supportive and let you go. With every fiber of me, I want to fight with you."

Pru wrapped her arms around Dom's waist, squeezing him tight. "You can't. With Slay gone, it makes way more sense for Mags to lead our forces."

"Because I'm the irreplaceable pride master."

"You represent stability," she corrected. "And yes, you're irreplaceable too."

"Be careful, kitten."

This time, when he kissed her, it felt like he meant it. He cupped her face in his hands and took her mouth with a sweetness and hunger that curled her toes, even under these circumstances. When Pru pulled back, she was breathless. She couldn't look at him, or she might not have the courage to play her role in defending Ash Valley. She ran to catch up with the rest of the pride warriors without looking back.

Magda welcomed her with a slap on the back as she slotted into formation along with the others. Their unit would be employing hit-and-run tactics along with the Noxblades and wolves while the war bears would try to hold ground alongside Prince Alastor's small unit of brutes. Apart from Callum, none of the other leaders would be fighting tonight.

This battle will make all the difference, either buy us the time we need or Ash Valley will fall before dawn.

The wounded in the med center, the surviving Latents, the kits who hadn't learned to shift yet... they were all counting on a successful assault. *And Dom. He's waiting for me to come home.* While their relationship might not be perfect, she couldn't brook leaving him alone again. Those thoughts firmed Pru's resolve as she shifted and fell in behind Magda, feeling incredibly small in ocelot form.

If she'd felt tiny compared with Mags, the bears loomed over her like titans. She'd never seen the Order of Saint Casimir geared for war, but they wore armored chest pieces, vambraces around their arms. Pru wished she could tell them how amazing they looked, how much confidence they inspired, but she could only snarl in approval. The wolves took up the call, howling their own battle cry, and soon the staging area echoed with Animari battle challenges.

"Let's do this," Gavriel bit out.

This had to be the largest war party that had ever slipped out of Ash Valley; certainly it was the most diverse. The Order of Saint Casimir exploded from the tunnel and hit the Golgoth from behind like a cluster of armored vehicles. For a moment, Pru just watched, stunned by such synchronized ferocity, then Mags bumped her, recalling her to their purpose, and she raced after the Noxblades, who had all but vanished in the dark.

For this fight, she chose a young wolf as her partner. She'd never have the size to take on a brute by herself, but she didn't need to be a killing machine to serve the pride well. *I'm doing this for everyone I love. I'm doing this for—*

Dominic. Because you want to fight for us, but you can't.

Somehow, her entire body felt lighter for that silent admission. With renewed determination, Pru leapt at a gray-skinned enemy, narrowly avoiding his razor-sharp claws when he spun on her. The wolf at her side went for the hamstring, and she bounded through the brute's legs, ready for action. All around her, the Order of Saint Casimir reaped the enemy like angels of death, silent in their violence. Noxblade silver flashed in the night, and each time one of Raff's wolves scored a kill, a howl split the silence. The taste of blood flooded Pru's mouth as she fought on. *For the pride. For my family. For—*

Dominic. Always.

PRU STILL LOVES *Slay.*

The devastation in her eyes haunted Dom. No matter what he did, he couldn't shake it—that moment of shock and pallor, where her freckles stood out like copper dots against skin like milk. She shook it off fast, covered up with a smile, but learning about Slay had fucking eviscerated her. Probably he should've expected that. Pru wasn't the kind of woman who could turn her heart so fast, but it felt like somebody had cracked his rib cage and scooped his out with a rusty spoon.

She'd said that when she was with him, she was *with* him, but that didn't speak to her moments alone, what she wished for in the silence of her own head. Somehow, he scraped those thoughts away and focused on the gunnery nest he'd constructed on the ramparts. If he couldn't be in the battle up close and personal, he'd be damned if he sat around waiting to hear how it went. As he set up and donned the goggles he'd borrowed from the Order of Saint Casimir, Princess Thalia joined him.

"I wish I was out there too," she said, her tone wistful.

"The lightning gizmo doesn't have good range?" he guessed.

"You impress me. So many people assume it's magic."

"By which I presume you mean humans? Give me a *little* credit. Even if I don't understand exactly how it works,

I can tell you have a small battery pack in your bracer."

"How?"

Holding up a hand, Dom shook his head. It wasn't the time to discuss his keen sense of smell, but if he'd wanted, he could've startled her with an account of everything she had eaten in the last twenty-four hours. The Eldritch princess apparently had a real fondness for pears.

He skated his fingertips across the lenses of his goggles to activate them; the tech augmented his natural night vision, making the action look like it was happening right in front of him. Though he told himself he wouldn't, Dom still tried to track Pru down below, scanning for an ocelot amid the melee. It was no use, though, so he flipped off the safety and powered up the beast of a gun. Most of the fighting was out of range, but when some dumb-ass Golgoth crept around the corner of the hold, Dom blasted him with great satisfaction. Even if the brutes were built like small dinosaurs, a hole that size in the chest had to slow it down. That one tried to get up, so he shot it again.

This thing has to be .50 cal.

That time, the brute actually exploded, chunks flying like shrapnel from a meat grenade. Killing took away some of the sting, so he locked on to the battlefield, firing whenever a Golgoth wandered in range. It drove him crazy not knowing how Pru was out there. More than once he thought, *Fuck being supportive. She'll be lucky if I ever let her leave the hold again.* But despite his visceral terror of losing her—a woman who shouldn't even be his—he'd never try to cage Pru or limit her in any way.

And if she comes back with Slay...if she finds him...

I'll set her free.

Pru would never break her promise or abandon him,

but Dom wasn't such a bastard that he could be fine keeping somebody beside him because he didn't want to be alone. *And she's propped me up "for the good of the pride" long enough.* It shouldn't have taken such a dire threat as Slay disappearing to wake him up, either. *I'll make it up to them somehow.* The mate bond *could* be broken; it would just be excruciating. He'd tried to convince himself that she belonged to him now, but as he knew better than anyone, wishing for something didn't make it true.

With a wicked hurt blazing inside him, he unleashed it on the cluster of Golgoth searching near the walls, probably for the hidden entrance to Ash Valley. He sprayed the ground, littering the wall with spent shells, and the enemy's anguished screams spoke to a sadistic streak he'd never even guessed at before now. *Heartbreak's making me mean.* It would be more satisfying if he could kill the invaders with his bare hands, but his status made that impossible.

"You hate it too," the princess said.

Dom started. He'd forgotten she was standing beside him. "What?"

"The limitations placed on us. Everyone acts as if we're incomparable, but the truth is, somebody else would rise up to lead."

"In time," he agreed. "But the chaos of the transition is a weakness we can't afford. I never dreamed I'd see the Pax Protocols broken in my lifetime."

"Do you feel as if...?" The princess trailed off, as if she wasn't sure she should ask whatever it was.

"It's fine. Finish the question." Dom shot another brute. Without their C-TAK, the opposition didn't have anything that could barrage the walls or he'd have sent the Eldritch royal below long ago.

"You failed. As if someone else could've stopped all this."

"Damn. You don't pull your punches."

The princess sank down on the chill stone walls and drew her knees to her chest, suddenly seeming unspeakably young, though she was probably five hundred, given what he knew about Eldritch lifespans. "It's not an indictment. I only ask because I struggle with it. If I'd acted sooner, if I hadn't given my father so many chances to turn back, if—"

"Yeah," Dom said softly. "I imagine how much better my dad would've handled things. Beren would still be alive, and we'd be signing papers instead of going to war."

"We should stop. Guilt only inhibits our ability to make rational decisions."

In the distance, something exploded. *Where are you, kitten?* Magda would keep her safe if at all possible, but Dom damn well knew in the scrum and filth of the battlefield anything could happen. His ears were keen enough to pick up distant echoes and snarls of challenge along with the wolves howling—because that was what wolves did—but with the radios down, he couldn't demand a status report. If something didn't give soon, he might chew off his own arm.

Hating himself for it, he took his impatience out on the princess. "There's nothing sane about any of this. Why the hell does this Tycho think he has the right to rule over us?"

"We have stories," she said. "I don't know if they're true."

That wasn't an answer, but before he could demand clarification, Raff raced up with a crackling comm unit. "We've got signal."

"Do you know how to shoot?" he asked Thalia.

Shitty apology, but... he shrugged mentally.

"I'm on it." Smoothly, she slid into position and went after the nearest target with great precision. Clearly there was more than swords and tech-lightning to this royal. When he handed over his goggles, her aim improved even more.

Impressive.

He snatched the radio from Raff and switched channels until he got Magda. "Can you read me? We stumbled on their jammers and took them out. The Golgoth are in full retreat. I'm awaiting orders. Over." From her frustrated tone, she had been repeating this for a while.

"Reading you loud and clear. Crush as many as you can, but don't pursue them into an ambush. If they get more than a klick out, circle back."

"Understood," Mags said.

He had to ask. "She's all right?"

"Fine. Fought like a tiny terror. The wolf she partnered with seems like he's half in love with her now." That teasing tone goaded him, just like Mags intended.

Relief swelled inside him so bright and sweet that Dom went lightheaded. *She's safe. But… not mine.*

When the connection dropped, he passed the unit back to Raff, who wore a roguish smile. "How much would it take to convince you to assign Magda to Pine Ridge permanently? Let's call her a diplomatic envoy."

Despite the sprawling shitfulness of his mood, Dom laughed. "She'd kill me if I agreed, so there's no bribe big enough to get that done."

"Then… could you put in a good word for me?"

"I've met you," he said. "So that would be a no. If you win Mags over, it'll be without my help. I like my head where it is." He turned to Princess Thalia, still eagerly gunning down the Golgoths below. "You got this?"

She nodded without glancing away from her ground targets. "If I get tired, the wolf lord will spell me."

"I will?" Raff feigned reluctance, but Dom had no interest in this exchange.

Leaving them to it, he headed for the staging area, as the strike force should be back relatively soon. *I'll hold Pru once more, just once, and then I'll tell her.* For at least an hour, he paced the chamber that was both inside the hold and beneath it, his strides echoing on the solid stone. At last, he heard the noise of the returning survivors.

Well, shit. It's time.

28.

PRU SMELLED DOM before she saw him, all cordite, winter wind, and… fear.

The latter quickened her step, and with an apologetic look for the injured wolf warrior leaning on her shoulder, she raced ahead. *Did something happen?* But it seemed that was Dom's worry too, as his gaze searched each face until he found her. Then his shoulders eased slightly, but his look skipped over her, as if he was seeking somebody else too.

Slay.

But she hadn't found him, not for want of trying. To make matters worse, she hadn't even caught a whiff of his scent. That failure left her shaken, despite their overall victory. *How can a person just vanish like that?* Something flickered in Dom's gaze as he met her look, a strange combination of devastation and yearning. Pru had never seen his face cast in exactly those lines before, and then she was in his arms, his face tucked against her neck.

"I'm filthy," she protested. "And people are watching."

"Let them."

"You're so relieved I'm all right? At this rate you'll give me a complex."

"That's not it. Just give me a minute like this. And then… we'll talk."

The successful strike team surged around them, likely heading off to celebrate. While they hadn't won the war, this strategic victory had turned the tide. *And I was part of it.* Elated, Pru wrapped her arms around Dom. *Tonight, I'll tell him. What the hell was I so afraid of, before? Even if he doesn't love me, he won't reject my heart.* She'd known this man long enough to be certain he would treat her devotion with as much respect and tenderness as possible.

"All right. I have something important to say anyway."

It might be her imagination, but he seemed to flinch a little, and his breath gusted against her skin, tickling her ear. Pru squirmed and rose to kiss him with a fresh, fearless enthusiasm. At first, he seemed too stunned to respond, and then he returned her passion with an intensity that made it seem like he expected never to touch her again.

"We get it, you're glad to see her," Magda said. "But take that show somewhere private before it gets *too* steamy. I heard from Raff that your old place is mostly livable now."

Deciding that was an epic idea, she laced her fingers through Dom's and tugged him out of the staging area. Tonight, the hold rang with laughter and the start of a party that would probably rage all night. Guards were dragging out the best booze that had survived the initial bombing, and musicians tuned their instruments in the park. In silent anticipation, she hauled her mate along with her, heart thumping with excitement.

I haven't felt like this since I first told Slay… Her heart ached over not knowing what had happened to her first love, but she couldn't let that stop her. For some reason, Dom didn't walk as fast, and she kept having to tug harder on his hand to keep him moving. She aimed a teasing glance over one shoulder.

"Lead in your shoes?"

"Something like that," he said.

At last the somber tone penetrated, but there was no point in questioning him before they got to the apartment. As with the other unit they'd borrowed, the keypad wasn't working, but the wolves had replaced the door, repaired walls and ceiling. The housekeeping left something to be desired, but she almost cried in relief at having a home again, no matter how dusty.

"If you don't mind, I'd like to talk first." Pru shut the door behind them and carefully turned the lock.

"If you prefer," he said, low.

The construction wasn't enough to block out all the festive noises from beyond the residential annex, but this atmosphere actually suited the moment. While the future of the pride might still be in jeopardy, tonight Pru meant to gamble everything. Since the power wasn't back on yet, she lit some candles while Dom perched on the edge of the tattered sofa, like this wasn't his home and he expected her to ask him to leave at any minute.

Finally, the strangeness of his attitude sank in. "Maybe you should instead? You're scaring me a little, if you want the truth."

Dom swallowed hard and tipped his head toward the ceiling, as if he could make out the patchwork of plaster scars left from the quick and dirty repairs. "I saw your face when we first heard about Slay."

Oh.

"I won't deny that I'm worried and sad, but that's how I'd feel if it was Mags or Arran, Joss or—"

"Stop. Please don't drag this out. Letting you go will be hard enough. I promise I'll devote all the resources we can spare to finding him, and I'll do my damnedest to give you the life you wanted all along. With him."

The onslaught hit her like a punch in the sternum. "Wait, so... you don't want me? You're giving me up?"

Dom closed his eyes like looking at her had become too hard. "Not from a lack of wanting, kitten. It's only right, now that I understand how you feel. I won't tie you to me forever because we made a deal."

I want forever. I want you. Forever. But with her throat tightening, she could barely breathe, let alone speak.

He went on, dogged in tone. "Besides... I have a confession to make. You never had to 'take me on', as I put it. Before, I'd already made up my mind to come home."

The silence went on for a thousand years. Or seconds. Whichever. Pru tried to process everything at once, but his words sliced like knives. She didn't know if he'd accepted her offer out of pity, or if she'd been tricked or—

No. Why this? Why now?

"You must really think I'm an idiot," she whispered. "I went on and on about the good of the pride and my s-self-esteem."

His gaze scraped down from the ceiling, lighting on her face with an anguished confusion. "*No.* That's not what I'm saying. Aren't you hearing me? You still love Slay."

"Bullshit. I don't understand *anything* anymore, and I don't think you ever did." She got up and paced by candlelight, stepping in and out of the shadows, silently playing a child's game to clear her head. "You know what's beyond ironic?"

"What?"

"I was going to tell you tonight."

"That you love him?"

"Fucking idiot. You. That I love *you*. I get that you didn't sign on for that, probably don't need or expect it from me. But I wanted to tell you because for once in my life, I felt powerful and brave, like nothing could..." *Damn.* She swiped at her cheeks, her eyes, hating the tears that made her look weak. "We don't have a great love, a destined one, like you and Dalena. I wouldn't even have asked for you to say it back. It's enough that you're good to me—that you treat me like I'm important a-and that you're proud to be with me."

"You... love me?" His voice broke on a note so hopeful that she stopped in astonishment.

"Try to keep up. Meanwhile, you're trying to—"

"Forget everything. Forget what I just said."

He dove at her like she was a wedding bouquet he had to catch, and Dom held her so tight and close that she couldn't get a breath. Confusion rioted in her head, echoed by the distant shouts from the park, the steady drumming that drove the music. He ran his hands over her back over and over again, as if he couldn't believe she was real. *What's happening here?* At least puzzlement dried her tears, and with the shocking pain of rejection receding, she started to sort things out. *He was... letting me go? Because he thought that was what I wanted?*

"What are you saying?" she asked, cautious.

Afraid to yearn, Pru had lived for twenty-seven years—quiet, unassuming, and endlessly helpful. For so long, she'd even been afraid to hope. But the spark flickered just like the candle flames dancing all around the room, impossible to extinguish.

"If you love me... if you love me, kitten, that changes everything."

SUDDENLY EUPHORIC, DOM spun her in a circle until she pummeled his shoulders, and he staggered to the sofa, dizzy. *I'm sorry, Slay. Wherever you are.* But he wasn't. Not really.

"How?" she demanded.

Even though he had misunderstood her in the worst possible way, she didn't fight him when he pulled her into his lap. "Because I was going by some old rule about how if you love something, you set it free, or I don't even know. I don't sleep a lot lately."

"I could kill you," she muttered.

"You'd miss me." Smiling, he kissed her temple. "Before, you said we don't have a great love, and that's bullshit. From where I'm sitting, our love is pretty close to miraculous."

"Our...?" she repeated in a wisp of a voice.

"Maybe we didn't fall for each other at first sight, but there's nothing inherently superior about instant attraction. Love can't be put in a pail and measured by volume. I wish to hell I'd told you how I feel first, but you're braver than me. Stronger too. In so many ways." Embarrassment swept him in a rush, but he didn't let it interfere with what he had to say.

She tried to speak then, but he pressed a soft kiss to her mouth. *She tastes like blood, my ferocious little war cat. Mine. Yes, mine.* He wouldn't rescind that claim for anything in the world now.

Dom went on, "Loss never broke you like it did me. Pru, you came along, swept me up like a window somebody put a rock through, and you made me feel like I had value again. I can't stress how important that is—you saw how I was on the mountain—and you *chose* me. That's worth a million magical first looks, do you understand? And I will spend the rest of my life working to be worthy of your faith. For that alone, it was fucking inevitable that I'd love you, even if you weren't you. Add in your sweetness, your dedication, your passion, and—"

"You're saying that I'm… lovable?"

"Eminently. Irresistibly. I fucking adore you, if that wasn't clear. Which is why I died a thousand times tonight, thinking I had to be a noble dickhead and cut you loose."

"Please don't," she whispered.

"Seems like we've both worried about the shadows other loves have left." He ran his palm over her cheek, her jaw, and didn't let himself wonder how often Slay had touched her. Somehow it was worse than it had been, now that Dom knew she loved him, because some small part of him wished she'd *always* been his. Except that wasn't only irrational but also impossible, because he didn't wish away the years he'd spent with Dalena.

"Now that I know I'm in your heart, it's fine." With endless delicacy, she traced his features, so that Dom fought and ultimately yielded to the urge to kiss her fingers one by one.

Nobody should be this sweet.

The desire to reassure her swept him. *I have to make her feel so safe, so cherished, that she never doubts us again.* "Some loves are like a fire, and they burn from the first spark." By her knowing eyes, she understood what he meant without additional context. "Our love, it's a tree, and you've been watering it for years. Dalena is and always will be my first love. But you, Pru... fate willing, you will be my last."

"Will you say it?"

He didn't tease or make her ask again. Now that he understood that she wanted his heart, she would never again need to request a glimpse of it. "I love you."

"I didn't want to be the one to break our bargain or ask for more." Gripping his shirt in her fists, she buried her face, and a few seconds later, the heat of her tears seeped through the worn fabric. "It's always me, you know? Begging for crumbs from a table at a party I wasn't invited to."

Fucking Slay. It was insane how he could want him back so much, but at the same time, he also wanted to punch him in the face. Repeatedly. *You have to be okay. Because I really owe you a beating.*

She must've read his mind because she raised her tear-stained face. "About Slay... I want him safe. I want him home. And that's where it stops."

"Promise me you'll never cry over that asshole again."

"Deal," she said. "Just so you know, I'd choose you as my mate every time. You were the best decision I ever made, even if you tricked me."

Dom averted his eyes, hoping she wasn't mad about that. *At least it's out in the open.* "Got it. Of course I'll keep my promise about finding Slay. Just... not so you two can pick up where you left off. In case you hadn't noticed, I'm possessive as fuck where you're concerned."

She rubbed her cheek against his, a slow glide back and forth that he recognized as Pru staking a silent claim. "It registered, but I wasn't sure how seriously I should take it."

"Put it this way. When I see somebody else's hands on you, I want to bite his face off."

"I hate how much I like hearing that."

"But you love *me*?" Okay, so it was a bit needy to make her say it. Again. But he felt like a dying plant in the desert that had been turned toward a cloudless sky for weeks waiting for rain.

Her mouth grazed his throat, making his heart skip. "I don't even know when it started, to be honest. You've always been so kind to me—"

Aggravated, he growled, "If that's all it takes, maybe I need to lock you up. From what I hear, Raff's plenty sweet to you, half his wolves, and maybe the Order of Saint Casimir too."

"They've all taken vows of celibacy," she pointed out.

"You're not helping."

"I'm not trying to. Plus, you've got me pegged all wrong. If I went astray, I'd chase after Alastor. He's all tortured and what-not, and who doesn't want to be a princess?"

Dom stared, unable to believe what he'd just heard. "*What* did you say?"

Giggling, she broke his hold on her and tumbled over the back of the couch, then peeped over the rim with such an impish smile that he fell in love with her all over again, even if she was fucking with his head. *I deserve it, considering everything I put her through tonight.* Somehow, he smiled, though that shit wasn't funny at all; that was Pru's magic.

"You know what I want to do?" she whispered.

"Abandon me for that Golgoth asshole?" Saying that with a straight face wasn't easy, and for a minute he had her fooled with the brooding expression.

Practice does make perfect.

"No." She legitimately sounded horrified. "I was teasing, love."

She's never called me that before. His every nerve crackled to life with delicious desire, but there was no reason to pounce on her straightaway. Tonight, they had some time to lavish on each other, before the endless demands kicked in again. *What did I ever do to deserve you?* That question had no answer, but he suspected he had been a big damn hero in some former life.

"Then tell me. From here on out, it's my job to make all your wishes come true."

"Yeah? Well, this isn't such a big one." She rose and rested her folded arms on the back of the couch, her chin, the sweet curve of her mouth only a few inches away.

His thoughts tumbled over one another like befuddled kittens. *Damn, I want to kiss her. I want to make love to my wife. Shit, we never even had a ceremony, never exchanged vows.*

Focus, dumbass, she's speaking actual words.

"...so that's why I want to plant a tree," she finished.

"Where?" *Please don't let her have covered that already.*

If he admitted all the blood had rushed to his cock so he hadn't heard a word she'd said, that would be hard to live down. *Pun intended.*

"At the retreat. I know it can't be for a while, but that's where all of this started. So I thought it would be special if we did that together when spring comes. As a symbol."

"Absolutely." If she'd asked for a solid gold bus, he'd have answered the same. "I don't know anything about arboreal whatever. What kind?"

"The apple tree represents beauty and love, but the alder symbolizes endurance and passion. So I'm not sure, but we have time to think about it." A sudden burst of merriment silenced her momentarily, as she cocked her head, listening. "But... this isn't urgent. Did you want to join the party? They seem to be having a blast."

With a grin, Dom pulled her over the couch on top of him, and his entire body trembled from the pleasure of it when he'd thought there would only be one more hug, one more kiss, and then only the endless sorrow of losing her. *But no. She loves me. Hell if I know why.* But he wasn't dumb enough to question heaven when she gazed down at him with such soft eyes.

"No thanks, kitten. I have a more private celebration in mind."

29.

"LIKE WHAT?" PRU asked.

As if I don't know.

Her heart was already racing like she'd run twenty kilometers, and she wanted to kiss him until neither of them could breathe. But he startled her by filling up a teakettle from the tap, then Dom had to light the stove manually. It took a ridiculously long time to heat up that small amount of water. Despite their recent declarations, shyness overwhelmed her when he peeled off her tunic. She had no idea why baring their souls changed everything; she only knew that it did.

He huffed with a sound somewhere between frustration and amusement. "You were completely shameless at the retreat. *Now* you're timid? And why do I always have to scrub blood off you before I take you to bed lately?"

"Because I'm ferocious?"

"Undoubtedly."

Closing her eyes helped, and somehow they managed to perform rudimentary ablutions. "Next time, we can shift and groom each other."

"I thought of that," Dom said. "But the prospect of

licking Golgoth effluvia from you kind of kills the mood."

She shuddered in reflex. "When you put it that way... I miss hot showers."

The scrape of the damp cloth over her skin distracted her—in the best possible way. There was no blood on her breasts, but he'd been circling there for a while. *Dom loves me. How can this possibly be real?* A small part of her simply couldn't fathom it; happy endings were for other people. But then he dropped all pretense at hygiene and pulled her close. For a long moment, she listened to his heart, thumping out a private message meant just for her.

He's really mine. Not a corner. All of him.

"I wish I had somewhere better to take you, but... this is home. We'll rebuild together."

"Just not tonight. Shall we inspect the bedroom?" It was nearly impossible for her to switch her brain off, so she unlocked the door in case her dad came home.

"Are you propositioning me?"

Pru smiled. With a fraction of her old insouciance, she sauntered away from him and took great satisfaction in Dom's muffled groan. She added a little extra swing in her hips.

Like the living area, their room was dusty, but someone had stripped the bed, at least. She unearthed a couple of blankets that had been bagged in storage and spread them on the mattress. With no heat, she was soon shivering, so she crawled between them and glanced at Dom still hovering in the doorway.

"Come to bed," she said.

"I'm not tired."

"Neither am I."

His grin threatened to crack his face open, and after

shutting the door behind him, he reached her in three long strides. "If you knew how hungry I am right now, it might scare you."

"For me?"

"No, for chocolate cake." Obviously amused, he slipped between the blankets, and everywhere his skin brushed hers, she shivered from the contact.

Breathless, she whispered, "It's... more now, isn't it? I'm not imagining that."

He sighed. "How am I supposed to cope? I already want you so much it hurts."

In answer, she wrapped herself around Dom and pulled him in for a kiss. Words like that were gorgeous and delectable, but she'd gorged on them until she might explode. Now she needed to touch him and feel him close. With a soft sound of appreciation, she admired the muscle he'd put on and tested the strength of him with eager hands.

Dom groaned. "Slow down. We have all night. Every other time, you've goaded me into rushing things. But not tonight. So just settle down and let me love you."

Her entire body melted. "Okay."

"Keep looking at me like that and this might go quick after all." His heated gaze lingered on her upturned face, her lips, the line of her throat.

"You say these beautiful things... and I'm so yours that it's ridiculous."

"I love hearing that." His voice dropped to a sexy rasp, and she shuddered when he kissed her throat, warm lips, soft and rough at the same time.

Pru closed her eyes in a silent affirmation of trust, fighting the impulse to writhe against him, all naked need. He didn't make it easier when he started at her shoulders and ran his hands over every inch of her body, light and delicate caresses that sensitized her skin. Impossible not to see it as her mate learning every dip, every hollow, memorizing her like a treasure map. Beneath his teasing palms her nipples peaked, but he skimmed away, down her belly.

Lower.

But he didn't linger there either, though he must sense her growing arousal. Pru made a tiny, frustrated noise, squirming against the blanket. He parted her thighs, and she thought she might get some relief, but no, he chose to massage instead in soft, circular strokes. The hypnotic pressure made her legs fall open as his thumbs worked ever closer to her core. Pru couldn't help but focus on the pleasure building in subtle increments, though he seemed determined to drive her utterly wild.

"Don't stop now."

"I'm not. I'm just admiring you. Do you know how pretty you are when you're turned on? You start with a gorgeous flush here... and it swells until you're all pink and glowing." With one fingertip, he traced the path from her chest to her cheeks.

"Dom, please." She pressed her palms to her face, both embarrassed and delighted.

"I could stand to hear you say that a hundred more times tonight. Only more breathless."

"You want me to beg?"

"Maybe a little."

"For what?" With his hands on her thighs again, it was all she could do to form such a short sentence.

"My fingers. My lips. My tongue. My cock. Whatever you want most, kitten."

"All of the above. Please?"

"Be specific."

She'd do practically anything to get him to step it up, let alone babble some words. "Use your mouth on me. Everywhere."

With a pleased growl, he started at her shoulders, licking and nuzzling until she grabbed at his head and pulled him to her breasts. The silent demand kindled something sharp and hot in him; she saw it in his avid eyes. When he sucked her nipple into his mouth, Pru's whole body locked, then she arched because he knew exactly how to use his teeth. Dom went back and forth, nipping and kissing, until her skin went tender from the scrape of his scruff, such delicious contrast to his mouth.

"Let's see how wet you are." Exquisitely gentle, he grazed her slick folds with thumb and forefinger, sending a shock of pleasure to her clit.

"I love you," she gasped.

There was no stemming the words, no reason to anymore, but their effect on him was profound. Though half-closed and dreamy eyes, she saw an answering flush bloom on his cheekbones, and she didn't imagine the tremor in his hands. Suddenly, he settled between her thighs and hooked her legs over his shoulders.

"Say it again."

"I love you, Dom. I love you."

Each time she whispered it, sometimes a moan or an outright cry, he rewarded her with a lavish sweep of his tongue, faster, sweetly rhythmic, until *love* and *Dom* was all she knew, apart from the fierce pleasure spiraling in her sex. He eased one finger inside her, then two, hooking them so her entire body bowed off the bed. Pru went rigid, so turned on she couldn't stand it, but somehow unable to come. No matter how she twisted or writhed, satisfaction hovered tantalizingly out of reach.

He rose over her then and took her mouth with brushes of lips and tongue. Pru tasted her own salt-sweetness and dove into his kiss, undulating against him all of her melted and yearning. Dom tormented her with little flickers of his damp fingertips, here and gone, grazing her nipples, the curve of her spine, and the softness of her pussy. Her breath came in runaway gasps, until she went lightheaded.

It took her a moment to process that *he* was holding her back, whispering, "Not yet, kitten. Not quite yet."

Their bond was so deep that his will drove her desire, kept her stretched and trembling, on the brink of an earth-shattering orgasm.

SHE'S MINE, DOM marveled. *Totally and completely mine.*

The world narrowed in scope to this woman—his wife—her body and their bed. In that moment, he stopped caring about taking his time, about control, and he spooned up against her from behind, so hard that he could burst the second her skin glided against his. At first, she didn't seem to get the position, but when he put his hand on her hip and tilted, she cried out.

That's right. This way will be slow and sweet. As he pushed into her, he wrapped his arms around her completely and set his lips against her shoulder.

Sheer pleasure overwhelmed him. He flattened his palm on her abdomen as the sensation of being part of her suffused him. When he let go of his tenuous control, her shivering reaction sank into him, their desire on constant loop. *It feels so good when she fucks me.* Something about that wasn't quite right, maybe, only it was, and his steady thrusts quickened as she pushed back, grinding on him until he could come just from the sweetness of it.

"You're so beautiful," he whispered.

Cupping her pussy, he strummed her clit as he worked into her from behind. She was all wet heat—*so hard. I'm so fucking hard.* Words melted out of his brain until there was only the rasp of him panting with each stroke and her shuddering sweat as a light orgasm pulsed through her. She squeezed his cock in delicious waves, but from the raw need still rolling off her, it wasn't enough.

"Take me."

"Can you feel how close I am?" He let go of everything except her, pushing deep and holding still, so she must feel the throbbing.

She answered with a deep groan, and the way she swiveled her hips drove him over. The orgasm that drenched him was hers, his, all tightening, arching sweetness, and he fell into her pleasure like it was an endless tropical sea, just as she swam in his. With careful fingertips, he stroked her to another orgasm after he came, and he would've gone for more if she hadn't pulled his sticky fingers away to kiss them.

"I'm on overload," she whispered.

With a smile that wouldn't quit, he held her close and licked the sweat from her shoulder. "I'd ask how you feel, but I already know."

"It's better," she said in a wondering tone. "I didn't really think it could be, but it is."

"Is that a compliment or a complaint?"

"How am I supposed to know? You just fucked me

senseless."

Though he was satiated for the moment, his cock twitched in response. "You're trying to get me worked up again."

"Feels like you're not quite done anyway." Pru gave a teasing squirm that locked him into a half-erection.

"Does it please you to be this filthy?"

"Endlessly," she purred.

"I think that's my line."

No matter what she said, Pru must've been exhausted because she dozed off in his arms. Dom caught a nap too, and when he roused, the music was still thumping away outside. Her skin smelled of him, commingled sex and sweat. He wished he could parade her through the hold as a possessive statement, but he doubted she'd be amused by such primitive inclinations. At some point, he'd slipped out of her, but having his dick pressed up against her ass was enough to get him going again.

If I'm not careful, she'll sex me to death. For some odd reason, he wasn't sad about it.

"You awake?" she whispered.

"Sort of. Barely."

"I feel like I owe you a blow job. Though you have a way of making my head fuzzy, it seems like you've done all the giving in bed lately."

Dom nearly choked on his own saliva. "You don't *owe* me anything. If that's something you want to do, however, I probably wouldn't say no."

"Probably, huh?"

"I'm pretty worn out, you understand. Near dehydrated at this point too."

"You make me sound like a succubus," she protested.

He smirked. "Sorry."

When he first woke up, he hadn't been contemplating round two, but it was impossible to deny that she had him stirred up. *Again.* Dom moved so that it wouldn't be so obvious, and Pru took the opportunity to face him. Her gaze went immediately to his stiff cock.

"You *do* want a BJ." She made this fact sound like an amazing discovery instead of an obvious truth.

Before he could say a word, Pru wriggled between his legs and settled like she meant to spend her life there. He swallowed hard, unable to muster a verbal response, but then his situation got worse, or better. Both, actually. From the teasing licks to his thighs, she intended to repay his earlier treatment in kind.

I won't survive this.

It's a good way to die.

She ran her tongue upward, nuzzling into the crease near his balls, and he lifted his hips, breathless. He fought the urge take control, shove her head where he wanted it, but this was about Pru choosing to give, not his ability to take. So he fisted his hands in the blanket and absorbed the relentless pleasure of her soft mouth. When she finally wrapped her lips around his dick, he opened his fingers and stroked her cheek, trying to focus on how it felt to her, how he tasted, as a means of slowing his urge to thrust.

I want to fuck your mouth.

As if she sensed that desire, she gasped, her breath hot against his skin. *Don't play. Suck me.* Ever so slowly, her head began to move, her suction gaining intensity as her gaze held his. Her nails scraped lightly against his balls in a tantalizing rhythm that matched the pressure of her hungry mouth. Her delight surged over him, nearly overwhelming in its wildness. His taste seemed to kindle her to greater eagerness, and she watched his face for each flicker of response.

She loves this. She wants it. She needs to lick me until I come apart.

Liberated by that realization, he tangled his hands in her hair, no longer interested in restraint. What she wanted wasn't his submission, exactly, but proof he ached for her so much that he could deny her nothing. Dom surrendered to the high, hard impulse to rock into her mouth; at first, her eyes widened, but she took his strokes with increasing excitement.

Since he'd come recently, it should've taken much longer to reach this state, but with each of her huffs and moans, it jolted him higher. When he noticed that she was humping her hips against the covers, he snarled in desperation.

"That's good," he bit out. "Get yourself off. But don't stop sucking me."

A high-pitched moan that was almost a whine vibrated against his shaft. Her round ass rose and fell in tempo with her head. The scent of her maddened him. If he didn't know she craved the hot gush of his juices, he'd spin her so quick and eat her until she came all over his face. Picturing that drove his hips faster, his cock flexing in her mouth.

"You're so sexy," he breathed.

And that was enough. She came with a ripple of her beautifully arched back, and her mouth clamped down in response. His own orgasm flooded him, deeper and stronger than should've been possible. Dom moaned her name and held her head still when she would've continued. Just the stillness and pressure was enough during the aftershocks.

Once his shaking arms steadied, he dragged her up to rest on his chest. Pru closed her eyes, exquisitely wrecked. He petted her sex hair and admired his own role in creating that dishevelment. *She loves me. She's all mine.* Incoherent glee ran amok in his bloodstream, along with serotonin and a cocktail of endorphins.

"What now?" she asked, sounding sleepy.

In a flash the answer came to him, but for optimum results, it should be a surprise, the best he could manage under the circumstances. Briefly he hesitated, considering what she'd said about needing time to brace. *It'll work out better than last time. I'll flip the script.* Somehow he kept his expression neutral when he answered, "I guess you'll just have to trust me."

"I do. Always."

Leaving the bed after she drifted off was one of the toughest things he'd ever done.

30.

A FEW HOURS before dawn, Pru woke alone in a tangle of blankets to the lingering scent of recently snuffed candles. Groggy, she stumbled out of the bedroom and found neither Dom nor her father. *This wasn't a dream. It all happened.* Yet it was hard to be confident, even though she suspected Magda had dragged him off to some critical meeting.

Her timing definitely sucks, though.

Then she noticed the sole candle flickering in the center of the room, well away from everything else, so it couldn't be considered a fire hazard. The wax had melted until the wick swam in a pool of it, and the glass was hot to the touch when she shifted it aside to dislodge the piece of paper beneath. Pru couldn't remember if she'd ever seen a note from Dom before. *Yes,* she decided, *a long time ago. And it wasn't to me.* Holding it to the light, she skimmed what he'd written once, twice, and tried to make sense of it.

My precious wife,

Consider this your heads-up. Something marvelous will happen soon (besides the obvious), so be ready. Brace yourself as needed, and then come find me. I'll be the one waiting for you, forever and always.

Your loving husband,

Dom

PS — Put on the dress hanging on the hook beside the front door. I've shaken it clean as best I could, and we'll make our own glamour from here on out.

Amused and reluctantly intrigued, she washed up in cold water and then donned the dress he'd chosen, a splendid yellow statement that defied the weather. As she put out the candle, someone knocked. Hurrying, she slipped into her cutest intact shoes and went to answer. To her surprise, it wasn't her mate, but Joss, beaming so bright that Pru checked behind her for a spotlight, as her cousin only ever looked this happy on stage.

"You know something," she guessed.

"No hints. He's told you enough that you can't call this an ambush. And I'm *so* happy for you." The last sentence came out as a joyful squeal.

"So you're my escort, then?"

"And me," her dad said, stepping out of the shadows.

She hadn't seen him dressed so nicely since before her mother passed away. Sheepish, he straightened his lapels and tugged at his tie, then he offered his arm. It was three in the morning, the music still playing, and she had *no* fucking idea what was going on.

I guess you'll have to trust me, Dom had said.

Time to prove that I do.

With a smile, she set her hand in the crook of her father's elbow, and Joss linked with her other arm. The floor was still uneven, but she didn't notice it as much with her family on either side. Even the broken steps didn't take as much navigating, and she didn't ask for explanations, content to be guided to whatever Dom had planned.

With the lateness of the hour, some of the initial wildness had settled, but a shocking majority of pride members and allied guests were still awake, and most were gathered in the park. Someone had strung fairy lights, and sleepy musicians plucked out a soft, heartfelt melody as her party approached the pergola. There was no snow any longer, only the damp, bare ground, where something beautiful would one day grow.

That's life, she thought.

Maybe it was because of the darkness, but the weight of so many eyes didn't feel punishing. Pru only wondered where her mate had gone. And then he stepped out of the crowd wearing a dark suit that fit him beautifully. The silver and black of his hair caught the twinkling lights, reflected in his eyes. There were no words to express how her heart swelled. As she feasted her eyes on him, she realized that the shadow that always lingered on him was gone.

With a flourish, he presented a bouquet of flowers rescued from the greenhouse, and she couldn't stop herself from clutching the blooms to her chest, no more than she could help breathing in their sweetness or the tears that spilled down her cheeks. *This is too much.*

But he was only getting started, apparently. Dom kissed her cheek and whispered, "You don't have to talk. Just listen, all right?"

The heat in her cheeks didn't come from embarrassment but a surfeit of joy. "Okay."

"We didn't get to have a proper wedding," he called,

signaling to the band for a pause. "So I thank those who stuck around tonight to celebrate with us."

People banged on tables, clapped and hooted. Most of them were more than a little booze-merry, so that added to her comfort. Who knew what anyone would even remember about tonight? *Except me. I'll never forget a second of this. Not ever.*

"First off..." He turned to her dad and dropped to one knee despite the wet pavement. "Better late than never, I guess. May I have your lovely daughter? Please, sir. I promise to love, cherish, and protect her for the rest of my days."

Pru might actually evaporate in a steam cloud if her father said anything but, "Yes."

And then she registered that terse assent had come from the old lynx, not her imagination. The crowd whooped in response, and Joss raced over to the band, where she took the mic and unleashed the most exquisite love song. *Without you, dear—without you here...* even the rowdiest of partiers settled, gazing at Joss like she was a goddess incarnate.

When the last note died away, applause rang out like thunder. Joss took a bow, and then she hurried back to Pru's side. She hugged her cousin tight and wanted to whisper to her as she had to Jase, *Thank you for surviving. Thank you for bringing such light to my world.* Over Joss's shoulder, Pru's teary gaze met Dom's.

Am I doing it right? he mouthed.

Pru could tell that he was ready to pull the plug right then if she shook her head, if she was tense or unhappy. Swiping at a tear, she said, "Perfect," loud enough for everyone to hear, but they didn't understand. They didn't have to.

Joss took it as a compliment on her performance. "I'm so glad. You deserve all of this and more."

"Then... it's time for our vows and the exchange of rings," Dom cut in.

He didn't exactly take her away from Joss, but he slid into their embrace and stayed until her cousin let go, wiping at her eyes. The first hints of panic kicked in, but with his arm around her, the terror-wings didn't take flight. *He said I don't have to speak. I trust him.*

"Tonight I spent an hour sifting through the rubble. And you know what I found?" Dom unfurled his fingers, revealing a very old ring. Though it was scratched, Pru could tell someone had once worn it with great devotion. *It seems like I've seen it before...*

"That belonged to your mother," someone called back.

Dom smiled. "I know. So it couldn't be more fitting that I put it on Pru's finger now. I clawed this out of the wreckage because I knew there had to be something worth saving. And that's how this incredible woman feels about me. I can only promise in front of these witnesses to treat her like the treasure she is. Henceforth we are one heart, one body, one life."

"Devil take you," Raff snarled from the back of the crowd. "Keep on like this and you'll have us weeping."

I am already. She understood what this meant and why he was giving it to her. This was more than just a ring; it was also a promise that belonged to her alone. *Me, not Dalena. Not anymore. Be at peace, my dear friend. I'll love him well.*

Dom's hands were steady when he eased his mother's ring onto the fourth finger of her left hand. Pru had no gift for public speaking, and no ring for him either. But receiving his adoration in silence could never be enough. If she had nothing else, she'd give him words.

Mustering all her courage, Pru spoke loud enough for everyone to hear. "If I'm a treasure, then you're the dragon who guards me. I trust that you will keep me safe, along with our friends and allies. There is no part of me that isn't yours completely. I love you with all of me. We are one heart, one body, one life. I only regret that I have no ring to offer in turn."

"But you do," her father corrected.

Then he pulled the wedding band from his finger, also scratched and worn, to proffer the greatest symbol of love she'd ever known.

Pru burst into tears.

FOR A FEW seconds, Dom hesitated, torn between comforting his mate and accepting this generous offer. When the other man nodded, he took the ring, the metal still warm from its tenure on his father-in-law's finger. The pride had a legend—it was said that if you used old rings passed down through each family line, it heralded a long and prosperous union.

I hope that's true.

Dom set her dad's blessing in Pru's hand, and she shook so hard she almost dropped the ring, but in the end, she got it on him. He pulled her close and jerked his chin at the musicians. Moments later, a cheerful song enticed the spectators to sing along, drink more, or dance. He held her until she calmed down, but he didn't think he'd gone terribly wrong this time.

"Should I be apologizing?" he asked.

"No. It's wonderful. Everything was better than I could've imagined, if I was prone to envisioning such things."

"You weren't?"

Hating himself a little for brightening over that, Dom still wondered why she never pictured the future with Slay. But he didn't—couldn't—ask. *I wish you were here, you arse. It's not right without you.* He also hated that he hadn't asked about the situation with Talfayen, about Slay's secrets, because now it felt like he might never get an answer, and that uncertainty fell like a stain on his second's memory.

No, not that. He's not dead. Just... gone. So... not memory. Reputation.

"Hardly. It would've meant that somebody wanted me forever, and I could never picture it. Until you said I had to take you on." Her bright eyes sparkled up at him in the moonlight, adorable, irresistible, all teasing sweetness.

I love this woman, head to toe.

"Kiss!" Raff shouted, interrupting the moment.

Soon other wolves took up the chant, and Dom didn't like to disappoint his audience. He swept Pru close, dipped her so it crushed her bouquet in a cloud of sweetness, and pillaged her mouth until her father actually had to haul him upright. But her smiling face made up for everything; her cheeks were pink with pleasure, and she pretended to pummel him with her flowers, showering them with petals.

"Don't destroy it!" Joss shouted.

At her behest, a score of single pride mates gathered in front of Pru, who couldn't seem to believe they expected her to toss it. In the distance, the dawn sky was lightening, pink and gold unfurling like a promise on the horizon. Dom nudged his mate and grinned; she argued with her eyes, but there was no stopping this tradition.

As Pru turned, the cranky-faced doctor strode into the plaza. "How long are you planning to keep up this racket? I have patients who haven't slept all night. And has anyone seen Prince Alastor? I need to—"

The bouquet smacked her square in the face, and she caught it with the excellent reflexes that marked her as one of Ash Valley's finest. Other singles groaned in disappointment as the Golgoth prince rose, slightly unsteady on his feet. "You have need of me?"

Sighing, Sheyla dropped the floral projectile like it might explode. "Come on. If you have the time to drink, you're free for an examination."

After a brief pause, the prince sighed and followed her when she stalked off.

"Not much for weddings, huh?" Joss said.

Surprisingly, the great bear, Callum, quietly requested another song. In a flash, Joss agreed, smoothing over the potential for awkwardness. Dom didn't want to let go of Pru, so he danced with her instead, and others coupled up around them, despite the faint chill. The sun would be up soon, burning off the mist and revealing the extent of the casualties on the field.

He didn't want to contemplate any of that.

Eventually, full daylight broke, and the musicians put away their instruments. Nobody seemed to know how an occasion like this should end, so Pru nudged him. "You should say something. Let them know they're dismissed."

Nodding, he vaulted onto a bench. Once, this sort of thing had been second nature to him, but that was before he was broken and spent years in silence. Now he scratched deep for the words like they were fruit he had grown specially for this purpose, and speaking them left empty furrows in his mind.

"I don't know what the future holds. If you have nowhere else to go, our walls will shelter you. We stand on the cusp of a great war, and while we've won a crucial victory, the battle isn't over. It won't be until peace is restored, until we've avenged those we lost and brought everyone home, either in our arms or their ashes returned to our earth. I will fight beside all of you, until that day dawns."

Unsurprisingly, Pru was the first to clap, but her enthusiasm drove approval from others, until his ears rang with it. With everything so fucking uncertain, he wished he could say more, make specific guarantees, but that would be irresponsible. Part of him felt guilty that he could be this happy with the hold still so disordered, but if he'd learned anything from Pru, it was the importance of moving forward. Respecting the past mattered, but he couldn't let it shackle him, and failure didn't have to be a cycle.

As the gathering dispersed, Callum strode up to him with his customary brusqueness. "We're marching north. I have matters to tend at Burnt Amber and a defense to mount. I suspect our departure will help you, as Tycho will find his concentration of high-value targets reduced."

"You don't call him 'king'," Dom noted with wry amusement.

The war priest curled his lip, barely perceptible amid the beard. "He's a self-styled lord, ruler of nothing but my foot up his ass."

"Colorful." Pru's dimpled, adorable smile actually made the great bear take a second look at her, and Dom checked the urge to set her behind him.

Need to get used to that. Somehow. But the feeling came

without an edge since she'd angrily admitted to loving him; the mere thought put a grin on his face.

Likely made skittish from the long silence, Callum took a step back. "Excuse me, then."

"Safe journey," Pru called after him.

Dom swore the man's shoulders actually hunched, and he dodged away from Joss, who was trying to say good-bye. Somehow the pretty cousins had the leader of the Order of Saint Casimir in full retreat. Amused, he turned to greet Raff, whose bloodshot eyes spoke of an incredibly long night, not confined to a single rise and set of the sun, either.

"How long since you slept?" he asked the wolf lord.

"This is where you expect me to say some rubbish, like *I'll sleep when I'm dead.*"

"Basically."

"Sorry to disappoint. Just FYI, these were the bloodiest peace talks I've ever been a part of. Pax Protocols, my ass."

"Thank you for staying," Pru said softly.

Raff gave her a long look, then he bent over her hand, kissing it with enough enthusiasm that Dom ground his teeth. *Fucking wolf.* "Despite everything, I don't regret it, little matron."

"I gather you're leaving as well?" If Callum was right, splitting up might confound Tycho enough to make it worth the risk.

"It's past time. Pine Ridge has its own problems."

Unexpectedly, the security chief came up behind Raff, close enough that Dom half-expected her to lock him down in a chokehold. But she lingered there, waiting. He made eye contact and cocked his head.

"What's up?"

"I'm heading to Pine Ridge with the wolves. Last night,

I… well, I'd rather not speculate until I know more. But I promise this mission is vital to the pride… and it's about Slay." By her somber expression, Dom understood that Mags wasn't making this request lightly.

"Understood. Stay in contact."

"Try not to wreck up the place while I'm gone. I'll update you as soon as I know more." With an elegant bow, she spun on her heel and followed the wolf lord.

When Dom glanced at Pru, she seemed too stunned to speak. Finally, she got out, "Everything is changing."

"And it's too fast," he finished.

She nodded, shivering in her absurdly thin dress. *I have to take better care of her.* Belatedly he shrugged out of his jacket and wrapped her in it. *Just like I did on the mountain. One day soon, we'll plant a tree together, and I'll never forget how fucking lucky I am.*

That she loves me. That she chose me. Aloud, he added, "Guess what will never change."

"What?"

"You and me."

The sun rose higher, yellow ripening to orange. Whatever happened next, they'd face it together. With Pru at his side, he might as well be bulletproof. When she snuggled deeper into his arms, Dom touched the ring she'd fixed on his finger and knew one true thing—she was his whole world—and always would be.

Author's Note

I'm so thrilled that you read *The Leopard King* and hope you're eager for more in the Ars Numina world. *The Leopard King* is the first book in a projected six book series, as follows:

The Leopard King

The Demon Prince

The Wolf Lord

The Shadow Warrior

The War Priest

The Jaguar Knight

In this first book, you've met all six heroes and many of the heroines. Would you like to know when the next book will be available and/or keep up with exciting news? Visit my website at *www.annaguirre.com/contact* and sign up for my newsletter. If you're interested, follow me on Twitter at *twitter.com/msannaguirre*, or "like" my Facebook fan page at *facebook.com/ann.aguirre* for excerpts, contests, and fun swag.

Reviews are essential for indie writers and they help other readers, so please consider writing one. Your love for my work can move mountains, and I so appreciate your effort.

Finally, as ever, thanks for your time and your support.

CPSIA information can be obtained
at www.ICGtesting.com
Printed in the USA
LVOW13s0233130717
541193LV00009B/168/P

7